MW01234026

The Heart of a Cult

Lena Phoenix

All the best,

Lena Phoenix

Garuda, Inc.

Published by Garuda, Inc.
PO Box 7018
Boulder, CO 80306
www.TheHeartofaCult.com

Cover design by Black Dog Design
Cover photography by Aaron Young

ISBN 0-9785483-0-2

Garuda, Inc. Presents for Review

Title: The Heart of a Cult

Author: Lena Phoenix

ISBN: 0-9785483-0-2

Pages: 234

Price: $14.95

First Printing: Trade Paperback

Cover Photo: request from garuda@garudainc.com

Publication Date: February 2007

Available From: http://theheartofacult.com
http://amazon.com
Boulder Bookstore

A copy of your review to the address below will be appreciated.

Garuda, Inc.
Reviewer Relations Department
PO Box 7018
Boulder, CO 80306
Tel: 303.447.3100; Fax: 303.443.0078
garuda@garudainc.com
http://theheartofacult.com

For all my teachers

Prologue

I never intended to join a cult. Like most people, I assumed that cults involved Kool-Aid and Nikes and dangerous madmen who would teach you that suicide was the most direct path to God. Cults were things that happened far away, to other people. People who were nothing like me.

I suppose none of us likes to think of ourselves as cult material. But there is in fact a type, a kind of person who is more susceptible to the influences of groups who may not always be what they first appear. This was the kind of person I suddenly became, just before my thirtieth birthday.

You see, one of the things that makes you susceptible to these kinds of groups is change. It happens all the time to everyone, but certain kinds of change can make you vulnerable. The job of change is to uproot us, to tear us away from the familiar so we can open our minds to the new. But in the space between shedding the old and discovering the new, the path is not always a clear one. It's easy to be tempted by the illusion of a group that seems to have all the answers that, ultimately, we need to find for ourselves.

For me, the catalyst was the loss of my job. It was such a simple thing, but it unleashed a cascade of reactions that undermined the stable framework of my life. In a very short period of time, I went from being a focused, levelheaded career woman to someone who was very confused about what to do with my life. I suppose I was just lucky that Heaven's Gate didn't find me first.

The group I hooked up with wasn't that bad, of course. There were no suicides, no surrendering of personal assets, no proselytizing on street corners. They would even deny that they were a cult—but then, people who are in these groups always do.

And at first, it all seemed so perfect. They offered me a wise and charismatic teacher, a loving and supportive community, and a sense of purpose I'd been sorely lacking. I truly thought this woman and her group were the answer to my problems, the light that would lead me forward into the next phase of my life. And in a way, that's exactly what they did. It just wasn't at all like I thought it was going to be.

You see, the cult I joined, the guru I found, all that was really just a doorway. They seduced me gently in, then shoved me brutally forward into the depths of real growth, into the white hot fire of transformation that burned away everything I'd ever known about myself until there was nothing recognizable left. It was not at all what I had signed up for. But by the time I discovered what was really going on, it was far too late to turn back.

One

We are in a train station—an arched, gray building filled with loud echoes of wheels on metal. A train has just arrived, and we are walking against a flowing crush of people. It is just my mother and me, alone in this huge crowd, and I cling tightly to her trench coat. She is walking quickly, and I have to take two steps for every one of hers.

She stops for a moment, craning her long neck to search the crowd. As she does, I spy a penny on the ground and reach down to pick it up. When I stand back up, my mother is gone.

I look around at the swarm of people much bigger than I am, searching for her in a sea of unknown faces. But she is not there. A moment later, I see her coat. I push my way towards her and yank on her sleeve, but the face that looks down at me is strange one.

I panic, turning every which way in search of her. Each time I see a familiar coat I run towards it and pull at the fabric. Woman after unfamiliar woman turns to look at me curiously before brushing me aside. But I keep trying—trying, and failing—to find her.

I awoke, drenched in sweat, to sunlight streaming through the wide glass window in my bedroom. I blinked a few times, trying to shake off the heaviness I always felt after having that dream. It just felt so vivid and real. I wondered sometimes if it was more a memory than a dream, if I really had gotten lost in a train station when I was little. But my mother had died when I was five, so she wasn't around to ask.

Disentangling myself from the covers, I stumbled out of bed and over to the window. It was another glorious Colorado day, not a cloud to be seen anywhere in the sky. My forehead smudged the glass as I looked down at the busy street three stories below, watching people driving purposefully this way and that, happily embedded in the rhythm of their lives.

I envied them.

I let out a sigh and turned away from the window. Just a few months earlier, I'd celebrated my five-year anniversary working as the senior web designer for a small graphics firm in downtown Denver. The husband and wife team who owned the company hosted a party for me at the office, indulging the staff with several bottles of champagne and a cake decorated to look like a computer screen. An hour into the party, Diana, the wife half of the team, who I'd never really thought liked me very much, lauded me with a toast praising not only my impeccable design skills but the overall fabulousness of my personality. Though I knew a good part of that toast was fueled by champagne, I was pleased. I'd worked really hard for them, and I knew I'd been instrumental in the growth of their business. It felt really good to finally be acknowledged for that.

Not even a week later, I was alone at the office, working late trying to meet a deadline for some demanding urologists when Mike, Diana's husband, came back into the office.

"Oh, Michelle, you're still here," he said, barely looking at me as he passed my desk on the way to his private office. Mike was usually a picture of composure, a fit, balding man in his early forties who always neatly dressed. But that night, his tie hung loose around his neck, and his blue shirt was splattered with what looked like red wine. I watched him as he fumbled with the keys and dropped them on the floor. As he reached down to get them, he knocked some papers off my neighbor's desk.

"Shit!" he said as he sank to his knees and tried to bring some order to the sheets scattered haphazardly around him.

I'd never seen Mike like this, and my concern grew as I watched him fumble around. I got up and came over to help him. "Mike, are you okay?" I asked as I knelt next to him and reached for some of the papers.

"Oh, God," he muttered, as he covered his face with his hands and fell against the desk. I realized in one horrible moment that my boss was both drunk and crying.

"Oh, my God, Mike, what is it?" I said. We were not close, but instinctively I placed my hand on his shoulder.

He didn't say anything for a while, his chest heaving in silent sobs. Then, suddenly, he said, "That fucking Diana."

"What?"

"She's cheating on me, Michelle," he said, choking out a sob. He looked up at me then, his eyes full of total anguish.

"What? Are you sure?"

He looked away, wiping his hand across his face. "It's been going on for months. Christ, what am I going to do?"

I stared at him, at a loss for how to answer. My mind was working overtime, trying to come up with some credible denial to make him feel better, while at the same time I was slowly nodding my head in understanding. Really, it made perfect sense. Mike was a workaholic; his wife had an overflowing need for attention. Surprise, surprise.

I was still trying to figure out what to say when he started speaking again. "I'm such an idiot," he said. "I knew I'd never be able to make her happy."

"Mike, I'm so sorry," I said.

He turned back to look at me, a half smile on his face. "It's not your fault," he said.

"I know. I just wish there was something I could do."

He looked at me a moment longer. Then he leaned over, pulled my face towards his and gave me a soft, lingering kiss.

My stomach flipped as I realized what was happening. A million thoughts rushed through my head simultaneously. One part of me was pointing out that this was really not a good idea because a) he was my boss, b) I wasn't even that attracted to him, and c) he was married to my other boss. But another part, the one that hadn't been kissed in longer than I cared to admit, was busy noticing how deliciously soft Mike's lips felt against my own.

After a few seconds, rationality won out. I reached for his wrists and pulled my face away from his.

"Mike," I whispered. "Please. This is not a good idea."

He looked at me, hungry longing in his eyes. "No, I guess you're right," he said as he turned away and reached for the edge of the desk to pull himself up. "Why do you always have to be so goddamned practical?" he muttered as he as walked out of the office without looking back.

I sat on the floor for a long time after he left, stunned by what had happened. My office mate, Lisa, had suspected for years that the reason Diana didn't like me was because Mike was attracted to me, but I'd never seen it. He'd been nothing but professional with me from day one.

Of course, I did tend to be oblivious to that kind of attention. I was okay looking, but my only really good feature was a rich mane of wavy, strawberry blond hair. My face was just average, and I was also ten pounds heavier than I should be, so I'd just never felt very confident around guys. So I usually missed any but the most obvious signs of interest in me.

It was hard to get more obvious than this. But I wavered, unsure what to think. He was drunk, and obviously hurting. It was likely just an unconscious reaction, probably trying to get even with Diana. But maybe it was something else.

I pulled myself to standing, and my eyes fell on the etched metal nameplate marking his door. He was kind of attractive, in a successful businessman sort of way. But I'd never really let myself think about him like that before.

Nor should I now, I reminded myself. Even if he wasn't my boss, a man in a troubled marriage was not a good risk. Even if my life could use a little excitement, this was not the way to get it.

I sat down at my desk, but was unable to focus on the work in front of me. My body was still tingling from the aftereffects of Mike's sudden display of passion. I gave up trying to work and went home, determined to put the whole thing out of my mind. It was a decision made easier for me by the fact that Mike barely acknowledged me for the rest of the week.

The following Monday, Mike and Diana called an office meeting. As Mike stood stiffly in the background, Diana informed us that they had decided it was time to take the business in a new direction. Meetings led by Diana tended to be long-winded and lacking in substance, so I was only half listening at first. I was thinking what an odd couple they made —crisp, professional Mike and flamboyant, overly made-up Diana. They were as mismatched as a Burberry suit and a hand-woven Guatemalan dress.

My attention was abruptly pulled back to the meeting by the word "downsize."

"As much as we hate to say goodbye to the family that you all have become," Diana was saying, "this is really what's best for Mike and I right now. We'd like you to complete your current projects, and we'll provide each of you with a severance package and whatever references you need. Our lease on the space will be ending at the close of the month, and we'll be moving the business back into our home at that time. If you anticipate that your current project will take longer than that to complete, please see me about that individually."

I couldn't believe what I was hearing. Downsized? But we'd been growing like crazy over the last year, and just a few weeks earlier they'd asked me to help interview yet another employee. I looked over at Susan, another web designer who'd been there almost as long as I had. She was staring at Diana with her mouth open.

"Why?" Susan said. "I mean, this just doesn't make any sense. We've been so busy!"

Diana looked over at Mike, who was staring intently out the window. She sighed and turned back to us. "It's really a personal issue. The growth in the business has put too much strain on both of us and we need some time to rethink our priorities. We need to get back to our roots. I'm sorry."

I knew then that this was all about Diana's affair. I felt a lurch in my stomach as I wondered if any of it also had to do with me. But neither of them looked at me as the meeting broke up; in fact, they didn't look at anyone.

I reminded myself that they were letting everyone go, so it probably didn't have anything to do with me. It made sense, given what was happening in their marriage, that they'd want to scale back. But still, I was completely unprepared for this. I'd never been fired from a job in my entire life, and I walked to my car that afternoon in a total daze. I felt like the proverbial rug had just been yanked out from underneath me and I was falling through space, just waiting to hit the ground.

It had now been almost three months since I'd lost my job. After finishing the urologist's website, I took a week off, and then threw myself into job hunting full time. But after weeks of diligent searching, I was still very much unemployed.

I was trying hard not to worry too much about it. There was a job I interviewed for last week that seemed promising, and I'd just sent off another resume for a position I'd heard about from a friend. But these were not good times, and there were an awful lot of people out of work. I'd already been passed over on four jobs I'd interviewed for, and it was hard not to take it personally. I knew I was a good designer, but apparently, there were plenty of people who were better than me.

The ring of the phone cut through the startled air of my apartment. I stared at it with hopeful disbelief—maybe it was about that job.

"Hello?"

"Michelle, it's me."

My body stiffened. It was my father. He and I were not on the best of terms, and he usually only called with bad news. Not at all what I'd been hoping for.

"What's happened?"

"Your brother's gone into rehab. Court-ordered program."

Danny. He was five years younger than I was, but a few centuries older from having lived on the streets since he was fifteen.

I let out a large sigh and sank onto the sofa. "Well, that's good news, isn't it?"

"Maybe. He's already tried to get out, though. I want you to go down there and see him."

My stomach tightened. "Me? Why do you want me to go?"

There was a long moment of silence. "He won't listen to me, you know. You're the only other family he's got, and he really needs someone to put his head on straight."

I closed my eyes and rubbed my fingers against my forehead. "Danny and I are not exactly close, Dad. We haven't seen each other in over three years, and I don't expect he's going to be excited to hear from me now."

"Your brother needs you right now, Michelle. Whether he knows it or not."

"What Danny needs is professional help. People who know how to deal with his problem and can help him through it—the kind of people he's going to find in rehab. What he doesn't need is you or me badgering him about straightening up his life. As you may remember, we've already tried that."

"Look, Michelle," he said, his voice softening as he spoke, "all I'm asking is that you go down to the center and visit with him a little bit. Is that really so much to ask?"

I didn't answer right away. It shouldn't have been too much to ask, I knew that. But the last time I'd seen Danny was just after he'd gone into rehab the first time. He was agitated as he paced back and forth across the chipped vinyl floor of the treatment center visitor's room. My dad had told him he could move back home if he took a job working for one of Dad's clients in some kind of factory, but Danny was having none of it. I was trying to help him see that it might be a good stepping stone while he got on his feet when he suddenly exploded. He screamed that he was sick and tired of my nagging attempt at mothering him and I should just go fuck myself. We hadn't spoken since.

"I'm sorry, Dad," I said quietly. "I just don't have time for this. If Danny wants to see me, he knows how to get in touch with me. But until then, I'm not going to run around chasing him. I'm still looking for a job, and that's taking up all my time."

"What? You're still out of work?"

"It's a really tough market, Dad. This career you thought would be so fabulous is just glutted with talented people."

"Well, what are you doing about it? You should be out knocking on doors."

"What do you think I'm doing?"

"What are you doing at home, then? You should at least get some kind of part time job. You've got to eat, for Christ's sake."

"Look, Dad, just calm down, okay? I've got unemployment; I'm not going to starve to death."

"You're living off welfare?"

"It's called unemployment insurance, Dad," I said, measuring my breath. "That's what it's for, remember?"

"Well, why aren't you—"

"Look, Dad, I've really got to go. I have to get ready for an interview."

I tossed the phone on the couch, wishing I'd never answered it. I was having a hard enough time staying optimistic about my current situation without any help from him. He'd always had a keen ability to make me feel worse about a bad situation. Once when I was eleven, I came home devastated because I'd gotten a B+ on a test. In spite of the fact that I was already crying, my father yelled at me for ten minutes about how lazy and stupid I was, doomed to a life of failure in spite of all his best efforts.

I felt a familiar anger begin to simmer underneath the surface of my skin. This was usually the prelude to an unpleasant headache, and I stood up from the couch, trying to snap myself out of it. My father was wrong about me, and he always had been. I was a talented professional, suffering from a temporary career setback. I'd find a job eventually; I knew that. I let out a heavy sigh, and just hoped I would find one soon.

The coffee maker perked at me and I went to the kitchen to pour myself a mug. My kitchen was open to the main room of my airy apartment, and as I looked up from the counter, my glance was caught by the sun's rays pouring in from a large, east-facing window. Light was spilling across the wood floor and the wine colored sofa, highlighting an easel I'd set up in the corner when I first moved in.

I surveyed the image carefully for a moment, my eyes automatically taking in the angles of the wood, the depth of the sun's glow, the shape of the shadows on the wall behind the easel. The image was a striking one.

I took a sip of coffee. I'd been thinking for a while now that I should really use this time to get back into painting. That's what I'd always really wanted to do anyway, ever since my aunt had given me a set of paints for Christmas one year. I'd been disappointed in the gift at first, since what I'd wanted was a Princess Dream Castle. But I soon discovered I could paint myself the castle my practical father refused to buy for me, and my whole world changed. There was just nothing like being able to create whatever you could possibly imagine, coaxing an image to life from a blank page with the magic of color and a steady hand. It brought some much needed joy to my otherwise dreary childhood, and I spent every spare moment I could in front of a canvas from them on.

I was good, too. I'd even gotten accepted at the Art Institute of Chicago after high school, but my father flat out refused to pay for what he considered a frivolous education. He had only agreed to pay for school at all if I majored in computers. You'll always be able to find a job in that field, he claimed. Oh, how wrong he was.

Despite the total lack of parental support, I did manage to keep painting through my time in college, though I could barely afford supplies. When I first got hired by Diana and Mike, I was ecstatic that I'd finally be making enough money to get an apartment with decent light and buy all of the painting supplies I could ever want. I'd been so motivated back then, planning to do a painting every weekend, get myself enough work to submit for showing.

But it hadn't worked out that way. The great job I'd gotten that allowed me to pay for the apartment and its amazing light started demanding more and more of my time, more and more of my creative energy. Designing web sites didn't take the same kind of creativity as doing a painting, but it took enough that when I wasn't working, I was often too tired to even think. So it had been years since I'd so much as picked up a brush.

I walked over towards my easel and settled onto the stool. The sun's rays perfectly framed the blank canvases resting haphazardly against the wall. I wondered briefly if someone was trying to tell me something.

Well, why not? It wasn't like I had anything else on my schedule.

I began prowling through the back of my closet, searching for my painting supplies. Behind a mountain of shoeboxes I found them, a couple of plastic containers filled with crinkled tubes and paint-splattered brushes. I ran my fingertips along the smooth wood of my favorite brush, a smile forming at the edge of my lips. I felt like a child again, awash in the infinite possibilities of pure color. I could create anything I wanted out of these materials, and I felt giddy with the excitement of it.

I reclaimed the small tray table I'd gotten for the easel from its current function as end table and arranged my paints carefully on it. I liked to be able to see as many colors as I could when I painted, to always know my options. Then I sat quietly on a stool in front of the blank canvas I'd chosen.

I always took a few moments to settle down before beginning to paint, to give the image a chance to come forth. The first thing that came into my mind was a landscape, a spring mountain scene, bright bursts of color against a still gray backdrop. I was just reaching for a tube of paint when I remembered a picture I'd wanted to do of a woman's body, bathed in layers of light and shadow. But then that got me to thinking about candlelight, and the image of a still life I'd considered years ago pushed itself forward.

As I sat there, more and more images I'd thought of and ignored over the past few years began jostling for attention inside my head. I felt suddenly overwhelmed, drowning in a vast sea of possible projects.

I got up, took a deep breath, and walked around my apartment to clear my head. One step at a time, I reminded myself, then sat back down.

Arbitrarily deciding to go with the landscape, I reached my brush for the paint. I was just about to dab some gray on the canvas, but then paused. I couldn't quite get the image in my head. I sat for another few moments, then looked at the canvas again. I still couldn't see it. My eyes turned to the clock, then back at the canvas, glaringly white and intimidatingly large.

I frowned. I should have started with a smaller canvas. A glance at my pile of frames informed me that I didn't have anything smaller. I sat there, stewing in uncertainty, for another few moments. The image remained just outside my visual grasp. Frustrated, I threw my brush at the canvas and gave up.

Two

Having been abandoned by my muse, I threw on some clothes and went off in search of Lucy. She was a dancer, and we'd met our sophomore year at the University of Colorado in a required Science-for-Artists class. That particular year the class had been taught by a psychotic visiting physics professor who experimented on us by teaching graduate level quantum physics. A third of the class dropped out, but by pooling our resources and staying up very late before the final, Lucy and I managed to squeak through. We celebrated our success by burning all of our books and papers from the class in a ritual bonfire fueled by a great deal of cheap Chilean wine. We'd been pretty much inseparable ever since.

Lucy made her living waiting tables at an expensive Italian place while she struggled to pull together a dance company out of her high-strung performing friends. This meant that she had almost as much free time as I did. In the early days of my unemployment, we'd met for coffee nearly every day at a funky little café just around the corner from Lucy's apartment called the Inner Room. The place was full of once rich velvet sofas with arms worn threadbare by years of use; quirky chandeliers made from multi-colored teacups shed soft light across the scuffed wood floor. It had been our favorite haunt for years.

It was almost noon when I arrived at the café, a good time to catch Lucy getting her wake-up coffee. But an initial survey of the customers was disappointing. My only companions were a woman with spiked green hair who was hunched over a laptop and whatever bits of the newspaper happened to be lying around. I dropped my things onto a worn, purple velvet chair and headed over to the barista to fortify myself with caffeine and chocolate.

Several hours later, as I struggled to keep my mind focused on a self-help book that discussed how my father's judgments of me might be impacting my choices of men, I caught a glimpse of Lucy's red suede jacket as she disappeared down the street in the direction of her apartment. I tried half-heartedly to get through the paragraph I was reading, but soon gave up. I gathered my things together and headed out the door after her, hoping I could talk her into having an early dinner with me.

Lucy's apartment was in a brown brick building rich in turn-of-the-century charms both good and bad, with leaded glass windows, built-in cabinets, peeling paint and deafening radiators. But her small one bedroom had a decent sized living room with relatively level wood floors that she could practice in, and the rent was cheap.

Her front door wasn't latched. I knocked twice, then pushed my way gently in.

"Luce?"

"Oh, hey Michelle, it's you," she said, stepping out of the bathroom, hairbrush in hand. Her hair was an utterly glorious mane of thick black tresses that she usually kept in a tight braid. The fact that it was down meant she'd be going out. "I thought you were Jeremy."

Jeremy was the new boyfriend. I hadn't seen much of her since they'd started dating a couple of weeks before, but we'd spoken enough for me to know that she was still all in a flutter about him.

I let out a sigh. "I was hoping I might be able to talk you into going to Tommy's with me, seeing as how I haven't seen you much lately. But it sounds like you've already got plans."

"Yeah, we've got a date," she replied, returning her brush to the sink in the bathroom. "I'm sorry I haven't been around much," she called out over her shoulder as she surveyed herself in an ornate tin mirror we'd found at a flea market years ago.

"We've just been spending a lot of time together. I'm not sure where it all goes, really," she said, turning back to me with an impish smile.

I smiled back, despite my pang of jealousy. Lucy was an extraordinarily beautiful woman, with rich olive skin, deep brown eyes framed by unbelievably long lashes, and a curvy sensuality that drew men to her wherever she went. I'd long since grown used to the fact that her love life was far more interesting than mine. Most of the time, it didn't bother me.

"Okay, well, another time then," I said. "You doing good?"

She took in a big breath of air, nodding. "Yeah. Really good. You?"

"Yeah, fine," I mumbled, feeling suddenly lame about the lack of anything interesting going on in my life. "But we can catch up later—you need to get ready." I turned towards the door, but stopped just before it. "Oh, hey, don't forget about next Tuesday, okay? I've made reservations for us at Cameo."

Her eyes widened and she covered her mouth. "Oh, shit, your birthday! I totally forgot. Ma's doing this special lecture and I promised Jeremy I'd go. I'm so sorry."

I gave her a look. "Well, can't you just cancel? It's my thirtieth birthday, for God's sake. Doesn't she give lectures all the time?"

"Yeah, but this is a special one she's doing on divine love relationships. It's specifically focused on walking a spiritual path with a partner. Jeremy thinks it will be really important for us."

"So you're blowing off my birthday?" I stared at her, incredulity on my face. It was our ritual, celebrating our birthdays together. We hadn't missed one in nine years.

She looked at me, an anxious expression on her face. "Can't we do it the day after? Or the day before?"

"It's not exactly the same, Lucy." I was getting angry. She knew how important the actual day was to me. Particularly since my father only remembered it about every third year.

She walked over to me and reached for my hand. "Look, Miche, I'm so sorry. If it was anything else, I would cancel, I swear. But you've gotta understand—I've never had a relation-ship like this before, and I think it's due in large part to Ma's teaching. I just don't want to screw it up this time, you know?" There was a pleading look in her eyes, one I was not good at resisting.

I steeled myself, eyeing her defensively and weighing my strategies. She did have a tendency to get in extraordinarily unhealthy relationships, and I hadn't seen her this happy in a while. But she also knew how important my birthday was to me. I couldn't imagine her not being there.

"Why don't you come with us?" she blurted out. "It's not just for couples, and the lecture doesn't start until seven. We could do an early dinner up in Boulder, and then you'd get a chance to see Ma in person. I swear, it's the best birthday present I could imagine having, a special lecture with Ma."

Before I had a chance to answer, there was a soft knock at the door. She brushed past me and opened it.

"Hi, sweetheart," she said, admitting a tall, blond man wearing khaki pants, a loose white shirt and an earthy, African print vest.

Lucy had told me a little bit about Jeremy—that he was British, gorgeous and a musician. But her descriptions paled in comparison to the very intense man who now stood in her doorway. He was at least six feet tall, thin but muscular, and moved with incredible grace. Though she'd told me he was in his forties, he looked so young I hardly believed it. Straight, shoulder-length blond hair framed his finely chiseled face, and his blue eyes were so clear they practically sparkled.

"Jeremy, this is my best friend Michelle."

"Hullo," he said with a slight nod as he looked me over with an intent gaze. Half the guys Lucy dated couldn't even look you in the face. But as I felt those icy blue eyes boring into my own, I realized this one was different. Unsettlingly different. In a kind of thrilling, maybe even a little bit dangerous sort of way.

"Hi," I managed to reply before I broke away from his gaze and looked back at Lucy. "Call me tomorrow?"

She nodded. "I promise."

* * *

As I stepped out of her dark building, the afternoon sun hit my face with a shock. It was a crisp day in mid-April, a touch of mountain winter still clinging to the air.

Lucy had met Jeremy a few weeks earlier at a party held by a mutual friend. For their first date, he invited her to attend a talk given by his spiritual teacher up in Boulder. The next day, she'd told me it was one of the most fascinating evenings she'd experienced in a long time. Now I understood why.

Having known Lucy for over ten years, I'd learned to listen to her raves about the new men in her life with a certain degree of reserve. When we were roommates, she'd gone through a phase where she had a new boyfriend almost every month. I'd met enough of them then to realize that she usually chose men who were either exactly like or exactly the opposite of her domineering father, and hardly any of them were worth her time.

I tried once to point this out to her, but it didn't go over very well. She'd picked up some hippie musician at a coffee house who ended up moving in with us almost right away, and my irritation at tripping over his drums in the kitchen of our tiny apartment finally drove me to speak. She told me flatly that I was in no position to be giving relationship advice (which was true) and if I didn't like Sun being there, I could move out.

It was the only real fight we'd ever had. I found a room with a woman from my graphics class and moved out three days later. We didn't speak for over a month, until Sun disappeared owing her six weeks' rent and over $100 in long distance from calls he'd made to his "spirit music man" in Costa Rica.

She apologized to me then, and asked me to move back in. I forgave her immediately, but declined her invitation. I adored Lucy, but she wasn't the best person to live with. Life was just a lot more peaceful without the constant stream of changing men.

I stopped at the curb, waiting for the pedestrian light to change. Jeremy was clearly in a different league than most of the guys she dated. She said he had some kind of trust fund, too, so he didn't even have to work. At least he wasn't likely to stiff her with the long distance bill. Who knew, maybe this one would actually work out for her.

By the time I got back to the café, someone had taken over my chair. I stood in the doorway, not wanting to go back in, but not really having anywhere else to go. The barista looked over at me with a frown.

"Don't let out all the heat," she said.

Embarrassed, I let the door swing shut behind me. I slid into a corner table covered with sections of newspaper. As I was gathering them up to move them out of my way, I noticed a page of personal ads from the local weekly.

I pulled out the page, my eyes casually scanning the "Men seeking Women" column. I had been single for the better part of two years, ever since my on-again-off-again boyfriend, Harris, had decided to move to California. We had been "on" at that point, so I was shocked when he told me flatly that he didn't want me to come with him. Something about needing a fresh start, he'd said.

I guess I shouldn't really have been that surprised when Harris moved on without me. From the beginning, we had struggled with an eighteen-year age difference. In addition to the wide gap in experience, his pressing desire to have kids was a constant source of friction between us. I just wasn't ready to give up my life for a family, and he felt he couldn't afford to wait.

We'd broken up twice over that issue, and the second time, I really thought that would be the end of it. But we'd decided to stay friends, and it wasn't long before we slipped back into being lovers. We had that kind of comfort with each other, that kind of ease. At first, we agreed it would just be casual. But at some point, it stopped being that way for me. It was only when he decided to move to California without me that I realized it wasn't that way for him.

I missed him greatly when he left. He'd been such a fixture

in my life for so long that he left an enormous, empty space behind him, full of questions about whether or not I'd made a mistake. I called him not long after he left, hoping to see if there was still any chance for us. But he was too full of news about his new job and new girlfriend for there to be space for any lingering questions about us.

I hadn't dated at all for close to a year after that. Since then, I'd gone out a few times, usually on dates set up by Lucy. But I hadn't met anyone I really connected with. It was just so hard to meet people, anyway.

I looked down the column of neatly typed ads. Lucy and I had decided a while ago that personal ads were for losers, but as I sat there, alone at my corner table, I had to wonder if maybe they might serve a purpose after all.

I scanned the list again. I immediately rejected anyone under the age of 28, or anyone who claimed to be a student. I wanted someone who was together, someone who knew where he was going with his life.

An ad for a 35-year old DWM caught my eye. Financially secure professional who plays music on the side. Into old movies and good food. Hmmm.

I pulled out my cell and dialed the 900 number. I pressed in his box code, and noticed I was holding my breath as I waited for the ad to begin.

"Hello," a high-pitched, nasally voice began. "Thank you for calling on my ad. My name is Stu and I'm a very successful financial planner..."

The tone of his voice made my skin crawl. I hung up, wondering what the hell I'd been thinking. I shoved the paper aside and went to the bar for a cappuccino.

I was just getting out of the shower when Lucy called the next morning.

"Have fun last night?" I asked as I pulled on my bathrobe.

"Mmmm. Just like always," she sighed.

I stifled a pang of jealousy. "So," I began, "are all the guys that go to this thing as hot as Jeremy?"

"Well, not quite. He's sort of the hottest. But there's still a ton of really amazing guys there, Miche, I swear. Healthy ones, too, who are in touch with their feelings and are actually capable of carrying on a conversation about them. Really, I think you'd find it quite refreshing."

I paused a moment, feeling my hesitation to go with her. She'd done nothing but rave about this group since Jeremy first took her there several weeks ago, and it was true that she seemed much more relaxed than I'd probably ever seen her. But still, there was something about it that made me uncomfortable.

"I dunno, Luce," I said. "I'm not sure this is really my thing."

"I know what you mean," she replied. "I was hesitant to go at first too. But Ma is just a really amazing person. I think you'd really like her.

"What is she, some kind of guru or something?"

"Oh, definitely not. She's really down to earth. She's just someone who's really skilled at helping people get to the next level in their lives. Most of her students are professionals, very career focused and all that. Meditation can be great for increasing productivity."

"That's what she teaches? Meditation?"

"That's a big part of it. There are other things, too, but it's all really pretty practical. I think you'd enjoy it a lot, Michelle, I really do."

Despite her testimonial, I was wavering. I had never been much of a group person, and I didn't know the first thing about meditation. I considered not going, but then flashed on what it would be like to face my thirtieth birthday entirely alone.

"All right, I'll come."

"I'm so glad, Miche. I know you're going to love Ma, really."

In spite of Lucy's enthusiasm, I regretted my decision the minute I hung up the phone. The idea of spending my birthday in the company of a group of strangers felt just about as depressing as spending it alone. I got as far as dialing the first three digits of her number to tell her I wasn't coming when my eyes fell on the canvas I'd abandoned the previous day. My flying brush had left one gray splotch in the middle of the canvas, surrounded by an empty ocean of white.

Three

I awoke the morning of my birthday to low clouds and heavy snowfall. It was not uncommon for it to snow in April in Colorado, but I'd been lulled into a false sense of season by the seventy degree temperatures we'd been having for the previous few days. I watched the heavy flakes hit the window ledge and found myself hoping that if it kept up, the lecture would be cancelled and Lucy and I could just celebrate here.

The first year we'd known each other, Lucy had held a surprise party for me on my birthday. I wasn't planning on doing anything to celebrate because I had so much end-of-semester work to do, so I nearly had a heart attack when the fifteen people Lucy had hidden in the women's bathroom in the basement of the Art building yelled "Surprise!" Vowing to get even with her, on her birthday a few months later I organized a pre-dawn raid on her bedroom. Half a dozen dancers and I all crowded around on her bed for a birthday breakfast of cake and champagne. I don't think she got out of bed that day before noon.

Our birthday ambitions had mellowed a bit since then, but not a year had gone by that we hadn't been together, even if we hadn't been able to actually celebrate. A few years back, Lucy's much loved grandmother died the night before my birthday. We had plans to go to Elitch Gardens Amusement Park, but instead we spent most of the day at her parents' house. Her family has always been incredibly volatile, more so in times of high emotion, and the constant arguing about funeral plans didn't take long to get to her. Eventually, I just pulled her into her old bedroom and wrapped my arms around her as tightly as I could, rocking her back and forth as she cried.

Regardless of what we did, being with Lucy on my birthday had become a valuable touchstone for me. Before my mother's death, she'd had a party for me every year with cake and candles and a few friends. But my father was not the celebratory type. On those rare occasions when he did notice the day, I usually got something practical. The year I turned 12, he gave me a box of maxi-pads and a two-year subscription to Seventeen magazine. It was a sad substitute for my missing mother, and I cried the entire night. So when Lucy threw that first party for me, it meant more to me than she'd probably every imagined.

My birthday snowstorm began tapering off around eleven, and by one o'clock the bright sun made it clear that I wasn't going to get my wish for a snow day. As soon as I realized that I would, in fact, be meeting a bunch of new people later that evening, I decided I'd better go shopping and see if I could at least find myself something interesting to wear.

Later that afternoon, Lucy showed up holding a bouquet of deep pink Gerber daisies and a plate of raspberry-chocolate brownies she'd made herself. We had first discovered this particular brownie recipe eight years ago, at a huge graduation party held by our friend Sam. I'm sure the pot that was in that first batch had a lot to do with why I thought they were the most amazing food ever created, but even since we'd abandoned the special herbal ingredients, they were still hands down my favorite food. Nobody could make them as well as Lucy, and she made them for my birthday every year.

"Don't you look cute," she said as she handed me the plate. I was wearing a pair of bright purple suede pants I'd found on sale with a white silk blouse and black sequined shoes.

"Yeah, well, I am turning thirty, you know," I said. "I couldn't start out my new decade with a boring outfit."

"Of course not," she replied. "God, I wonder what I'm going to wear for my thirtieth?"

"I wouldn't worry about it too much," I said. "You've still got a few months to figure it out."

"So," she said, perching herself on a stool by my breakfast bar, "how does it feel?"

I shrugged. "Not much different than twenty-nine and three hundred and sixty four days," I said.

"Oh, come on. You've got to be feeling something!"

"Honestly, Luce, I'm kinda trying hard not to," I said. "I mean, I'm single, unemployed and haven't gotten anywhere with my art in the last five years. I really thought things would be better than this by now."

She watched me silently, a thoughtful look on her face. "Well, how do you know this isn't exactly what you need right now?"

I raised my eyebrows at her, unsure what she was getting at.

"I mean, maybe this is just a perfect opportunity for you. Don't you always say you work best with a blank canvas? Instead of being tied down with an exhausting job, you've got total freedom. Who knows what can come out of that?" she paused, a mischievous grin on her face. "Honestly, to me it actually sounds kind of exciting."

I stared at her, surprised by the insight. "I hadn't really thought of it that way."

"See, that's what you need me for," she winked. "C'mon, let's get going. It's rush hour, and I don't want to be late."

We were supposed to meet Jeremy at a Caribbean restaurant just off Boulder's Pearl Street Mall, but we'd barely been seated in the brightly colored dining room when Lucy's cell phone rang.

"He's not going to make it," Lucy said a moment later as I debated how risky it would be to order conch fritters a thousand miles away from anything resembling an ocean. "They're having technical hang ups and he needs to make sure everything's working before the lecture."

I decided I wasn't feeling adventurous enough for the conch fritters and ordered a vegetable dish. "I thought he was a musician," I said as I handed my menu to the woman who'd taken our order.

"He is, but his primary job right now is handling all of Ma's sound work. He's good at it, and it's really an honor to be able to work with her so closely."

I eyed Lucy warily, unaccustomed to hearing her speak with such deference.

"Why is she called Ma?" I asked. "Doesn't she have a real name?"

"Of course she does. I think it's Carmen, or Carlotta, or something like that. But once she started teaching, people just started spontaneously calling her Ma. I think it's fitting, really —all great female spiritual teachers are called Ma."

I felt my previous sense of discomfort growing. Meditation was one thing—Harris had even done a little bit of that as a stress reduction technique. But the phrase "spiritual teacher" gave me pause. It conjured up images of the red robed Tibetans and fawning disciples I'd occasionally seen wandering around Denver, or the ditzy Hare Krishnas I'd run into who were trying to beam you with love or whatever it is that they do. It was a subject that just seemed so foreign and weird to me.

"So what is it, exactly, that she's teaching?" I asked, hoping for some kind of answer that would make me feel more at ease.

"Well, it kind of depends on the level that you're at. A lot of what she teaches is about how to be a better person, you know, more loving and centered and all of that. It's a really great foundation for everyday living. But her primary focus is really on helping her students develop their own direct experience of God."

I stared at her, not quite believing what I was hearing. "Since when have you been interested in that stuff?" I asked, knowing full well that much of Lucy's childhood had been spent rebelling against her Venezuelan father's ridged Catholicism. "I thought you hated all that religious crap."

"I do hate all that religious crap. But this isn't about religion. It's about mysticism. It's a totally different thing."

"Different, how?" I frowned at her.

"Most religions are designed to come between you and God. They're based in beliefs and rules and hierarchy. But if you dig a little deeper, you'll find that every major religion has a group of people who weren't satisfied with the intermediaries and wanted their own direct experience of God. For the Christians, it was the Gnostics. In Islam, it's the Sufis."

"So this Ma person is some kind of modern day Gnostic?"

"No, not exactly," Lucy shook her head, "though she's studied their teachings extensively. What she really is, is a pioneer. She's one of those people who are looking to help forge a new mystical path."

I stared at Lucy, wondering at what point my best friend had morphed into an esoteric spiritual scholar and how on earth I had missed it.

"Funny how your sudden interest in this blossomed about the same time you met Jeremy," I said.

Lucy ignored my comment, her voice softening as she spoke. "I've always had a hunger for something deeper, you know? I just didn't really know what it was. Until I met Ma, that is."

There was dreaminess in Lucy's eyes that I was unaccustomed to seeing there. It made me uncomfortable, and I shifted uneasily in my chair.

Just then, the waitress arrived with our meal. I'd ordered an experiment, a Jamaican invention called callaloo. The perfectly browned pastry was stuffed with a savory leafy green that was utterly delicious.

Not long after our food arrived, Lucy stood up abruptly and went to the bathroom.

"So, listen," she began as she sat back down in her chair a few moments later. "I have something to tell you."

I looked up, concerned by the seriousness of her tone.

"I've decided to move to Boulder."

My jaw dropped. "You've got to be kidding," I exclaimed, feeling a lurch in my stomach as I stared down the enormous hole her move would leave in my life. I had other friends in

Denver, but no one I was as close to as Lucy. And though Boulder was only 30-odd miles away, it was just far enough that I rarely saw the friends who'd moved there.

"I can't believe you would want to live in this place," I said. "It's like everything we hate about this country."

"I know, it's such a white bread town," she said, shaking her head, "but I'm spending like half the week up here already, and the commute is killing me. If I get a job up here, it will be much easier for me to study with Ma, and it won't put such a strain on my relationship with Jeremy."

"Are you moving in with him? It hasn't even been a month!"

"No, no, it's too soon for that. I'm renting a room in a group house with some other students of Ma's. It's a really amazing place, actually— I was super lucky to find it."

I pushed my food around my plate. "We will never see each other."

"Don't be silly, of course we will. You always talk about getting to the mountains more—think how much easier it will be when I'm up here. And then when I come to Denver it will be so much more relaxed because it will be like a vacation for me. Really, Miche, it will be fine."

I didn't believe her for a second. But before I had a chance to protest, the waitress returned carrying a small, round loaf of ginger cake in which she'd placed three candles.

"Happy Birthday, hon," Lucy said with a smile.

As we headed back towards Lucy's car, I couldn't help cringing at the Disneyland feel of the town around me. Boulder's pedestrian mall was a cheerful, red-bricked zone of upscale shops and designer eateries. Toddlers wearing more expensive clothing than I could ever hope to own ran giddily in circles around a giant stone fountain. Nearly every person I saw was young, healthy looking, and white. I was convinced Lucy was going to hate it here.

We headed north out of downtown in her red Subaru. Sometime in the past month, she'd taped a photograph of an elegant, middle-aged woman to her dashboard and surrounded it with dried flowers and a long string of sandalwood beads. It seemed out of place in Lucy's car. I wondered what had happened to the plastic Hula dancer that had been there before.

I turned away from the photo and stared out the window. It's true that Boulder had a cute downtown, but as we drove past Target, Burger King and a series of chain store strip malls, I failed to see why it commanded real estate prices that were so much higher than Denver's. Maybe it was the mountains that ran impressively along the western edge of the city, and the fact that a progressive open space policy severely limited growth. Whatever the reason, when Lucy turned the car into an exclusive subdivision near the Boulder reservoir composed of custom built homes on two-acre lots, I realized that whoever the hell this Ma person was, she clearly had a great deal of money.

We left the car in a gravel parking area off to the side of the main house, a sprawling two-story with a slightly dated air of upper-middle class grandeur. I followed Lucy down a flagstone pathway to what appeared to be a large, white barn.

As we stepped inside, I felt like I had suddenly entered a different world. Even in the small coatroom, the smell of incense and the soft, ethereal music had a tranquilizing effect. I watched as Lucy kicked off her shoes and dipped her fingers in intricately carved silver bowl filled with water and rose petals. She then traced her fingers slowly across her forehead.

"It's to clear the sight," she told me, gesturing towards the bowl.

I didn't really want to, but she was watching me patiently. Deciding it was easier not to argue, I tentatively dipped my fingers in the bowl and tried to mimic her actions. It felt very silly, and I was glad no one else was watching.

Lucy pushed aside a rose-colored silk curtain and we stepped into a spacious room with a high, curved ceiling cut by wide beams. Plush white carpeting cushioned our feet as we headed towards the rows of round, blue meditation cushions lining the center of the room. The numerous windows were framed in wispy curtains of gold and white fabric, and a series of abstract, ethereal paintings in blues, pinks and purples lined the walls. At the front of the room, a slightly raised stage played host to an overstuffed white chair flanked by a potted ficus tree and two large vases filled with fresh flowers.

In the back of the room, Jeremy was staring intently over a table covered in purple fabric and sleek black sound equipment. He glanced up when Lucy turned to him and flashed her a dazzling smile, then nodded in my direction.

Lucy had wanted to get there early to get seats up close, but there were still a dozen people in front of us when we landed on our cushions. An overweight, middle-aged woman draped in a batik tent dress and no less than five different kinds of crystals turned to greet Lucy as we sat down.

"Are you just so excited that she's finally giving this lecture?" the woman said as she gave Lucy a tight hug. "I've been waiting two years for her to do this. Who's your friend?" she asked, turning to me.

"Melinda, this is Michelle. This is her first lecture."

Melinda's eyes widened. "I can't even tell you how much you are going to love this," she said, gripping my hand tightly as she spoke. "Ma is just the most amazing teacher. You'll never be the same after being in her presence."

I bit my tongue to keep from laughing. Melinda was a New Age caricature, the kind of person Lucy and I would have made fun of had we seen her anywhere else.

"I can hardly wait," I replied, stifling a smirk and hoping Lucy didn't notice. My sense of unease began to dispel, and I found myself relaxing. The whole thing was just impossible to take seriously.

"So when are you going to move in?" Melinda asked Lucy.

"It'll be the end of May," she replied. "My boss asked me to stay until then." She turned to me. "Melinda is one of my new housemates."

"Really," I replied. Knowing Lucy as I did, I imagined she would not last long living with the likes of Melinda. Lucy was too edgy for all this airy stuff.

"You should really come by on Sunday," Melinda continued. "Ma's encouraged us to re-do the altar space, so we'll be doing a ritual in the afternoon. You really should be there, since you'll be a part of the house and all."

"Oh, I'd love to," Lucy said. "Do you know what needs to be done?"

"She wanted us to really focus more on the Earth element. I guess Simon and I are not grounded enough—too much meditating," she said with a grin.

"You know, I have some heart-shaped rocks. Do you think that would be a good addition?" Lucy asked.

As the two of them went on discussing interior spiritual decorating, I couldn't help feeling left out. I didn't like this vivid reminder that Lucy was moving away.

Over the next half an hour, the room began to fill with several dozen more people. Quite a few were like Melinda, but there were some people in our age category and, true to Lucy's word, a couple of halfway-decent looking guys.

At exactly seven o'clock, Jeremy picked up a golden-colored Tibetan bowl. Using a polished wooden wand, he rang it three times. As the high, clear tones sang out through the room, the chatter instantly dissolved. Everyone closed their eyes.

"We meditate before she comes in," Lucy whispered.

Never having meditated before, I wasn't at all certain what to do. I snuck furtive peeks at my neighbors, all of whom appeared to have developed sudden breathing problems as they struggled to take in as much air as possible. Grinning to myself, I crossed my legs, closed my eyes and took a deep, labored breath. At least I could look the part.

I sat that way for I don't know how long, semi-impatiently wondering how on earth I'd let Lucy talk me into this. My thoughts were drifting between casual judgments of the goofy people around me and anxiety about finding another job when suddenly, I had the eerie sensation of being watched. The hair stood up on the back of my neck and my eyes flew open.

Sitting in the white chair at the front of the room was the woman from the picture. Dressed in an elegant pantsuit of silky, deep blue fabric with a long, matching coat, she sat in that chair with the commanding presence of an ancient queen. Her hair was shoulder-length, deep black woven with streaks of white, and framed a startlingly youthful face dominated by full lips, a sharp nose, and penetrating blue eyes that were staring directly at me.

"Welcome back," she said, a soft smile playing around the edge of her lips.

The moment the words left her, I felt as though I'd been hit by a lightening bolt. My stomach did a triple somersault and my skin felt electrified. I reached for the ground to steady myself, breaking away from her gaze as I did so. Totally unnerved, I struggled to regain my composure as the people around me opened their eyes, stretched and shifted on their cushions. By the time I had calmed down a bit and looked back at the woman on the chair, she was staring off into the distance with a pleasant smile.

"You've come here today to learn about love," the woman began in a gentle, yet strangely hypnotic voice. "It is your very nature, this love, the core of who you are, but you have forgotten that. You have forgotten," she paused, staring intently for long moments at several people in the crowd, "that you are this love, and so you think you need to learn about it. In reality, there is nothing you need to learn. You simply need to remember. But, since you don't remember," she said with a generous smile, "I will teach you. Until you do."

A slight chuckle went through the crowd. The joke was lost on me, as was the majority of what she said for the next twenty minutes. I was still reeling from the impact of her pointed welcome statement. Had she really been talking to me? What did she mean, welcome back? I'd never seen this woman before in my life. True, there was something strangely familiar about her, but I was certain I'd never met her. Why on earth would she be talking to me?

I looked back at her, trying to figure out what it was about her that was having this effect on me. On the surface, she looked very relaxed, and her face radiated an inviting warmth.

There was a nurturing quality to her, something very comforting about her smile and her grace. But at the same time, she brimmed with a focused intensity that was so strong it was almost frightening. It was as though she somehow had access to more energy than the rest of us.

Lucy had told me over dinner that Ma was enlightened, but I knew so little about the concept that it hadn't really registered for me. Watching her now, however, and seeing how palpably different she was from anyone I had ever met before, left me with a suddenly powerful curiosity.

"In our dualistic Universe," Ma continued, "love seems to exist only in relationship to hate. They are opposites, and they give each other life. So, we go back and forth between them, forever back and forth. That's how duality works," she paused again, continuing her focused survey of the crowd. "But when you learn to transcend duality, then," she paused yet again, "then, you exist only in love. And that is God."

I looked over at Lucy, who was staring with rapt attention at Ma, nodding every now and again with a sense of new insight. I felt envious of the ease with which she seemed to understand all of this. I turned back to Ma, and tried to pay closer attention.

"You know," Ma continued, leaning forward as though she was about to share a great secret with us, "if you want to understand your relationship with the Divine, all you need to do is look at your relationship with the opposite sex. The issues you experience with the opposite sex are a mirror for how you experience God. And if you have not resolved your issues with God," she stressed, "how do you think you will ever be able to experience peace in your human relationships?"

As I listened, I felt a sudden current of electricity prickle under my skin. Aside from Harris, I'd never dated a man for more than a few months. My history of abandoned relationships flashed before my eyes as I surveyed my non-existent connection with anything even remotely divine. Could that really be it? Was having so much trouble in relationships with men because I had no relationship with God?

If I'd felt off balance before, I felt even more so now. I had been raised entirely without religion, and I barely even had a concept of God, let alone any idea how to have a relationship with Him. Or Her. Or Whatever. I wondered nervously if God would even be interested in a relationship with me.

I spent the rest of the lecture in knots of internal confusion. Ma's comments about using love relationships as a spiritual path—seeing the beauty in your partner even when you were angry, becoming aware of the tendency to project negative emotions onto your partner, and embracing all conflict as an opportunity for growth—all of that seemed remarkably logical to me. But underneath everything, her high-minded path seemed dismally unattainable. How on earth was I supposed to see God in another when I barely had any idea what that even was?

When Ma completed her lecture, she leaned back and closed her eyes. As if on cue, the class settled into a deep, reflective meditation. When Jeremy rang the Tibetan bowl signaling the end of the sitting period, Ma was gone.

A serene Lucy stretched out her legs in front of her before turning to me. "Well? What did you think?"

"Um, I'm not sure," I began. "I mean, it was pretty intense. Especially the beginning, the way she was looking at me like she knew me or something."

Lucy smiled. "She probably does know you."

"But how can she know me? I'm sure I've never seen her before."

"Oh, it's not like a surface thing. She may not know your personality. But she knows your soul."

I watched Lucy as she said this, wondering how she could be so at ease with all of this. "I dunno, Luce. I mean, she said some interesting things. But this is all kind of new for me, you know? I'm not really sure what all of this means."

"I totally understand," she said with a reassuring nod as she rested a hand on my arm. "I was completely overwhelmed after my first lecture. But Ma is truly an amazing teacher. It gets much clearer the more time you spend with her."

I let out a sigh, feeling grateful for her understanding. It seemed like it had been a long time since I'd felt her emotional support, and I realized how badly I'd missed her these last few weeks.

"So, like, this God thing makes sense to you now? I mean, you never even talked about it before."

"It wasn't a part of my life before," she said solemnly. "But Ma is just like a doorway into the divine. She's really helped me connect with the spiritual side of life in a way that I never imagined was possible. My life is so different now, I can't even tell you. I was so unhappy before, always searching outside of myself for things. Now, I'm learning how to look inside."

Her comments struck a deep chord in me. I flashed on how many times in the last few months I'd found myself wandering around downtown Denver, fueled by the gnawing feeling that I was looking for something. But as I left each shop or café as empty-handed as when I'd arrived, I was never quite able to figure out what it was.

"You know, Ma's doing a workshop this weekend," Lucy began tentatively. "Jeremy and I are doing it, and it might help you get clearer about some things."

"A workshop, huh," I said. I looked up into the room, taking in all of the people laughing and hugging around us. I still felt kind of shaky inside, but I felt calmed by the fact that everyone around me seemed to be radiating this kind of peaceful happiness. Honestly, it was the most pleasant place I'd been in a long time.

Jeremy asked Lucy to stay with him that night, so I took the keys to her Subaru and drove myself back to Denver. I was distracted as I drove, my mind wrapped up in questions it had never even occurred to me to ask before. The whole question of God—what it was, and how whatever it was related to everyday life—seemed to press on me from all sides.

Unfortunately, I didn't have much in the way of background to draw from. We had never gone to church when I was a kid, and, as near as I could tell, God didn't make house calls. It wasn't that I didn't believe in God, or even followed the there's-no-proof-so-I-can't-decide agnostic thing. It was more that all that God stuff just didn't seem to have much of anything to do with me.

But it was true that, like Lucy, I didn't have to look hard to find a sense of deep longing lurking quietly in the background of everything I'd ever done. Existential angst, my philosophy-major boyfriend had labeled it in college. He'd given me the impression that there wasn't anything to be done about it, that you just had to live with it until you were dead. I'd never been a particularly demanding academic, so I just assumed he was right.

Now, though, I found myself entertaining the idea that maybe it wasn't necessary to walk through life with the feeling of a gaping hole inside of me. That maybe it really was possible to fill that hole, not just temporarily with good sex or choco-late, but permanently, with something more spiritual. What, exactly, I had to admit, I didn't really know. But I was in-trigued by the idea that it was something that this Ma person seemed to know all about.

When Jeremy dropped Lucy off at my apartment the next day to pick up her car, I grilled her for information about Ma. I wanted to know everything about this woman, why she was so different from anyone I had ever met before.

"Really, she was born that way," she said. "But it took her a long time to accept her talents. She used to be an actress, when she was younger."

"An actress? Would I have seen her in anything?"

"Mostly she just did commercials, I think." Lucy was in the kitchen now, poking through my cabinets, looking for my junk food. "But Jeremy did tell me that she had a small part in one of the James Bond movies, as a cocktail waitress or something like that."

It was hard to imagine Ma in a cocktail uniform. It was hard to imagine her as anything other than what she was right now.

"That's a pretty big jump, from actress to spiritual teacher."

"Well, she worked as a psychic for a while first," Lucy continued, turning towards me with a bag of pretzels in her hand. "She started out doing readings for friends to support her acting career, but I guess it wasn't long before the word got out about how good she was. I guess she was one of the biggest psychics in L.A. in the eighties."

I thought about the way she had looked at me at the lecture, the way she seemed to be able to see right through me.

"But then she had her awakening," Lucy continued. "I mean, she'd always been interested in transformation, but she had this experience one day when she was walking on the bluffs overlooking the ocean and was just totally changed by it."

"Do you know what happened?"

"Well, not exactly. But what Jeremy told me is that she became one with everything, you know, the sky and the sand and the sea. That she saw through the illusion of our separateness, and received a calling to help others achieve the same understanding. That's when she started teaching."

"When was that?"

"I think it was in the early 90's, 1992 or so?"

"Wow. No wonder she has such a big following."

"I guess it used to be much bigger, when she was still in California. She had such a good reputation that things just really took off when she started doing workshops. A lot of her students followed her when she moved here in 1999, but not everyone could. So we're kind of lucky now that it's smaller, since I guess it used to be a real zoo."

"Why did she move here?"

"I don't know. But a lot of the California people still fly in for the weekend workshops, so if you want to come, be sure to get there early."

"How much is it?"

"$550."

"Wow. That's a lot of money."

"Yeah, tell me about it," Lucy said. "I'm picking up lunch shifts just to pay for it. But it's going to be so worth it, I can't even tell you." She paused a moment, chewing thoughtfully on a pretzel. "I bet it would just be the perfect thing for you right now, with all this change in your life. Oh, crap, is it really 10:15? I've got to get to work!"

As Lucy grabbed her coat, she turned back to me suddenly. "You know, you might want to listen to this," she said as she handed me a white cassette tape she pulled out of her pocket.

"What is it?"

"It's a recording of one of Ma's lectures. I borrowed it from Jeremy because he said it was a really good one, all about spirituality and art. But maybe you should listen to it first."

After Lucy left, I dropped the tape on the coffee table and sat on the couch. I stared out the window, trying not to think of the empty day spreading out ahead of me. Maybe the workshop would be a good thing for me right now. But $550 was a ton of money, way more than I felt like I could spend with my small savings and meager unemployment benefits. There was no way I should even be considering it.

Letting out a sigh, I reached for the pink flyer I'd gotten at the lecture that had all the information about the workshop. In the center was a large black and white photo of Ma. I stared at it, thinking about how much she seemed to know. Maybe she really could help me. I was feeling pretty stuck where I was, that's for sure. And Lucy really seemed to be benefiting from all this.

Still, I found myself hesitating. $550 seemed like a pretty large fee for just a weekend. Wasn't spiritual teaching supposed to be free? Or maybe on a donation basis, like a church or something. Charging so much money for this kind of thing seemed odd.

I took another look at the flyer. Boulder was a pretty expensive place to live, so I guess she had overhead like everyone else. But would it really be worth it? What could she really teach me that would be worth giving her a huge chunk of my very limited cash?

As I sat there debating, I was startled by the appearance of a sudden thought.

"Just sign up."

The thought appeared inside my head, in my voice. But it seemed to have come out of nowhere. It sliced right through all my normal chatter until it occupied the center stage of my brain, where all of my reasons for not taking the workshop had been just a moment earlier.

An involuntary shudder passed through me. I couldn't remember ever experiencing anything like that before. It was really weird.

It was also very strong. Signing up for the workshop suddenly felt enormously important. This was exactly what I needed right now, I was sure of it.

I took a deep breath, and reached for the phone.

The woman who took my registration was named Kali. She was very abrupt with me as she took my information, almost to the point of being rude. I was off the phone in only a few minutes, surprised at how unfriendly she was.

Despite the certainty of a few moments earlier, I wondered immediately if I'd made the right decision. I'd expected more of a welcoming response for signing up, not to be treated like an annoying interruption in someone's day. I got up and paced around my living room, more agitated than I could remember feeling in a long time. Maybe this wasn't the right thing to do.

I sat back down again, thinking I'd call right back and cancel. But that would be pretty embarrassing. I'd probably never even meet this Kali person, but I was concerned about looking like a total flake. The urge to sign up had been such a strong one. What if I cancelled, but then changed my mind again?

My eyes fell on the cassette tape. I decided to listen to it before doing anything else. If it was stupid, I'd know what to do.

The tape began with the ringing of the gong, and then a period of silence. I was too agitated to sit still, so I fast-forwarded the tape until I heard Ma's voice.

"How many of you are artists?" she began. "Raise your hand if you regularly work in a creative medium. All right, that's ten, twelve, thirteen, fourteen of you. Fourteen out of a room of sixty or so. Tell me, what do you do?"

There was a blank spot on the tape. I couldn't hear the reply.

"Pottery. Good. And you?" Another pause. "Acting? All right. Susan? Poetry. Good. Another? Watercolors? Lovely, yes.

"Now, all of you who did not raise your hands, I would like you to take a close look at those who did. Take a look at your neighbors who have opened themselves up to the creative force and who are expressing themselves through the arts. Look at them closely, because there is something that I would like you to see."

There was a long pause. "What I would like you to notice," Ma continued, her voice taking on a commanding tone, "is that there is no difference between you and them. Each and every single one of you is an artist, whether you are aware of it, or not.

"Now, let me clarify what I mean when I say artist. When most people think of art, they think of the tangible productions of the creative process—paintings, sculpture, dance, poetry. But these things are only a few of the manifestations of the great creative energy that moves throughout this universe. God is always at work in our world, creating art with every breath. If you do not believe me, just go outside and look at the lilacs blooming on the side of the barn. Look up, and see the masterful strokes of God's brush in the clouds that so beautifully decorate the sky. The world is his canvas, and he is painting on it every single moment.

"But it is not only nature that God is working on each day. We've all heard that mankind is one of God's greatest creations. But many people do not realize that this applies to them personally. I want to you to understand this. Each and every one of you is a creative expression of the divine thought of God, unlike anything that has ever been on Earth before.

"But, as with the rest of the world, God did not create us and then disappear. No, he continues to work on all of us, perfecting the human work-in-progress as he goes. Those of you who have worked in tangible artistic mediums should understand this best. No true artwork is ever done, it is always evolving. And that is true of human beings as well.

"Now, here is the part where it gets most interesting. Not only is God creating us in every single moment of every day, he is doing it with our help. We are made in the image of God, and that means we possess all of the creative talents that he himself does. As God creates the world around us, we use our creativity to create ourselves along with him. So your life is your own unfolding creation, directed by you, but inspired by something much larger."

There was a pause in the tape before Ma continued speaking with new strength in her voice. "Both you and God are holding the brush that is painting the strokes of your soul. You are both the creator and the created. The art and the art project of God. So don't be fooled if you've never sat in front of a canvas in your life. You are the canvas, and the artist who is painting upon it. Whether you know it, or not."

Tears had begun welling up in my eyes, and as I clicked off the tape, they began rolling down my face. Everything she was saying spoke directly to me, touching those parts of my soul that I only felt when I was holding a brush in my hand. As a painter I had always marveled at the feeling of something else painting along with me, an energy I could feel but knew was something other than me. To hear Ma speak about this directly was almost more than I could believe. I knew then without doubt I had made the right decision about the workshop. Whoever Ma was—whatever she was—I wanted to know more.

Four

By the time I arrived at Ma's property on Friday night, both sides of the street in front of her house were lined with cars. I parked a good quarter of a mile away and started walking. The night was touched with a hint of spring chill, and a sliver of moon hung over the mountains.

I found Jeremy before I saw Lucy.

"Oh, brilliant!" he said with a warm smile as soon as he saw me. "I'm so glad you've decided to join us." He was wearing a silky white shirt and his blond hair was down, making him look almost like an angel.

"Lucy's so happy you're here," he continued in that delicious British accent. "It's really hard, you know, when you start moving forward and your friends don't choose to come with you. It means a great deal to her that you've made this commitment."

I nodded, not sure what to say. I hadn't realized I was committing to anything. Before I had a chance to fret about it, though, Melinda swept up to me.

"I'm so glad you came back!" she said. "Isn't it just the best thing you've ever experienced? Being in the presence of all this love—there's just nothing like it."

She had a point. The atmosphere in the room was festive. People were standing in groups, talking and laughing. As I looked around me, I couldn't help notice how together everyone seemed to look. Though a wide range of ages was represented in the room, the vast majority of Ma's students seemed to be tanned, well-dressed and in their forties. Most of them looked like they would be quite at home behind the wheel of a BMW.

"Oh, we've got to get going," Jeremy said as he glanced at his watch. "See you on break," he added, touching my arm as he said goodbye.

I looked around for an empty cushion, noting with a start that there didn't seem to be any. I was wondering what to do when Lucy snuck up on me from behind.

"Hi, Miche!" she said as she wrapped me in a tight hug. "C'mon, I've saved you a seat." She took my arm and led me up to a cushion in the third row she'd claimed with a water bottle.

A few moments before seven, a dark-haired, dark-eyed woman came out onto the stage. She looked to be in her late forties, and was impeccably dressed in beige pants and a white blouse.

"Who's that?" I whispered to Lucy.

"That's Kali. She runs Ma's office."

"Oh, right," I nodded. She was the abrupt woman who had taken my credit card information.

"Good evening," Kali began. "Before we start the weekend, I have a few items of housekeeping to go over. First off, Jenny from California needs a room for the weekend. Jenny, could you stand up?" A small Asian woman rose up in the back of the room. "If you have extra space, please let her know.

"Second, we've been having a lot of trouble with people not keeping their commitments regarding the tape library. The library is a resource for everyone, but if people don't return the tapes, it hurts all of us."

Lucy rolled her eyes. "Kali's got such a power trip going on," she whispered. "Just because she works for Ma, she thinks she can boss us all around."

"To encourage people to return their tapes on time, we are instituting a system of late fees. If you don't want to be fined, make sure you return your overdue tapes to Jeremy by the end of this weekend. Thank you." She turned and disappeared through a door at the back of the stage.

This time, when the clear tones of the Tibetan bowl rang through the room, I had a better idea of what to do. I settled into my cushion and focused on my breathing.

It wasn't long before I'd forgotten all about my breathing and was lost in my thoughts. The practical part of me was nervous, worrying that this might be a big waste of time and I'd just thrown away $550. But another part of me was excited, convinced that there was something really different about all of this and it was going to change my life in ways I couldn't even imagine.

Oh, right, my breathing. I turned my attention back to my breath, trying hard to focus on the gentle in, out, in, out.

I wondered how much Ma already knew about me. Obviously she'd noticed something that first night I was here, otherwise why would she have been looking at me? What did she know about me that I didn't know myself?

Lucy rustled next to me, and I realized I'd forgotten all about my breathing again. She'd warned me that thoughts would come up, but told me to just let them go. It was a practice, she'd said.

Some agitated moments later, I let out a sigh of relief as the sound of the bowl signaled the end of our meditation. I opened my eyes to see Ma sitting in her chair, eyes closed. She looked as intense as I remembered her, as though some invisible current pulsed around her. Yet her face was completely serene. She sat that way for several long minutes, then abruptly stood up.

"Over the last ten years I have been teaching you," she began, "you have grown a great deal. These classes have served as a foundation for your ever widening explorations of Spirit, and we have had a great deal of fun together." She smiled with a benevolent air as she said this, and a murmur of agreement went through the crowd.

Suddenly, her smile faded. "It is now time, however, to get to work. The world can no longer wait for anyone who is sitting on the fence. Those of us who have chosen to walk the path in service to the evolution of humanity must now be willing to surrender ourselves totally to God without hesitation. And we must hurry," she stressed, "because we do not have much time left."

The atmosphere in the room was deathly quiet.

"I did not expect this moment to come so soon, so I am as surprised by this as you. But the message is loud and clear." She paused a moment, surveying the crowded room carefully. "I have been asked to do everything in my power to help you make this change. So, starting this weekend, I will be holding open the doorway. Those of you who are ready to make this leap will now have a clear pathway. There will be nothing holding you back anymore. It is now entirely up to you," she said, staring intently into the eyes of several students in the front row.

There were several gasps in the room, and I looked around in confusion. I wanted to ask Lucy what this was all about, but I dared not break the silence.

"In contrast to our normal format," Ma continued, "we will spend a great deal of this weekend in meditation. The pathway is within you, so that is where you must look. I will simply be holding open the door."

She returned to her chair. She sat silently for a few moments, her eyes occasionally scanning the crowd. At one point, she looked right at me. I felt as though she was reading the book of my soul, and I fought the urge to hide.

A moment later, she broke her gaze from me and returned to the crowd. "Some of you have questions. Let's get them out of the way so that your minds will be clear."

A few hands shot up around me. She nodded towards an attractive, dark-haired man in the back. "Thomas."

"Why now, Ma? What's happening that this has become so urgent now?"

"We all know the danger that the Earth is facing. Human consciousness must evolve before we destroy ourselves or are destroyed from without. Over the last year, the planet has begun to reach critical mass. There is an enormous amount of support for this evolutionary leap pouring in to Earth from many dimensions. What's different now is that the planetary alignment that started last week is opening up an entirely new set of portals, including a portal directly over these mountains," she said, gesturing in the direction of the Foothills as a few more gasps escaped the crowd. "We have an opportunity now that we have never had before. We owe it to God to make the most of it."

The crowd sat in stunned silence, contemplating the weight of this statement.

After a few silent moments, Lucy's hand wavered timidly in the air. Ma nodded towards her.

"I want very much to make this leap," she began, her voice shaky, "but I am so new to all of this. I don't have the foundation that so many of your other students have. What can I do to make myself more ready?"

Ma smiled gently at her. "If you are here, you are ready. The mind does not have to understand." She looked away from Lucy and back out at the crowd. "Every person in this room incarnated with the commitment to help this planet evolve. You are all light workers, whether your mind knows it or not. Just surrender to your soul," she said, looking back at Lucy. "Your mind will catch up eventually."

I wondered if what she said was true. My own mind was certainly reeling from the implications of what she was saying. I had never heard of any of this before, though if you'd asked me a few days ago, I'd certainly have agreed that the planet seemed to be in a pretty bad way. But that I was a light worker? And always had been? I felt myself flipping back and forth between deep doubt about the sanity of these people and the strangely seductive idea that I was a member of a multi-dimensional team who had come to Earth to help the planet evolve, and that there was in fact a great deal more to my mundane life than I had ever dreamed.

As I drove back up to Boulder on Saturday morning, my stomach was knotted in a mixture of trepidation and excitement. It was kind of like how I used to feel as a kid before

Christmas, full of hope about what gifts the morning might bring, yet not wanting to get my hopes up too high in case I didn't get what I wanted. I still didn't know very much about the magical realms waiting to be explored in Ma's room, but I did know that the world outside of that room now seemed strangely dull by comparison. I could hardly wait to get back.

In contrast to the festive air of yesterday, the morning atmosphere at Ma's house was much more serious. Though the workshop didn't officially start for another fifteen minutes, many of the participants, including Lucy, were already meditating. I tip-toed across the rug and took my seat on the cushion next to her.

Ma spoke to us briefly after the opening meditation to let us know that we would be sitting in meditation for most of the day. I settled into my blue cushion, ready to give it my best. And at first, I found the focus in the room really helped me to calm down. But it wasn't long before the physical discomfort of sitting in one position for such a long time made concentration exceedingly difficult. I fidgeted frequently, embarrassed by my inability to sit still when everyone around me seemed to have turned into rocks. Even Lucy, whose love of dance and movement had caused her to choose an unpredictable and low-paying career, seemed to have no trouble being in one place for almost two hours.

Midway through the morning, we took a silent break. A metal urn with hot water and various types of herbal teas had been set up on a long table in the back of the room. I stood in line behind an older woman with dyed red hair; behind me was a cute guy with curly brown locks. As the woman was soaking her teabag, I managed to knock over a stack of paper cups. She smiled softly at me as I tried to get things back in order, then turned silently and went back to her cushion. Mortified, I didn't dare look at the guy as I picked up my cup and walked away with my eyes on the floor.

Not ready to sit back down, I leaned against the back wall with my tea and watched people moving meditatively between their cushions, the tea table and the bathroom. In spite of my own agitation, there was a calmness in the room that I'd rarely experienced before. It seemed like only a few minutes passed before the gong rang again, but I felt better at the end of the break. I hoped the rest of the morning would be easier.

By the time lunch mercifully arrived an hour and a half later, I had a serious cramp in my leg, my back was killing me, and the most spiritual thought I'd had all morning was that maybe death wasn't such a bad idea compared with the torture of meditation. I was convinced that there must be something I was doing wrong, that there was some instruction that I'd missed and there was something else to do besides just sit there in agonizing pain. As we'd been given instructions to remain in strict silence over lunch, however, I had no chance to seek clarification, or vent my growing sense of frustration to Lucy or anyone else.

In spite of the fact that we couldn't talk, I watched with dismay as Lucy disappeared through a back door with Jeremy at the beginning of the lunch break. Not knowing anyone else well enough to sit with, I picked up my sandwich from the coatroom and followed a group of students outside.

Behind Ma's house was a large, grassy field. I spied a fallen log near the back corner of the property and headed towards it. I picked at my sandwich, anxiously wondering how I was going to make it through another day and a half of this. As I watched the other students, calmly enjoying their lunch under the warm spring sun, I felt certain I was the only one who was having trouble.

I tried harder that afternoon. I diligently focused on my breathing, and I even offered my first tentative prayers to God to help me survive the weekend and understand what this was really all about. But the harder I tried, the worse it got. Self-judgments about everything from my difficulty with meditation to my inability to find a new job swirled around the inside my head like a tornado, ripping any momentary shred of peace I might happen to touch upon right out of the ground. By the end of the day, I was near tears. I had already decided I wasn't coming back.

I waited, feeling antsy, as Ma advised us on how to keep the pathways open while we slept. Then, just as she was about to close, she looked over at me. "Don't be fooled by how bad you may feel," she said. "Sometimes, tests are necessary."

I felt like a deer caught in the headlights, too stunned to look away. She looked at me for what seemed like a long, long time, then settled into the closing meditation. As soon as she broke eye contact, I bolted.

There was a call from Lucy on my answering machine when I got home, wanting to know what happened to me. But I erased it without calling her back. The tension of the day had built up into a nasty headache, and I wasn't sure I could talk to Lucy without taking all of my frustration out on her. I swallowed a couple of Advil for dinner and went straight to bed.

Though the drugs worked well enough on the physical pain, they did nothing to relieve the mixture of anxiety and anger that grew inside me as I lay awake well into the night. I wasn't even sure what it was I was anxious or angry about—it was as though some kind of emotional storm had been let loose in my soul and all I could do was stay low, trying to protect myself from the flying debris.

Finally, just before dawn, I slipped into my nightmare. The train station was bigger and more crowded, my fear of being lost beyond intolerable. I pull on coat sleeve after coat sleeve, until finally, finally, I found her. Ma.

My alarm went off just before eight the next morning, still set from the previous day. I banged groggily around my night table until I found it. I pulled myself to sitting, blinking hard at the sun streaming in through my window.

I was exhausted beyond belief. At the same time, though, I felt strangely calm, more peaceful than I could ever remember feeling before.

I looked at the clock, automatically calculating the time it would take me to get back up to Boulder. Then I remembered I'd decided not to go back.

I threw off the covers and sat on the edge of my bed. The decision I'd made to not return had lost a lot of its power during the night. Yesterday had been very unpleasant, but all that seemed far away now.

I stumbled into the bathroom and splashed some water on my face. I didn't particularly want to go back to the workshop, but there was a persistent little feeling inside me that I should. I looked at myself in the mirror, surprised that I looked rested, even if I didn't feel that way.

I considered my options, how nice it would be to go back to sleep. Then I remembered the $550 I'd paid for the privilege of confronting my own personal hell. Well, the worst of it had to be over. I might as well get my money's worth.

Ma smiled warmly at me at the beginning of class. I had the sudden feeling that she knew exactly what I'd been through, and I felt a burst of pride for having had the courage to return.

The morning's meditation was a great deal easier than yesterday's. Too tired to fight, I simply rested on my cushion, often sitting up with a start as I slipped in and out of that space between waking and sleeping. It was kind of pleasant, in a dreamy sort of way.

By the afternoon, it was all I could do to keep myself from falling over. I struggled to stay awake, a battle I realized, with diminishing consciousness, that I was losing. Surrendering to the inevitable, I let go.

As I did so, my normal sense of my physical body receded, and the next thing I knew, I was drifting among the stars. The collection of anxieties that usually occupied my mind seemed to have dissolved with my body, and in their place was nothing but awareness. No thoughts, no feelings. Just awareness, floating lazily through the vastness of the universe, both connected to and separate from it at the same time. It was an odd sensation, but a familiar one. Strangely, calmly, familiar.

I had no idea how long I remained in that place. I only knew that when the gong finally rang, the sound seemed to come from very far away. As its sweet, metallic echo floated through the room, I struggled to reconnect with my body. I opened my eyes and looked down at my hands and legs. It was as though they belonged to someone else. I closed my eyes again, trying to center myself with a deep breath. But in the place where my center had been, all I could find was an infinite black universe scattered with twinkling stars.

"Oh, my God," Lucy began, standing and gathering her things as the room began to clear, "that was unbelievable. I've never felt energy like that before." She paused, looking down at me as I sat rooted to my cushion. "Hey, are you okay?"

"Um, I think so," I muttered, my voice sounding strangely distant to me. I kept opening and closing my eyes, thinking I'd snap out of it in a moment or two. But that didn't seem to be happening.

Jeremy came over and kissed Lucy lightly on the lips. "Hey, that was amazing. I've never seen her ramp up the energy like that before. God, it's just outrageous."

"Apparently Michelle thinks so, too," Lucy said, a semi-worried expression on her face. "How are you feeling, Miche?"

"Um, kind of infinite, actually," I said. My mouth seemed to be working okay, but I heard my words as though they were being spoken by someone else.

"Extraordinary, isn't it?" Jeremy said. He was smiling at me, but there was an appraising look in his eyes.

"Hey, are you girls hungry?" he continued. "I've still got some clean up work to do here, but I can sneak out for a quick bite if you like."

"That sounds great," Lucy nodded. She turned back to me. "What about you, Miche? Are you hungry?"

"I have no idea. Does infinity eat?"

I followed Jeremy's black Pathfinder down the road away from Ma's house. I couldn't say how I actually managed to operate the car—I was so out of it that it felt like I was swimming through a dream. As we drove through the back streets of Boulder, I focused intently on the spare tire hanging from the back of his SUV, afraid that if I lost sight of it I would simply float away.

After being seated in a bright red booth at a busy Vietnamese restaurant, I stared uncomprehendingly at the menu. The letters formed into words, but the words didn't make sense. Or rather, they made sense, but all the meanings I had traditionally associated with them were gone. Though I vaguely remembered that I didn't like cilantro, I could see no reason to protest when Lucy asked about adding an extra helping to a noodle dish. Personal preferences just seemed unimportant.

Our food came quickly. The brightly colored vegetables the waitress delivered seemed to vibrate with an energy all their own. After placing a few of them on my plate, I sat quietly, floating in infinity, as I listened to Lucy and Jeremy gossip about other people in the class.

"I couldn't believe when Delia brought that crystal up to Ma for a blessing," Lucy said. "It's like, could she be any more obvious?"

"She's nothing compared to Kevin," Jeremy replied as he loaded up his plate with glistening noodles. "He was actually complementing Ma on the quality of energy in the bathroom. It's just unbelievable."

"I don't know why Ma puts up with it," Lucy continued.

"Of course, she sees right through them," Jeremy replied. "But that's part of her compassion—she knows they have to have the lesson."

"You're not eating much, Miche," Lucy said. "Not hungry?"

"Um, no, I guess—well, I don't know, really," I mumbled as I stirred my food around on my plate. There were sensations in my stomach, but they didn't seem to belong to me. What I was mainly aware of was a growing feeling of unease. While this kind of altered state experience I was having was not altogether unpleasant, I was still in touch with enough of myself to know that it wasn't normal. Some part of me, somewhere, was starting to worry about that.

"So, how long is this going to last?" I blurted out.

"Is what going to last?" Jeremy asked.

"This feeling of not being able to find myself," I said, grasping my forearm with my other hand, wondering if holding onto myself solidly might help me come back. "I mean, it's interesting and everything, this feeling sort of infinite," I continued, distracted by the sensation of my hand against my arm, "but at some point I'd like to feel normal again."

Jeremy and Lucy exchanged glances.

"If you're lucky," Jeremy said, "you'll never feel normal again."

"What?" I said, more loudly than I intended. "What do you mean?"

"The path of surrendering to God is the path of giving up your familiar sense of self, the small identity," Jeremy said. "It's all just ego, really. But the mind does seem to protest when it has to let go," he added with a sigh. "It's easier if you don't resist."

I stared at him. "Do you mean to tell me that this is permanent?"

"It's hard to say," he said. "The path is different for everyone. But it's not uncommon to feel disoriented for a while when you have a major spiritual opening."

Confusion washed across my face. I hadn't really considered that this was a spiritual opening, though I certainly had no idea what else it might be.

"But shouldn't I be feeling different?" I asked. "I mean, shouldn't there be some bliss or something?"

He shrugged. "Not necessarily. That's the problem, you know, everybody is always so focused on the bliss. But it's not always like that. There's a lot of empty space between the you you're used to and the you in God. It can be uncomfortable, moving through that empty space."

I was only slightly reassured by this. The idea that I was experiencing some kind of opening was certainly an appealing one. But it was overshadowed by the fear I felt at the idea that I was permanently dissociated from my familiar sense of self. My anxiety must have shown on my face, as Lucy looked at me with open worry.

"You know, Miche, maybe it would help if you had a private consultation with Ma," she said. "She can see what you are going through better than anyone, and might be able to help you with what you are experiencing."

"She sees people privately?"

Lucy nodded. "I haven't been able to afford it, yet, but as soon as I've got the money, I'm going to start seeing her myself."

"She charges money," I repeated.

"Oh, she has to," Jeremy said. "Otherwise every lame brain wanna be would be wasting her time. The money is a way of screening out those people who aren't really committed to the work."

"How much?"

"Three hundred," Jeremy replied, adding some pepper to his noodles.

"Wow," I replied. "That's pretty committed."

He shrugged. "Money is just an illusion, really. It's impossible to put a value on God."

By the time I returned home, I was completely exhausted. I dropped my clothes on the floor and fell into bed.

I was asleep almost instantly. Or rather, my body seemed to sleep. While the tension unwound from my muscles and my body slipped into a resting state, some part of my mind remained fully awake. I had no dreams—only a quiet awareness at the back of my mind, calmly watching over the infinite darkness of sleep.

The sensation of waking in the morning was more than odd. Something was different after I opened my eyes. But the part of me that hadn't slept slipped seamlessly from night to day as though they were one and the same.

I felt deeply disoriented as I got out of bed, unsure of what to do with myself. The momentum that usually dictated my morning routine was conspicuously absent. My stomach growled, but I had no desire to eat. My hair was a mess, but showering seemed unimportant. I stared into my closet for what must have been a half an hour, trying, and failing, to find the mechanism by which I made decisions about what to wear.

Finally I just sank back down onto my bed, considering that I could very easily have sat there for the entire day, and every day after that.

It wasn't long, though, before the anxiety I'd begun to feel the previous night returned from the back corners of my mind. Though there was nowhere I had to be, I was disturbed by my inability to follow any thought through into action. I feared I was becoming entirely non-functional.

Forcing myself to stand, I decided to go for a walk, hoping the fresh air might help me snap out of it. It took enormous effort to push through the inertia that seemed to have wrapped itself around me. I grabbed last night's clothes from the floor and threw some water on my face. Then I went outside.

The spring air felt delicious against my face. I stood in the doorway in front of my building, taking a few deep breaths. The sun peeked through the clouds overhead, teasing me with its light.

After a few moments of this, I let the door swing shut behind me. I took a step forward and then stopped, uncertain which direction to go. My stomach turned uncomfortably as so many possible options spread themselves out before me. The criteria by which I usually made this kind of decision—the filters through which I focused the information in front of me to make a clear choice—were completely gone. I had no idea what to do.

Behind me, I heard the door to my building open, a rushed "Excuse me!" in the voice of one of my ruder neighbors. My mind was still trying to process what those words meant as he roughly shoved passed me.

"Jesus! You gonna stand there all fucking day?"

Somewhere in what was left of my mind, I realized that the world had little patience for a person suffering from spiritual disorientation. I turned around, went back up to my apartment, and made an appointment with Ma for the next day.

Five

Ma's private sessions were held in an office inside the main house on her property. I was seated in the foyer until she was ready for me. Almost everything around me was white—the walls, the floor tile, and the cushions of the bench I was sitting on. A bamboo fountain gurgled softly in the corner, and a large hunk of rose quartz decorated a cherry wood table. The whole place had a magical, otherworldly feel to it.

Though I still felt dissociated as I sat there, nervousness vibrated through my body. The idea of having a private, one-on-one conversation with Ma was intimidating. I'd never met an enlightened person before, and I had no idea what to expect. Or what would be expected of me.

A moment later, Kali appeared in the doorway and nodded at me to follow her. She led me down a long, white hallway into a large, sun-drenched room with a floor-to-ceiling view of the Flatiron Mountains.

Ma sat quietly in an overstuffed white chair in front of the window. She nodded to me to sit in a matching one across from her.

She looked even more radiant than I remembered. She wore a long, flowing dress in a soft shade of lilac, two strands of small pearls intertwined around her neck. Her perfectly manicured hand rested lightly on the arm of her chair.

Up close, I was amazed at how young she looked. She wore no make-up aside from a light brush of mascara, yet her face was vibrant with life and color. Her skin was perfectly smooth, not a hint of wrinkles to be seen anywhere. Based on what Lucy had told me about her history, I'd guessed she was in her fifties. But as I sat in front of her, I didn't see how that could be possible.

She simply watched me for a while, her eyes sparkling. She had this beautiful, feminine elegance, yet at the same time, a silent power seemed to surround her. I felt humbled in the presence of it, too awed to speak.

After a few moments, I shifted uneasily in my chair. I was profoundly uncomfortable with the silence, but I was still too nervous to actually say anything.

After another small eternity, she spoke. "You are feeling frightened by the change that is happening within you."

I nodded, feeling the tears begin to well up. Her acknowledgement allowed the fear that had been simmering underneath the fog of my disassociation to surface, and I felt a rush of gratitude for her understanding.

She leaned forward. "You are an interesting case, Michelle. You have an enormous capacity for God—one of the greatest I have seen in a long, long time." She paused for a moment, watching me closely. "Yet it is very undeveloped. And this will be your challenge."

I stared at her. Me? An enormous capacity for God?

"But I'm not really a spiritual person," I said. "I've never even been to church."

Ma let out a high, clear laugh. "We are all spiritual people, whether we know it or not. For some, church can help in the path to God. But God speaks to each individual in his own unique way, and you are not one to be satisfied with conventional platitudes. You must find your own pathway to the Divine.

"A person like you has both a great gift and a great handicap," she continued, staring not so much at as through me. "On the one hand, the door for you is wider than it is for most, so you are more likely to find what your heart seeks. But because your capacity for the Divine is so great, you are likely to often be overwhelmed by the power moving within you. The mind is not prepared to cope with that much God. Other people, they get smaller doses, so they have more time to adjust. You will have to learn to accept much more than your mind can handle. It is not an easy path."

My eyes widened as she spoke. I could hardly believe what I was hearing.

"What you are experiencing now is your mind's first taste of surrender. This weekend, you made a shift from ordinary human consciousness to a wider cosmic consciousness. It is a small step, but a significant one. And your mind is having trouble adjusting."

I found myself nodding. "I don't know what to do," I whispered. "Nothing seems to make sense anymore, I can't figure out what I'm doing or why, or anything. I feel paralyzed," I added, surprised at how clearly I was able to talk to her about it.

"You are discovering the fundamental meaninglessness of the actions of the ego. In the past, your choices have been driven by the base emotions, either running from things you fear or reaching for things you think you want. But the truth is that all of these things that we obsess about, from what to eat to where to work, all of these things are but irrelevant distractions on the spiritual path. Your soul knows that now, and knows that it must respond to a higher mission. But the rest of you is still bound by habit, still seeking to live unconsciously."

She paused again, surveying me. "Eventually, you will learn to listen for and hear the higher call of the Divine. Then, all action will be obvious because you will only ever choose that which will bring you closer to God. For now, you must fight the urge to regress." She leaned forward again. "I should not tell you this, but I will because I can see that your mind needs to hear it. In all my years of teaching, I have never seen anyone make such enormous progress in one weekend. You have a gift, Michelle—a greater gift than many of my students combined. Do not waste it by caving into your fear."

Her words affected me like strong caffeine. As she spoke, I felt something inside me snap to attention. For so long, I had wandered through my life without any real conviction, always taking the easiest choice, the path that seemed the safest. But now, Ma's words burned through me like a purifying fire, washing away the fog and pointing in a new direction. The direction of all the things I'd never even known I wanted. I felt a sudden urge to leap forward, to get started, to stop wasting any more time.

"How?" I asked. "How can I—"

"Have you signed up for the Seminar Series?"

I shook my head. The Seminar Series was a full commitment to Ma's weekly lectures and monthly workshops, with a special bi-monthly class only for Seminar Series members. At $12,300 per year, it had seemed an extravagant expense when Lucy first told me about it.

"Do it," Ma commanded. "I will help you, but I can only do so if you are willing to work. To do this work, you will need support. The energy of the Seminar Series will help you a great deal."

I felt my stomach leap into my heart. I knew she was right— I needed her support with a desperation I'd rarely felt. But I didn't have anything close to that kind of money. There was no way I could afford the Seminar Series without a job, and I didn't even have any decent prospects.

"You are hesitating," she stated. "Why?"

I shifted uncomfortably under her penetrating gaze. "I want to, I mean, it seems like exactly what I need. But I don't have $12,000 right now. I mean, I don't have a job."

"There are payment plans," she said, waving her hand. Kali will help you with that."

I nodded, feeling my stomach tighten.

Ma was watching me closely. "Do not let your fear stop you. Money is only an excuse. This is really about fear."

I looked back up at her, my eyes wide. How could she see right through me?

She kept me locked in her gaze as I sat there, turmoil churning inside me. I was aghast at the idea of spending that kind of money when I didn't have it, but I was equally afraid of what might happen to me if I didn't. I had no frame of reference for the experiences I was having, and I was terrified of what might happen to me if I didn't have her support.

"All right," I said softly.

"Good," she said with an approving nod. "Commitment is everything."

I felt a rush of warmth through my body as the tension in my stomach instantly relaxed. Relief washed over me, as though I'd just come frighteningly close to missing my train.

"All right, yes," I repeated. "But the next workshop isn't for a month. What do I do in the meantime? I'm not even sure how to function from this state."

She smiled at me. "The lectures will help. Come to as many of them as you can. Then, when you are home, practice just observing everything that happens within you. You will feel frightened; you will feel confused. But these things are just momentary sensations. Observe them and let them go. Eventually, you will cease to be distracted by your own personal drama."

She leaned forward then and cupped a hand softly around my cheek. Tears formed in my eyes as I felt a lurch of longing, overwhelmed by the enormity of my desire for the love she was offering me.

"Do not worry," she said softly. "God and I will be watching out for you."

After my appointment with Ma, I sat down with Kali in the office to sign up for the Seminar Series.

"There's a couple of ways you can do it," she began. "If you pay the whole thing in advance, there's a $600 discount, so that would be $11,700. Or you can pay a deposit of $3,000, which will cover the Seminar Series classes, and then pay for everything else on a monthly basis, which would be about $750 each month. You can miss one class and not pay for it, but you have to pay for everything else even if you don't show up. Or you can just pay half now, $6,150, and then pay the rest in six months. It's really up to you."

I stared blankly at the sheet she held out for me outlining the three options. I couldn't realistically do any of them. I'd paid most of my expenses for the month, and I had maybe three thousand dollars left in my savings. Even to just pay the smallest deposit would leave me with only my $400 unemployment check to live off of, and that wouldn't even come close to covering my everyday bills, let alone another $750 on top of that.

I felt the fear surge back up inside my body. "I'm sorry," I muttered to Kali, who was watching me impatiently. "I'm just not quite sure how to swing this."

"You've got credit cards, don't you?" she said.

I nodded.

"Well, you can just use one of those, too. Then your payment would be just a few hundred dollars a month, and you'd still get the discount."

"Oh, right." That could work. I could use my unemployment check to make the payment. If I got a job, I could start paying it off early. But I'd still have some cash to live on for the next couple of months.

"Okay," I said. "Let's do that."

I left Ma's that day with my receipt for the Seminar Series and a tape series of her lectures entitled "The Spiritual Path for the Modern West." I'd asked her for some books I could read to help me better understand what it was that was happening to me, but she said that there were none. She told me that the Eastern texts about spiritual growth don't really make sense for Americans because the cultural differences are so vast. Books written by Westerners about their discoveries on the path to God aren't any help either, she said, because every person's journey is so unique. She warned me that individual experiences of transformation can vary drastically from one person to another, and reading about someone else's experiences can be dangerous because it can set up unrealistic expectations that can then interfere with an individual's own natural process of development.

I turned my car off of the Foothills Parkway and onto the highway that led back to Denver. After my experience in the gentle peace of Ma's sanctuary, the sensation of cars zooming loudly past me was almost painful. I pulled my car into the right lane and tried to focus on my breathing.

Boulder lay in a valley at the foot of the mountains, and as I drove past the open grazing fields at the south edge of the town and back into the urban density of greater Denver, I found myself feeling more and more oppressed. The buildings around me seemed grey and heavy; the people who passed me all looked desperately unhappy. The 35-mile drive home seemed to take forever.

When I finally made it back to my apartment, I dropped my keys on a chair and slumped, exhausted, onto the couch. But instead of relaxing, I found myself looking around my flat with distrust. I'd lived in that apartment for over five years, and I loved its high ceilings and wide windows. But now, instead of feeling beautiful and homey to me, the place felt vaguely threatening.

Ma had warned me about that. She said the places we lived held patterns of energy that affected us in ways that most people weren't aware of. She told me that I'd made such a big shift that I might feel uncomfortable there, as my new energy configuration conflicted with the patterns entrenched in the space. It would be very important for me to do an energy cleansing of the place, to clear out the old patterns so that they wouldn't start pulling me back.

When she'd told me this I didn't think too much of it, but as I sat on my couch, feeling this kind of constricting pressure, I realized this was what she must have been talking about. I didn't know much about cleansing energy, but I knew I had to do something before it got any worse.

I'd seen Lucy use a sage stick once, after one of her hippie boyfriends said our apartment had some bad vibes in it. At the time it had seems sort of an odd thing to do; I failed to understand how smoke could do anything except make a room dirtier. But it was the only technique I'd ever heard of. I headed out the door in search of some.

I walked in the direction of a small health food store about a half a mile away, turning onto the wide avenue that served as the main commercial thoroughfare for this part of town. It was mid-afternoon; the first burst of rush hour traffic rolled noisily down the street.

I'd grown up in a sleepy Denver suburb on the edge of Colorado's eastern plains. I'd moved downtown for college when I was eighteen, and I'd immediately fallen in love with the thrilling rush of activity in a real city. It had always felt so alive to me, so much more dynamic than the homogenous streets of my childhood. But as I walked along the pavement that afternoon, I cringed against the noise, the fumes, and the rush of energy moving past me. There was too much happening, too much angry chaos swirling in the air. I couldn't believe I'd never noticed it before.

As I stepped into the health food store, I immediately relaxed. The place didn't feel nearly as good as Ma's, but it still felt like a small sanctuary from the world outside.

A basket of sage sticks sat on a small counter right in the front of the store. I took this as a good sign. There were fat sticks with thin leaves wrapped in multi-colored thread and short, thin sticks made with wide leaves wrapped in solid threads.

"Can I help you?" A girl in a paisley blouse and long skirt was looking at me.

"Um, I need some sage. To cleanse a room. What's the best kind to use?"

"Well, they all work well. But it's really best to just tune in and choose a stick from there."

I stared at the basket, unsure how to do this. I picked up a stick and looked it over carefully, then looked at another. They all seemed about the same.

As I poked around the basket, a hint of purple thread caught my eye. On the bottom, there was a thinner stick of fat leaves. I pulled it out and breathed in the rich, earthy scent. With nothing else to go on, I picked that one.

As soon as I got home, I opened all the windows and lit the sage. Lucy had said some kind of chant when she smudged our place, but I couldn't remember what it was. So I walked around the apartment as meditatively as I could, waving smoke through the center and the corners of each room. I wasn't really certain what I was doing, but soon the place was so smoky I figured that was probably enough.

I turned on a fan, trying to blow the excess smoke out the windows. When the smoke cleared, the apartment did feel better to me. I found myself relaxing, able to breathe a little easier. But though the sense of constriction had lifted, the place still felt strange. It was as though I didn't belong there any more.

I wandered over to the window, looking down at the street below me. My apartment was in a three-story, faded brick building surrounded by others that were nearly the same. A plastic grocery bag was wadded up at the base of the only nearby tree; the concrete was littered with bits of paper and cigarette butts. I couldn't imagine how I had ever found it beautiful here.

In that moment, I realized that what I really wanted was to be living in Boulder. Someplace open, with grass and sky and trees. Someplace much closer to Ma.

"So how did it go?" Lucy asked me when I called her later that evening.

"It was pretty amazing. I can't believe how well she was able to tune in exactly to what was going on for me. It was such a relief, to know that I wasn't just going crazy, you know?"

"What did she say?"

"Just that I'd made a shift and was having some trouble integrating it." I thought about telling her more of what Ma had said, but held myself back. I didn't want Lucy to feel jealous.

"So, listen," I continued, "I signed up for the Seminar Series. And I'm thinking that moving to Boulder might make sense for me."

"Oh, Miche, that's awesome! I would love it if you moved up there!"

"Yeah, it just seems like the right thing to do. But I was wondering—how did you find your room?"

"I was really lucky, actually. I happened to be getting a drink of water as this guy was talking about being abruptly transferred back to California. It happened just like that."

"I see. So, is there any other way to find out about open rooms, other than standing by the water jug?"

"You know, I'll ask Jeremy if he knows of anything. But I've heard it's pretty hard, that there's not much turnover in the group houses. Usually what happens is new people live on their own until there are enough people to get another house. I think a new one just started, though, so you might have to wait a while."

"So I should look for a place on my own, huh,"

"Yeah, probably. It's so cool, though, that you'll be so close!"

Jeremy hadn't heard about any other house openings, so I set about looking for a small one-bedroom. I wanted to be in the northern part of town, near Ma and Lucy. I was also hoping that by moving up to Boulder I'd be able to cut my expenses a bit, but I was dismayed to find out that what I'd been paying in Denver for a spacious one bedroom apartment with a nice view might, if I was lucky, get me a closet in North Boulder. If I wanted to save money, I was going to have to seriously down-size.

After a week of relentless searching, I managed to find a small studio apartment in the basement of a North Boulder house that was slightly cheaper than what I had been paying in Denver. I hated basements, but the place was south facing and partly above ground, which made it bright. The location was good, too—just a few blocks away from a cozy little lake, and I could walk to the mountains from my front door. Since it was the only thing I'd seen that came close to being workable, I took it.

I signed the lease late on a Friday afternoon, just before one of Ma's lectures. I stopped briefly to eat an overpriced sandwich from the gourmet market on the corner near my new place, then headed over to Ma's.

I was standing in the back by the tea table when Lucy arrived. Jeremy wasn't there yet, so she came straight over to me.

"Well?" she began. "Any luck?"

"As a matter of fact," I said, a smile slipping out between my words, "I signed a lease this afternoon."

"What? Where?"

"On Quince. A couple of blocks west of Broadway."

"Oh, my God! Melinda's house is just like four blocks the other direction. You'll be so close! That's so awesome!" she gushed.

"What's so awesome?" Melinda asked as she walked up and began filling her water bottle from the cooler.

"Michelle found a place just a few blocks from us. We'll be neighbors!"

"Congratulations!" Melinda beamed. "Isn't it amazing how everything just falls into place as soon as you commit to Spirit?"

I smiled again. It did seem to be a real stroke of luck.

"When does your lease start?" Lucy asked.

"June first."

"That's perfect! We can move up together. Hey, Matt!" she said, calling out to a rugged, sandy-haired man who had just walked in the door.

"What's up, Luce?" he asked, crossing the room in large strides.

"I need your body," she said with a flirtatious smile.

He raised his eyebrows. "Well."

"Jeremy had promised to help me move up at the end of the month. But now my friend Michelle," she said as she turned and pointed to me, "is moving up with me, and I think we'll need reinforcements. Any chance you might be interested in helping us out?"

Matt followed Lucy's gaze and looked at me. He was a little on the scruffy side, dressed in worn khakis and a torn flannel shirt, and hadn't shaved in a day or two. But he was also very attractive, with a strong jaw and wide, deep brown eyes. As he stood there, looking me over with a friendly gaze, I found myself feeling suddenly shy.

"I can never resist a damsel in distress," he conceded. "Not to mention two of them."

"That's really nice of you," I said.

He shrugged. "It's just part of living in community."

"Matt's Jeremy's roommate," Lucy said.

"Ah," I said. "Nice to meet you."

"Likewise," he said.

"So you're both moving up on May 31st?" Melinda broke in. "Well, we should have a party to celebrate! Sort of a house blessing/welcome to the neighborhood kind of thing. What about that next weekend?"

As Matt, Lucy and Melinda began discussing party details, I felt a rush of warm energy wrap itself around me. To be so welcomed, to be so embraced, by people I hardly knew was something I'd never before experienced. I felt my eyes begin to tear, and I quickly turned away so no one else could see them.

I spent the next few weeks up to my elbows in boxes and packing. Since my new place was significantly smaller, I had to get rid of a lot of stuff. But it felt good to clean things out. As I started this new phase of my life, it seemed important to travel light.

The intense focus on packing also helped me to better manage the discomfort I felt with the fact that the new state of being I'd been experiencing since the workshop didn't seem to be changing. I tried hard to follow Ma's instructions, to just observe my experience without judging it. True to her word, it did seem to get easier. I continued to feel a kind of weird disassociation, like there was this part of me that was simply enormous and empty, all the time. But I also continued to have the same kind of emotional reactions to my life that I always had. It was just that now they seemed to be happening in a part of me that was somewhat farther away.

Even after several weeks, this new state of awareness showed no signs of changing. Eventually, I got used to it.

A few days before the move, I took a break from packing to meet my friend Jodi for lunch at the pannini place not far from my apartment. She was one of my oldest friends in town, but a couple of years ago she'd started working nights in this group home for schizophrenics, so I rarely got to see her anymore.

"So how's the job?" I asked as we took our seats in a smooth wooden booth next to the window.

"'Bout the same, really. There's a rumor that we might be getting a new director, so I'm kind of on edge to see what happens with that."

"Do you think they might consider you?"

"I've been there the longest, but I don't have the Master's Degree, so they really can't. So I'm toying with the idea of going back to school."

"That would be great, Jodi."

"Maybe," she said with a shrug. "I'm getting a little burned out on the home, though, so I'm kind of on the fence. It gets to you, living with crazy people all the time."

I smiled in sympathy. She worked harder and got paid less than anyone else I knew.

"But enough about me," she said. "Any luck with the job hunt?"

I shook my head. "Nope."

"How frustrating."

"Yeah, it has been," I said.

"So what are you going to do? You've been out of work for a while."

"I'm okay for a couple of months yet. They gave me a pretty good package when I got laid off. But I guess I'll start looking in Boulder, see what I can find."

"Why did you guys decide to move up there, anyway? It's so expensive!"

"Yeah, I know it is. But Lucy turned me on to this woman up there, this teacher who's pretty amazing. We've both been studying with her several times a week, and the commute is getting to be a drag. Since I'm not working down here, it seemed like it would just be easier to move up there."

"What, is she like some kind of art teacher or something?"

"No. She's a spiritual teacher, actually."

Jodi's fork paused mid-air. "What kind of spiritual teacher?"

"Well," I paused, trying to figure out how to talk about it, "I guess her focus is on helping people connect with God in their own way. She's sort of a pioneer, I guess."

Jodi was looking at me with an expression I couldn't quite read. "Since when have you been into that kind of thing?"

"Just the last few weeks, actually. Lucy turned me onto her, and she's pretty cool."

She leaned back and let out a heavy sigh. "Please don't tell me you're turning into one of those Boulder New-Age flakes. I'm not going to be able to deal with it if you start talking to me about my aura."

I smiled at her, but inside I felt a twinge of defensiveness.

"It's not like that, Jodi. She's pretty grounded, into meditation and stuff like that. Besides, not all New-Age stuff is bogus, you know. A lot of what her teaching is about is well documented in Eastern traditions."

She raised her eyebrows at me. "I'm trained as a biologist, remember? If you want me to believe that God is blue and likes to sleep around with milkmaids, you're going to have to prove it to me."

I rolled my eyes back at her. "Ma's not a Hare Krishna, Jodi. Don't worry—I'm not going to shave my head and start hanging around airports. Really, she's quite normal. One of her primary teachings is about integrating spirituality and everyday life."

"Whatever," Jodi replied, leaning forward and beginning to poke her fork around her salad. "Just don't become some kind of freak on me, okay?"

"Don't be silly, Jodi. That's not going to happen."

As I walked home from lunch, I found myself feeling progressively more disturbed by Jodi's reaction to my involvement with Ma. I was really surprised by her resistance to it—I'd always thought of her as an open-minded person. But she just didn't seem to have any room to even hear what this was all about for me. A comment Jeremy had made about your friends being threatened when you start to grow away from them popped into my mind. Maybe that's what was going on.

I arrived home to the controlled chaos of neatly stacked boxes. I was getting close to being done—all I had left to do was pack up the rest of the kitchen, then do all the last-minute stuff. And to make one more phone call.

I sat in front of the phone for a while before I dialed. I hadn't spoken with my dad since hanging up on him several weeks ago, and I had no real desire to speak with him now. But I needed to tell him I was moving.

"Hi, it's me," I began.

"Did you get a job yet?"

"No," I said, taking a deep breath, "I'm still looking."

"You know you can't afford to be picky, Michelle. In this economy—"

"I'm moving to Boulder. I wanted to give you my new information."

"Why the hell are you moving to Boulder?"

It was the question I'd been dreading. My father had never been a very religious person to start with, but he had become a devout atheist the day my mother died. There was no way he would ever understand Ma and her community and what it meant to me. And after what had happened with Jodi, I wasn't about to even try to explain it.

"I need a change," I said. "I can't handle all the congestion in Denver any more. Lucy's moving up there, too. And I'll be closer to all those companies in the Tech Corridor," hoping I sounded more logical than I felt.

"Do you know how expensive it is up there?"

"Yes, Dad, I know. But I'm getting a smaller place than I have here, so I'll actually be saving money. Believe it or not," I added, unable to keep the edge out of my voice, "I've actually thought this through."

"Well, that sounds like a big waste of time to me."

I counted to ten before replying.

"Do you want my new phone number or not?"

I hung up the phone and began rubbing at the tension that had crawled into my neck while I was speaking with him. I'd learned a long time ago that it didn't really matter what decisions I made in my life; my father would always find something wrong with my choices. I'd given up hoping it would be otherwise. But I still wished it didn't get to me so much.

I stared at my pile of boxes, unable to muster the energy to continue. It was a gorgeous day, and a light breeze blew in from my open kitchen window. I grabbed a sweater and my keys, deciding to head downtown to the 16th Street Mall. I hoped some fresh air might help me clear my head.

For a time when I was little, my dad had worked for an accounting firm a couple of blocks away from what is now the Mall. Once a month my mother and I would take the bus downtown and meet him for lunch at a restaurant that was supposed to look like an English pub. I would sit quietly, eating my grilled cheese sandwich, while my mother and father talked about grown up stuff. But as soon as lunch was over, she and I would go shopping in the department stores nearby.

I loved these afternoons downtown with my Mom. It was always so exciting, even kind of scary to go downtown. But she made me feel safe wherever we were, holding my hand tightly as we walked between the giant buildings towering overhead. Whenever we went into a shop, she would ask my opinion of this towel or that sweater. I felt so grown up then, helping her make decisions about her purchases. At the end of the day, she would thank me for my help and repay me with a piece of chocolate she'd buy at a small candy shop across the street from our bus stop.

That candy shop has been gone for years, but there's a drugstore next to where it used to be that has a pretty good selection of chocolate. I've never been able to walk past it without getting something. This time I selected a small ball of Lindt wrapped in blue foil.

I stuck the chocolate in my mouth and stepped outside. The day was getting warmer, and I took off my sweater so I could feel the sun on my arms as I strolled along the pavement.

It had been another really warm spring day, not long before my sixth birthday, when my mother's sister told me that my Mommy was not going to be coming home from the hospital with my new brother. Tears were streaming down her face as she said something about a better place and her watching down on me from above. In my mind I saw the giant buildings that made up the core of downtown, the tiny windows that towered high above my head. Even as I began crying, I was certain that's where she must be. For years afterwards, whenever we went downtown, I would look for her there. I'd crane my neck upward, squinting my eyes against the sun's glare as I tried to catch a glimpse of her in one of the windows until my father would yell at me to stop dawdling and watch where I was going.

Six

Jeremy, Lucy, and Matt arrived at my apartment in a beat-up U-Haul on the last day of May. It was a glorious morning, and after I propped open the front door to my building I stood for a moment, letting the warmth of the sun soak into my skin.

I was already tired as I climbed the stairs back up to my apartment. I'd been up half the night re-packing things after discovering around ten that the few boxes I had left were water damaged. When I finally did get to bed, I was so wired I just lay there in the dark, worrying about whether or not all of our things would fit in the truck we'd rented. I'd probably gotten no more than three hours of sleep, and even the double latte I'd had for breakfast couldn't mask the tiredness. But in spite of my exhaustion, I felt almost giddy. I hadn't felt this excited since I first moved to Denver years ago.

"I think we should load the bed first," Matt was saying as I stepped back into my apartment.

"Oh, my God!" Lucy exclaimed as she poked through an open box of framed prints. "I can't believe you still have this!" She held up a black and white photograph of the two of us from our junior year. It had been taken the morning after we'd stayed up all night studying for our History of the Arts final, and we both looked so strung out you could barely recognize us. It had hung on the wall of our first apartment together.

"Is that you?" Jeremy asked, taking a closer look. "I'm glad I didn't know you then."

Lucy elbowed him in the ribs. "I told you I had a dark side."

After a few more sips of coffee, the boys set to work loading my furniture as Lucy and I ran up and down the stairs hauling boxes. The atmosphere was playful, and my apartment was cleared in no time.

Before we left, I took one last look around the empty space that had been my home for the previous five years. I felt a pang of sadness as I said good-bye to the windows I'd fallen in love with the first time I'd seen the place. I told Lucy on the day I moved in that I wouldn't leave this apartment until I moved in with my husband. Well, that hadn't turned out to be true. Nor had the art gallery showing I was convinced I'd have within my first year. I let out a sigh, trying not to let that get me down. As I shut the door for the last time, I felt glad I was at least starting to move forward in my life.

Lucy had even less stuff than I did, so it barely took any time at all to empty out her place. Close to the end, the four of us were awkwardly struggling to get her futon down the stairs. Trying to negotiate a tight stairwell curve, I lost my balance and fell into Matt.

"Oh, God, I'm so sorry," I sputtered as I pushed against him to right myself.

"Hey, no worries," he said as he helped me find my feet. As I stood, I caught his eyes briefly. There was a smile in them, an invitation.

"Would you two please stop fooling around and help me get this bloody futon off my foot," Jeremy grumbled.

"Sorry, Jeremy," I said as I tried to regain my grip on the awkward bed.

Half an hour later, I collapsed on the curb as Lucy and Jeremy rearranged the last of her things in the truck. The next thing I knew, Matt was sitting beside me.

"So, are you excited?" he began.

"Yeah, I am," I nodded. "It's a big change."

"Boulder's nicer than Denver, I think," he said. "It's great being so close to the mountains. So will you be working up there?"

"I hope so," I said. "But I'm still looking for a job."

"What do you do?"

"I'm a web designer."

"I didn't know you did web design," Jeremy said, hopping off the back of the truck and wiping the sweat off of his brow. "I'll have to mention that to Ma. She needs someone to do a web site for her."

"Really?" I asked.

"Wow, that would be cool, being able to work on a project like that with Ma," Matt said.

"No kidding," I agreed, not imagining for an instant I'd be able to get a job like that. "So what about you? What do you do?"

"I work at the climbing gym."

"That sounds fun."

"Yeah, it is. Doesn't pay much, but at least I get to spend a lot of time doing stuff I love."

I nodded. "I've heard rock climbing was sort of a cult up there."

He smiled. "Yeah, we're a pretty dedicated crowd. Have you ever been?"

I shook my head.

"Would you be interested?" he asked. "I could take you out on a real easy, intro climb."

"Um, well," I stumbled, "I don't know anything about it."

"That's okay, I could show you everything you need to know in about twenty minutes. Boulder's got some really nice spots for beginners, too."

"Well, okay, I guess," I shrugged, trying to hide a smile.

Before he could say anything else, Jeremy interrupted us. "Okay, I think that's it. Let's go."

Lucy's group house was a cute frame two-story, gray with purple trim. Melinda had bought the place after following Ma out here from California and paid the mortgage by renting out rooms to three other people in Ma's group.

The interior of the house looked a lot like Melinda herself— the couch was covered in ethnic-print pillows and nearly every flat surface had some kind of crystal on it. A small, poofy white dog she'd shut in the back yard yapped at us through a sliding glass door.

Lucy gave us a tour of the place before we started unloading. At the top of the stairs hung an enormous dark wood crucifix, a bloody Jesus looking despondently over the railing into the living room below.

"What's with this?" I whispered to Lucy after the guys had gone back to the truck.

"It's Melinda's."

"What's it doing here?"

"Melinda's pretty into Jesus."

"You mean she's Christian? Then what's she doing studying with Ma?"

"I guess she's sort of a New-Age Christian. The conventional church didn't do much for her, but she really relates to Jesus. And some of Ma's teachings do talk about finding the Christ within, so it works for her."

I looked at the unhappy King. "I didn't know Ma had a Christian base."

"She doesn't, really. She embraces all traditions as paths to the one true source. Melinda has a Christian background, so that's the framework she can best relate to. It's all so individual, really, it doesn't matter which door you use. Hey, do you guys need help with that?" she called down the stairs as Matt and Jeremy struggled to get her futon through the front door.

"The more the merrier," Matt said.

I took one last look at Jesus, then followed Lucy down the stairs.

I awoke the next morning to the sound of a garbage truck. I blinked, confused as to where I was. I rolled over into a box and sat up. I'd been so tired when we finished the night before that I'd fallen asleep in my clothes in the only empty spot on the bed.

I surveyed my new home, yawning as I did so. Sunlight was pouring in the bank of windows that ran along the upper third of the south and east sides of the apartment. Saltillo tile floors gave the place a warm, earthy feel, and if I leaned over far enough, I could even see the Flatirons.

I decided to start the day by hanging the housewarming gift Lucy had given me after we'd finished unloading last night. It was a single piece of long, faceted crystal that had once been a part of a chandelier. Ma had told us that these kinds of crystals were a good reminder of the true meaning of life on Earth. She said that many people criticize the material world because they see it as inferior to a life lived in pure union with God. But what they don't understand is that only when the light of God is focused through prism of Earth does the full spectrum of experience become available to us, in the same way that a crystal fractures a clear beam of light into a dazzling rainbow. Life on Earth allows us to experience all the color and beauty and magic of the rainbow in such a way that we can then experience the oneness of God even more deeply upon our return.

Having no idea where my thumbtacks were, I slid the crystal onto a curtain rod and adjusted it until there were rainbows covering half a dozen surfaces in my new home. It seemed an appropriate baptism.

I turned back to my studio and surveyed the chaotic pile of boxes, wondering what had happened to my toothbrush.

The quest to clean my teeth threw me straight into unpacking. I had most of the bathroom put away before I found my toothbrush. I was so revved up by then I paused only a moment to clean my teeth, then dove straight back into the chaos. By the time the sun had passed from one side of the apartment to the other, I was almost done.

One of the last boxes I opened contained a set of framed photographs. They were of my family—a glamorous, black and white high-school picture of the mother I barely remembered, a picture of my father and I fishing when I was twelve, a snapshot of my dad, myself and Danny on a rare vacation we'd taken to Mesa Verde, the summer before I'd first discovered my little brother was smoking crack.

I sighed, tracing my finger through the dust on the edge of one of the frames. I'd had these pictures on top of the bookshelf in my old apartment, but I felt reluctant to set them up there now. They just didn't seem to fit, somehow. I looked down again at the picture of my dad and me. We were both smiling, but just before the picture had been taken, he'd yelled at me for forgetting to tie down the cooler.

I put all of the pictures back in the box and shoved it into the back of the closet.

Lucy and I had set up a shopping date for the next day, to stock up on food and get all those things you inevitably need from Target whenever you move into a new place. We met for breakfast at a funky diner a few blocks north of our new neighborhood. The walls were covered in rusty farm implements and large stuffed fish.

"Weird place," I commented.

"Yeah, but the food's awesome," she said. "Jeremy and I eat here like constantly." She reached over towards the paper I'd bought on my way in. "Can I look at that?"

"I thought you'd already gotten a job," I replied as I slid the paper in her direction. Lucy had years of high-end restaurant experience. It would be easier for her to find a job than anyone else I knew.

"I did, but then they called me and said that the person I was supposed to replace had decided not to leave," she said as she opened the paper to the employment section. "I've checked out a few other places, but I guess I just missed the big turnover that happens when CU lets out. Oh, how depressing. The only thing listed in here is Denny's and the brew pub. Do me a favor—if I get that desperate, please shoot me in the head, okay?"

I smiled at her. "Sure, no problem." She tended to be dramatic about stuff like that, but I wasn't worried. Not about her. But I was very nervous about my own job prospects. The main reason I hadn't even begun looking in Boulder was that I was afraid I wouldn't find anything.

"Oh, look, there's some web design stuff in here," she pointed.

"Really?" I took the paper from her. Sure enough, a local company was seeking experienced designers. No phone or address, just a fax for a resume.

"That's a good sign," she said.

I hoped she was right.

I spent the next day working hard on my resume and cover letter. Late in the afternoon, I drove over to Kinko's to fax it off.

It was Tuesday, and Ma was giving a lecture that night, as she did almost every Tuesday and Friday nights. It was only five-thirty, but I decided to head over to her house early. I didn't have anything else to do.

I was surprised to see that there were already three older women waiting outside the barn when I got there. I knew that some people got there early so they could sit in the front row, but I hadn't realized they would wait so long to do so. The doors weren't even unlocked yet, so the four of us just stood there, waiting. One of the women smiled at me, but nobody said anything.

By 6:00, when Kali came out of the main house and unlocked the door, several more people had arrived. I made my way towards the stage and managed to get two seats in the front row, just to the left of where Ma usually sat. I saved one for Lucy as well; Matt was working at the climbing gym, so he wouldn't be there, and Jeremy was always working sound in the back.

Ma had barely sat down before I realized why those women had been waiting by the door for so long. Being close enough to actually feel her energy while she was teaching was unlike anything I'd ever experienced before. As I sat in front of her, my skin would often tingle or grow warm, and I began to have the feeling that I was physically absorbing her teachings as much as I was hearing her words. I decided from then on to get there early whenever I could.

I wasn't sure if it was because I was right in front of her, but halfway through the evening, Ma addressed me personally. She was speaking about the difficulties of walking the spiritual path when she turned abruptly to me. "What I am saying is particularly important for you, Michelle," she said. "If you are serious about walking this path, you need to become serious about meditation. God can only come to you if you make the space for him to do so."

I was so embarrassed I nearly fell off my cushion. I had seen her address people directly a few times before, but I was shocked she had chosen to single me out in this way. What she said, though, was unquestionably true. Outside of her lectures, I had only meditated once or twice since the workshop. It was so hard for me to sit still, and I still felt like I didn't know what I was doing. But it was eerie to discover she could see that.

After that, I began each day with as long of a sit as I could stand. I asked Ma for some kind of instruction to help me get started, but she didn't really say much. She just told me the main thing was to learn to stay present with everything that was happening inside, to experience it as fully as possible, and then to let it go.

I can't say I actually began to enjoy meditation, but it did get easier after a little while. Though I continued to feel like I wasn't really doing it right, I noticed that just taking some time to slow down in the morning and pay attention to what was happening inside of me did seem to help me relax a bit. Which was good, since I'd heard nothing from the people I'd faxed my resume to, and nothing else even remotely interesting had shown up in the paper.

Lucy was in a similar situation. She'd been turned away at a half a dozen major restaurants in the first week we'd been there. At least she had Jeremy to distract her some of the time, but when he was busy working for Ma, she'd come over and hang out with me.

"I brought some of Ma's tapes to listen to," she said as she pulled a handful of audio tapes out of her bag and dropped them onto my bed.

"You got these from Jeremy?" I asked. One of Jeremy's other jobs was managing Ma's tape library. They'd started recording all of her lectures over seven years ago, and there were thousands of hours of tapes. Some of them were dated and titled, but a lot of the early stuff was only labeled by date. So in addition to acting as librarian, he was working on creating a master index of all of the tapes.

She nodded. "Since I have all this time on my hands, I figured I'd just go through as many of her tapes as I could. He said these were some good ones to start with. There's 'Soul and Mind,' 'Finding God in your Heart,' and this one's not titled but he said it's a really good one about the challenges beginners face on the spiritual path."

"Let's do that one. God knows you can't be much more of a beginner than me."

The tape was interesting. It talked about how stepping forward on a spiritual path can be one of the most difficult things a person does in life. Not only are you moving into an unknown realm, which we've been so strongly conditioned to avoid, but doing so often creates fear in the people around you, who don't want you to disturb their own comfortable notions of a more limited reality. After witnessing Jodi's reaction, I could really relate to this. It made me realize just how lucky I was to be able to do this with Lucy.

"You want to take a break?" she asked me after we'd finished the first tape.

"Yeah. I need to stretch my legs."

We stepped outside into a particularly beautiful June day. It was only a couple of blocks to the lake near my house, and soon we were walking the gravel footpath around the perimeter of the water. I hadn't quite gotten over how stunning the setting was—the foothills began climbing right out of the edge of the lake, and the enormity of the mountain towering over us never ceased to take my breath away. As the sun's reflections sparkled in the surface of the water, I realized, for the first time I could remember in I don't know how long, that I was happy.

* * *

Melinda kept her promise about hosting a community housewarming party for Lucy and me the first weekend after we moved up. She said it was a potluck/barbeque, and asked me to bring something vegetarian. I mixed up a large bowl of guacamole and headed over there late in the afternoon.

The door was open, so I pushed my way in and went back into the kitchen. There were already a half a dozen people milling about, but aside from Melinda and Jeremy, I didn't know any of them, though most looked familiar from Ma's lectures.

"Michelle!" Jeremy said as he set down a loaf of bread and came over to give me a kiss on the cheek. "Everyone, this is Michelle," he continued, pointing to me. "Michelle, this is Joseph, Summer, Lila, Michael, Dakota and Shadowdancer."

"Hi," I said.

"Nice to meet you," Lila said. "So, you've just moved up from Denver?"

"Uh huh," I said, "Just a few days ago."

"Here, let me take that from you," Jeremy interrupted, whisking the bowl out of my hands and setting it on the counter. It was still early, but the island in Melinda's kitchen was already crammed full of food—small triangles of spanikopita, kebabs composed of onions, bell peppers and tofu, fresh baked bread, a selection of cheeses worthy of any gourmet market.

Lucy came up from behind me and gave me a big hug. "Welcome home, sister!" she said. "Punch?"

"Yes, definitely," I said, taking the small glass of bubbly pink liquid gratefully. I had never been very comfortable at parties, particularly when I knew so few people, but alcohol usually helped. I took a sip, and was dismayed to discover the glass contained only a blend of juice and sparkling water.

I looked around for a bottle of wine, or even a beer, but didn't see anything. I followed Lucy out to the back deck, where she was grilling her way through another enormous plate full of kebabs.

"There's just juice in this punch," I said, a frown on my face.

"Yeah, I know," she wrinkled her nose at me. "Ma's crowd isn't really into alcohol. She says it clouds your higher perceptual abilities. It's kind of a bummer."

"No kidding," I said. "How am I supposed to talk to all these people on my own?"

"Oh, just be yourself," she said. "You'll be fine."

Matt stuck his head out the back door. "You ladies need any help out here?"

"We always like the company," Lucy replied. "Makes the food taste better, don't you think?"

"So, you all settled in?" he said to me as he took a seat in one of the wooden chairs encircling the teak patio table.

"Pretty much," I nodded.

"Cool. I can't wait to see what you've done."

I smiled. "You'll have to stop by soon."

"So, now that you're all unpacked and stuff, you think you might have time for that climbing lesson?"

"Um, yeah," I said. "I guess I do."

"Great. How about Thursday?"

"That should be okay. Unless by some miracle I actually have a job by then," I added.

"I'll take my chances," he said.

From behind Matt's head, I caught a glance from Lucy. She had a very wide smile on her face.

A half an hour later, Melinda poked her head out from the kitchen. "C'mon, everyone—it's time for the blessing!"

I looked over at Lucy with a questioning gaze, but she wasn't looking at me as we headed back inside. There were now over thirty people in the house. Melinda surveyed the crowd for a moment, then said, "Let's do two circles. Lucy, Michelle, you should stand on either side of me in the inner circle."

I followed Melinda to the middle of the living room as people formed two irregular circles around the coffee table, their hands linked together.

"Okay," Melinda began. "Everybody, let's start by closing our eyes, centering ourselves and taking a deep breath." Deep sighs began escaping the people around me as I tried to relax. I had no clue what this was all about.

"Let us start by taking a moment to give thanks for this incredibly bounty of nourishing food that God has given us for this meal," Melinda began. She paused for half a minute before continuing. "Today we are extraordinarily blessed to have our community brightened by the new arrivals of Lucy and Michelle. We welcome them into our spiritual neighborhood with all the love in our hearts. Please take a few moments to silently send them your blessing. As you do so, please think of one word you'd like to share with them out loud."

I stood there, unsure what to do. Then I felt a nudge from Melinda. "Open your eyes!" she whispered. As soon as I did so, the first thing I saw was a man I'd not yet met looking at me with a soft, loving gaze. His hands were pressed together in prayer position, and he smiled at me.

"Love," he said softly.

I felt tears form at the edge of my eyes. From next to him I heard someone else say, "God."

I turned to the next person, who said "Joy." My heart began to ache, and I struggled to keep from crying as each stranger I turned to wished me more from life than I had ever thought I deserved.

When my eyes met Matt's, he wished me grace. The tears finally escaped my eyes and I started to cry in earnest.

Melinda wrapped me in a tight hug. "Welcome home, honey," she whispered. "We're so glad to have you back."

A few days later, Matt picked me up at 7:30 for my first climbing lesson. After months of living without an alarm I had to protest, but he insisted the mountain air was best in the morning and it would help to beat the crowds. I relented when he promised to feed me first.

He took me to Lucille's, a Cajun-inspired breakfast place that had been a Boulder institution for close to fifty years. The yellow clapboard house which housed the restaurant showed signs of wear, but the cramped dining room, with its floral curtains and little ceramic pots of homemade strawberry-rhubarb jam, was cozy and cheerful.

It didn't take long for the richly scented spiced tea Matt recommended to wake me up a bit. Still, I was nervous. It had been a long time since I'd been out on a date. Even if it was only a breakfast date.

"So, how did you first hear about Ma?" I asked, attempting to break the silence after all that remained of my tea was a melancholy puddle at the bottom of the mug.

"From a friend of mine in California. He called me up as soon as Ma moved here and told me she was the real thing, that I had to check her out. I'd thought he'd gone a bit off the deep end at first," he said with a shrug, flashing me a smile, "but when I finally got around to checking her out last year, I realized he'd been right on."

"She's really amazing."

"Yeah. I couldn't believe such an evolved teacher just up and moved into my backyard. I just wish I'd figured that out sooner."

I looked at him quizzically. "How come you didn't check her out right away?"

"Well, you know, there are so many flakes out there calling themselves spiritual teachers these days. I had kind of a bad experience when I first started out, hooking up with someone who wasn't really for real. It left kind of a bad taste in my mouth."

"What happened?"

He rolled his eyes. "It's kind of embarrassing, really. When I was in college, I was introduced to this guy who claimed to be the re-incarnation of this Indian saint I'd read about when I was a teenager. I'd always felt this calling towards Spirit, and I guess I was too young to know any better. Eventually I realized the guy was just flat out crazy, but not until after my own head had gotten seriously messed with."

"That sounds awful."

"It was," he said, nodding. "It's hard, you know, when you put your faith and trust in someone and they abuse it. That's why I was really careful with Ma, really checking her out before I got involved. I had to make sure she was the real thing."

I sat for a moment, relieved to hear Ma passed the test. But I still felt vaguely unnerved. "So, like, how did you find out this guy was a fake?"

"Well, the longer I was with him, the more I started to see these inconsistencies. Like, he'd be teaching one thing, about peacefulness and non-aggression and all that, and then he'd just blow up at some student who didn't properly line up his shoes against the wall. I tried to ignore it at first, you know, thinking that he was coming from a place of higher wisdom, responding to things based on information that I wasn't capable of understanding. But after a while, I had to get real and face that the guy was a total poser."

"That must have been really hard."

"Yeah, it was. I was pretty disillusioned for a while, just kind of gave up on the whole thing, actually. But then I met Ma, and I realized that not all teachers are just jerking your chain."

He looked at me with a soft smile. "You're lucky, you know," he said. "Most of the people in Ma's school have walked other paths before finding her. Most of what we learned, though, is just garbage, and you end up with tons of stuff you have to unlearn before you can even move forward. But for you, it's great, 'cuz you're starting out right, with a real beginner's mind. You have no idea how lucky you are."

After breakfast, Matt drove me in his beat-up Cherokee to a beginning climbing spot in Boulder Canyon. It was the first time I'd been up into the mountains in years, and the Colorado sun shone brilliantly on the ragged, pine-covered foothills.

As Matt untangled his mass of climbing gear, I marveled at the rugged beauty of the trees and boulders around us. I'd never been much of a nature person, but for the first time I realized how alive the forest was. It seemed like everything around me was pulsing with this intense life force that was so palpable I was amazed I'd never noticed it before.

I would have been content to just sit there, watching the squirrels playing in the trees, but eventually Matt got everything sorted out and went about giving me my first climbing lesson. As he spoke, he slipped into the role of teacher, sharing with easy grace the benefit of his years of practical wisdom. He was clearly a master of his subject, and I was much more fascinated than I expected to be.

In spite of my attention to his lecture, the majority of what Matt taught me fled from my brain as soon as I found myself hanging from the side of a cliff suspended by a rope and a harness. In spite of Matt's reassurances about load strength and redundant safety locks, never mind the fact that I barely a few feet off the ground, it took a Herculean effort on my part to follow his instructions and actually move. With a great deal of coaching and encouragement, I somehow managed a simple rappel, and by the end of the lesson had actually experienced some real joy as I felt the freedom of moving across the rock for a few seconds before I banged my knee into the side of the cliff.

"Not bad for a first timer," he nodded in encouragement as I tried to catch my breath after finally getting safely back down to the ground. While I was up on the rock I'd been too terrified to be embarrassed, but now that we were done I realized that doing an activity in which there was no way I could look anything except ridiculous with a cute guy was probably not one of my better choices.

"Sorry I'm such a chicken," I said.

"Aw, hey, don't be silly. You did great. You're just learning, and everybody's awkward when they start out. But that's the only way you get any good."

I nodded, not particularly reassured. So I was surprised when he asked me if I wanted to get together on the weekend when he dropped me off a bit later. Surprised, but pleased. We made another date for Saturday.

"Miche?" I heard Lucy's voice call out through my open door the next morning.

"Hey," I looked up from my sink, surprised to see Melinda behind her.

"Listen, Mel just told me about this great clothing sale that's happening across town. It's this woman who designs really cool clothing in Indonesia and then imports it back here. Everything's, like, ten dollars. We're heading over there now—want to come?"

"Um, I don't know," I hemmed. "I don't really have a lot of money to go shopping right now."

"Michelle, everything is so cheap at this place you can't afford not to go," Melinda said, a stern look on her face.

"Besides, you don't have to buy anything if you don't want to," Lucy said. "I don't have any money either, but it sounds like so much fun!"

"Yeah, okay," I nodded.

We headed east in Melinda's green Forrester, towards the closest thing Boulder had to an industrial park. Sandwiched in between a small, local brewery and a ski repair shop was a narrow storefront with long, brightly colored flags waving in front of it.

Inside, the place was crammed with rack after rack of handmade batik clothing. I did a double take as I looked around at the patterned fabrics, many of which I had seen on members of Ma's group.

"So this is where everybody gets all those cool dresses," I said.

"It's the best place in town to shop," Melinda said. "This stuff goes for fifty and sixty dollars retail, but this is the warehouse and twice a year the owner has these incredible sales."

I ran my hand along a rack of light rayon tank tops. It felt like I had just been let in on a huge secret.

I began poking my way through the rack closest to me, marveling at the array of bright, gorgeous patterns. I'd always been a very subdued dresser, living most of my life in khaki pants and neutral tops. So at first, I couldn't quite see myself actually wearing any of these things.

"Miche, you have *got* to try this on!" Lucy interrupted me, holding up a pair of rayon pants with a matching tank top.

The fabric was a light sea green, decorated in a delicate pattern of curling white streaks. The bottoms of the pant legs where trimmed with an inch of crazy lilac-and-white batik that was mirrored in a large patch on the front of the top. It was beautiful.

I made my way into the group dressing room. Though it was only mid-morning, the place was already packed, with a dozen women of various sizes and states of undress crammed into the tiny room.

I did a quick change, then tried fruitlessly to get a glimpse of myself in front of one of the mirrors. Since it was too crowded to see, I stepped outside for a second opinion.

"Oh. My. God," Lucy exclaimed. "That is *perfect* for you!"

"You think?" I asked, taking a peek at myself in the outside mirror. It did look good, I had to admit. But it was so different from what I normally wore.

A woman I didn't know came up from behind me in the mirror. "It really suits you," she nodded.

"You know," one of the shop girls began, "I have a matching jacket for that."

Two hours and way more money than I should have spent later, I climbed back into Melinda's car with two pairs of pants, a skirt, three tops, and a dress. I fingered the light fabrics in my lap, wondering just who it was who was going to wear all of these things.

My plans for a weekend date with Matt had morphed into a joint dinner with Lucy and Jeremy at the small house the two men shared on the very north edge of the city. I decided to wear my new sea-green outfit for the event and headed over there with a bottle of Pellegrino.

On the outside, their skinny, wood framed two-story looked like any neat suburban home, but the minute I stepped through the doorway, I felt like I was in India. Intricate tapestries depicting various Hindu gods hung on many of the walls, metal statues of Shiva, Ganesh, and Buddha covered the tops of bookshelves and windowsills, and the scent of sandalwood incense permeated the air.

"This is outrageous," I said as Matt took me on a tour of the house.

"Yeah, it's not bad for a tract house."

"How long have you lived here?"

"Mmmm, 'bout four years now?"

"And you can do it with just one roommate?"

He nodded. "This neighborhood is all affordable housing, so my payment's pretty low. And then we rent out the extra bedroom and the basement to the Seminar Series people who come in from California. So it works out pretty well," he added as we headed back down stairs.

"Hey, easy on the chili powder," Matt chided Jeremy as we returned to the small kitchen where he was mixing red powder into an exotic, Asian-style sauce for a stir-fry. Lucy had taken up residence at the large wooden table that dominated the room and was chopping neat piles of bok choy and onions.

"What can I do?" I asked.

"Can you slice the tofu?" Jeremy asked, nodding in the direction of a couple of thick, white cakes currently being pressed between two cutting boards under the weight of a cast-iron skillet.

I perched on a stool across from Lucy with an enormous knife and set to work. The smell of sizzling garlic exploded from the wok as Jeremy began cooking. Though I didn't know Matt and Jeremy all that well, I was surprised to feel so comfortable with them. It felt like I'd known them almost as long as I'd known Lucy.

"I guess there's nothin' left for me to do, huh," Matt said, stifling a yawn and sitting down at the table.

"How come you're so beat?" Lucy asked. "Hard day at the office?"

"I dunno," Matt shrugged. "I haven't been sleeping well since this whole portal opening. I think my body's just not used to the energy of it."

"Yeah, I know what you mean," Jeremy agreed. "I keep feeling this buzzing feeling in my veins, like I'm being super-charged or something."

Though the topic of portals had come up in Ma's lectures several times since I started going, I still wasn't entirely certain what a portal really was. I'd been hoping to discover it in one of the tapes, but I'd had no luck so far.

I debated asking them about it for a moment, weighing my fear of looking stupid with my desire to know what was going on. "So, um," I ventured, "what, exactly, is a portal?"

"A portal is an opening to a different dimension," Matt replied. "It's like a doorway, except it's not physical."

"Oh," I replied, wondering if that was supposed to mean more to me than it did. "And so there's, like, energy coming through it?"

Matt nodded. "This one I think is just an energy portal. Some of them are for actually traveling to other dimensions, but I didn't hear Ma say anything about that with this one. I think they're just using it to send energy to Earth right now."

I looked at him with a puzzled expression. "They?"

"Yeah, you know, the aliens who are helping humanity evolve."

I stared at him, not quite believing what I was hearing. Aliens? Was he out of his mind? He certainly looked normal enough as he leaned back in his chair, as relaxed as if he was talking about the weather. What on Earth was going on?

I turned to Lucy in alarm, but she was absorbed in an attempt to get her fingernail underneath an onionskin. She appeared completely nonplussed by the whole conversation.

"Aliens are helping humanity evolve," I said, trying unsuccessfully to mask the edge of disbelief in my voice.

Matt and Jeremy exchanged glances.

"I know, Miche, it sounds kind of weird," Lucy said. "But they're not bad aliens or anything, not the kind that kidnap people. They're just races of beings that have already moved past the evolutionary stage that we're now in, so they're just helping us out a bit with some energy."

"You're kidding me," I said, not at all liking the way this conversation was going. "Are you telling me that Ma's teachings are based on information from little green men?"

"No, don't be silly," Lucy said. "People have such misunderstandings about aliens. Most of them look just like us. Well, actually more like Scandinavians, I guess. But they're not that different from us, really—just more evolved."

I stared at her. "And you know this how?"

She shrugged. "Through Ma."

I looked from her to Matt to Jeremy. They all seemed completely at peace with the idea that there were other-dimensional Norwegians transmitting energy to us on Earth through a hole in the sky over the mountains. My God, could that possibly be true?

Jeremy was watching me carefully, as though he could see my brain struggling to make sense out of all of this. "You know, Michelle, as you spend more time with Ma," he began, "you'll start to recognize that this planet is infinitely more complex than most of us realize. Most people are content to live out their lives within a narrow range of consciousness, letting other people decide for them what is and isn't real. But when you start opening up and expanding your mind, you can have experiences that are beyond the range of normal perception. Because Ma is so evolved, she's been in contact with these other races for many years. I know it seems hard to believe, since you're new and this is sort of an advanced teaching, but as your own perceptual filters start to open up, you'll get hip to it. Trust me."

He was watching me closely as he said this, and I felt myself grow uneasy under that penetrating gaze. What he was saying had a certain strange logic, but I wasn't at all sure I was ready to just accept the idea of aliens in my reality. It was true that Ma had already opened the door for me to some things that I wouldn't have believed just a few months ago, but this—well, it all just sounded so weird to me.

"So what's happening with that stir-fry?" Lucy asked. "I'm so hungry I'm about to fall over!"

I let myself be distracted from my discomfort by Jeremy serving up heaping plates of brown rice covered in a succulent and spicy stir-fry. As soon as the conversation turned back to more mundane matters, it almost felt like it had never happened. A part of me somewhere was still uncomfortable, but I ignored it and turned my attention to Lucy's lamentations of her troubles finding a job in a decent restaurant. By the time Matt started telling stories of hilarious stupidity at the rock gym, I'd forgotten all about it.

Jeremy and Lucy disappeared upstairs not long after Matt and I set about cleaning up from dinner. As we moved around each other in the small kitchen, I found my attraction to him growing. It was true, he was very different from the more career-driven types I'd dated in the past, but there was an honesty and a sweetness about him that was appealing. And, while he may not have been the most externally successful guy I'd ever met, he was clearly committed to walking the spiritual path, something which I was beginning to realize was much more important to me than an impressive business card.

He'd told me when we'd made plans for the evening that he had an early climbing date the next morning, so as soon as we were finished cleaning up, I made motions to be on my way. He offered to walk me out to my car.

As we reached my Honda, I turned to him.

"Well, thanks for dinner," I said. "I had a really great time."

He nodded. "Yeah, me, too," he replied, stuffing his hands into the pockets of his jeans.

We stood there silently for a moment, looking into each other's eyes. It was that moment of tension before the kiss, and I felt the butterflies swimming in my stomach.

But instead of kissing me, Matt looked away. There was a pause, then he cleared his throat and looked back at me. "Uh, so, listen, Michelle," he began softly. "I really like you a lot. But, uh, I'm kind of nervous about starting up anything new. I mean, I want to, but I haven't really had the greatest history with women, so I'm kind of cautious. You know?"

I didn't know, but I nodded as sympathetically as I could. Whatever he was trying to tell me was clearly difficult for him, and I was touched by his earnestness.

"I have this tendency to just sort of lose myself in new relationships," he continued. "In a not really healthy kind of way. You know how Ma talks about displacing your feelings for God into relationship?"

I nodded. Ma had spoken about that in depth at my first lecture, and Lucy and I had just listened to a tape on the subject.

"Yeah, well, I do that," he said. "And I've totally screwed things up with that, by having all these unrealistic expectations and everything. So I'm trying to do things differently now, in a more balanced kind of way. So I can still see the God in the other person, but not, like, give myself up to them."

I nodded again, surprised to hear almost the exact words I'd heard on the tape coming out of Matt's mouth.

"So I was wondering," he continued, looking down at the ground for a moment, then back up at me, "I was wondering if maybe we could just take it slow, like maybe hang out as friends first, and, you know, just take it slow?"

He phrased it as a question, but there was obviously only one answer I could give.

"Yeah, sure, Matt, of course," I nodded. "Taking it slow is probably really good for me, too."

He sighed, visibly relieved. "That's so cool, that you understand and all," he smiled, then leaned over and gave me a feather light kiss on the cheek.

As I made the short drive home, I considered that I was really lucky to have met someone who was really committed to being so conscious about relationships. So it was hard for me to understand why I also felt so crushingly disappointed.

I woke up the next morning with the day stretched emptily ahead of me. I knew Lucy wouldn't be over—she and Jeremy always spent Sundays together. I felt a pang of loneliness as I sat down to meditate.

An hour later, after making a meager breakfast consisting of my last remaining egg, I went to the grocery store to stock up. On my way home, I just missed the stoplight at Broadway. As I sat in my car, waiting for the green light, I looked up at the mountains in front of me. The brown peaks contrasted sharply with the infinite sky, and only a wisp of cloud here and there marred the perfect blue palette.

My eyes began scanning the sky above me, down towards the south end of the range, and then all the way up to where the mountains disappeared in the north. Nowhere did I see anything that looked like a portal.

The light changed and I drove forward. If it were visible, then everyone would know about it. So of course it wouldn't be visible to the naked eye. If there even was such a thing at all.

I pulled my car to a stop in front of my house. As I stepped out onto the curb, I paused for a moment, my eyes again taking in the rugged mountains and the sky above them. Despite having grown up in Colorado, I'd never spent much time in the mountains; my father was too busy to ever take us there except on the rare vacation. So the mountains had always seemed deeply mysterious to me. I was both thrilled and frightened by the stories I heard from friends about bears and mountain lions—exotic, dangerous animals so close to our doorstep, yet moving secretly through a world of their own.

I'd never seen a mountain lion, but I was pretty certain they really did exist. So I guessed maybe it was possible that there were other things in the mountains that I'd never seen either, like a portals or aliens.

I frowned at the mountains, not sure this line of reasoning made me feel any more comfortable. It was all just a little too unfamiliar for me to relax into. I reached in my car for the bag of groceries and pushed the whole idea out of my mind.

When I ran into Matt at the following Tuesday's lecture, I was at a loss as to how to behave. I would have known what to do if we were lovers, or what to do if he'd blown me off. But this sort of in-between thing, this place where we'd acknowledged our attractions but weren't acting on them, was very confusing to me.

He greeted me with a warm hug. We chatted briefly about something, I can't remember what. I was too distracted, trying to stem the undercurrent of longing that flowed through me as we spoke. I wanted us to be Lucy and Jeremy, snuggling in the back over the sound table.

By the time Ma began her lecture, I was feeling pretty depressed. Emotions swirled through me like lost children, each one searching for something to attach itself to, but finding nothing. I thought back about what Matt had said about displacing your feelings for God onto a relationship, and wondered if that's what I was trying to do with him. My feelings were certainly feeling displaced.

I looked up at Ma, who seemed particularly radiant as she spoke with infinite tenderness to a woman in the class who suffered from terrible anxiety attacks. It never ceased to amaze me how constant her affection for us was, no matter what we were going through. It was as though she had a limitless reservoir of love that she dispensed without prejudice to us all.

I wished that I could be that way. I wondered what it was like, to just love another person for who they were without wanting anything in return. It made me realize just how conditional my own love had been, always based on what I was getting from the other person, instead of what I could give them.

The awareness was a sobering one. I thought about Matt, realizing just how annoyed I was with him for not giving me the security of a familiar kind of attention. I felt suddenly grateful for his restraint, and also a real appreciation for his commitment and courage to do something different. As I sat there, watching Ma bathe us in the kind of love most people can only dream about, I vowed to make a practice of learning how to do that myself.

I woke up the next morning with an urge to paint. I did a brief meditation, then pulled out a canvas. I wanted to do a painting of Matt, to look at him with the detached eye of the artist as a way of helping myself see the magic in him as a person instead of just seeing what he could do for me.

I pulled up his face from my memory, letting my eyes wander over the lines and contours that composed it. He had a beautiful strong jaw line, and well-defined cheekbones lightly dotted with freckles. His nose was perhaps a tiny bit large for his face, but it had a nice, balanced shape. And then there were those lovely, wide set eyes, big and open, brown with just a hint of green.

I considered whether to portray him with razor stubble—he was haphazard about shaving, and was often a little fuzzy around the edges. But I decided against it. He did try to keep it smooth.

I knew from the start that I'd have the most fun painting his hair. It was longish and untamed, its natural wave defying any attempt to control it. He told me he'd been trying to grow it out for a while, but then it would reach that stage where it would get in his face while he was climbing, and he'd trim it back again. At the moment, though, it was on the longer side.

I stifled a desire to run my fingers through that hair, and turned my attention to finding the right shades of brown to portray it.

Later that day, I called Matt up at work and asked him if he'd be willing to have dinner with me. It was a warm summer evening, so we decided to meet early and see if we could get an outside table at one of the sushi restaurants on the mall.

Though it was just after five o'clock when we met, the outdoor patio was almost full. I looked over the collection of mostly young, mostly trendy people and was surprised to be reminded that Boulder contained many different worlds besides Ma's community.

A very thin, black-draped hostess seated us at the last remaining spot. The chairs were made of bright orange plastic; the table sparsely decorated with napkins, chopsticks and soy sauce. I felt oddly out of place, and was glad Matt was with me.

"So, listen, I have to tell you," I began as soon as the waitress had taken our order, "I've been having a hard time with the whole 'taking it slow' thing, because I've never done that before. I've always just dove in headfirst, and then tried to figure out what was going on later, you know?"

He nodded, his gaze intent and earnest.

"So this has been really strange, because I'm attracted to you, but I can't express it in any way that's familiar to me, so it's been really frustrating. But then, it's also been really great, because it's given me a chance to get in touch with my own neediness, and all the places where I want to use you to fill this hole inside of me, and do things other than just really love and appreciate the person that you are, you know?"

He laughed, nodding. "Boy, do I know."

"Yeah, I thought you would," I said, grateful for his understanding. "So I just had to thank you, because it would have been so easy for me to start this unconscious thing with you and make this big mess, and I'm really grateful that you were so clear and honest about where you were at, because, you know, I'm not sure it would have worked out so well otherwise."

He smiled and nodded again. "God, I'm so relieved to hear you say that. I was worried that you were just going to think I was some kind of nut-case."

I laughed. "Well, I sort of did, actually. But I'm not exactly perfect myself, so it's okay."

He grinned at me across the table. "Well, I guess that makes us a good match then, huh?"

"I guess so," I smiled. "Of course, that doesn't give me any better idea what I'm supposed to do with you."

"Yeah, well, there's that," he nodded, looking thoughtfully at a young couple who passed by, their fingers entwined. "I can't say that I really know myself, since this is new for me as well. But I think for me," he confessed with a tentative air, "the place where I tend to get in the biggest trouble is when it gets physical really fast. So that's why I want to start with more of a friend thing."

I considered this. "I think I know what you mean," I said. "But how are we supposed to do that? The friend thing, I mean."

He thought for a moment. "Well, uh, maybe we could start by seeing a movie. That shouldn't be too dangerous."

"Well, as long as it's not a tortured romance."

"Good point. Okay, how about a comedy?"

"You've got a deal," I said with a smile.

Seven

A few days later, Jeremy pulled me aside at the end of an evening and said that Ma was very interested in my web skills and wanted to set up a meeting between the three of us and Kali to find out exactly what I could do for them. I had to remind myself to breathe as he told me this—the chance to work closely with Ma on any kind of project was a decidedly rare honor.

Jeremy's invitation came at an interesting time, as I'd spent the last few days toying with the idea of getting out of web design altogether. Since breaking open my paints a few days earlier, I'd wanted to do nothing but sit in front of my easel. In addition to the painting of Matt, I'd started both the landscape and the nude that had been floating around inside my head for what seemed like forever, and I was experiencing a kind of deep satisfaction I hadn't felt in years.

While I knew that it was unlikely I'd ever be able to support myself as a full-time painter, I also knew that doing design work for others took just enough creative energy that I never had anything left over for my own artistic projects. I was wondering if my inability to find a job might be because I wasn't supposed to be working in web design any longer, and I'd spent much of my meditations the previous days wondering what else I could do for money that would leave my creative energies free for my own work.

So when Jeremy approached me, my gut reaction was to say no. But as I listened to him talk about what Ma was looking for, a battle began brewing inside me. Though I had zero desire to do any more design work, it was such a strange sign, being offered this opportunity right when I was thinking about quitting. Hardly anyone was ever offered the opportunity to work directly with Ma on a project. To be able to spend time with her like that would an amazing gift, and I began to wonder if my recent ideas about finding another kind of work might in some way be flawed.

A few days earlier, I'd listened to one of Ma's tapes in which she'd spoken about the importance of finding meaning in your work, no matter what you were doing. At the time I'd first heard it, I took it as support for the idea that any kind of job could work for me, and leaving web design was the right thing to do. As I considered Jeremy's offer, though, I began to wonder if maybe what I needed to do instead was embrace web design from a more spiritual perspective. Since I had always viewed my design work as an annoying distraction from my real artistic interests, I found myself wondering if God was giving me another opportunity to experience first hand that any work could be sacred work.

So I told Jeremy I'd help in whatever way I could.

I arrived at Ma's house a few days later more nervous than I'd been the first time I went there. Then, at least, I wasn't really expected to know anything. But this time, Ma would be evaluating me on an entirely different level. Though I had designed dozens of web sites, I was concerned about what her expectations were and whether I'd be able to meet them. Not to mention what she would think of me if she had the chance to work with me up close.

"Ma's just finishing up a meeting," Kali said in as she led me down the hall into the dining room-turned-conference space. "She should be done shortly."

I waited alone for about twenty minutes. The room was dominated by a large portrait photograph of Ma on the California coast, smiling peacefully as she overlooked the ocean. She was dressed in shimmering white, and looked so radiant she practically glowed.

Finally, Kali returned with Ma and Jeremy. Ma sat at the head of the elegant, frosted glass table and observed me thoughtfully for a moment before beginning. I took several deep breaths, trying to calm myself under her scrutiny.

"So, Michelle," she finally began, a warm smile on her face, "Jeremy tells me that you can make a web site for us."

"Ah, well, I hope I can," I replied. "Maybe you could tell me a little bit about what you want, and then I could let you know if I can do it for you."

Ma nodded and looked over at Kali.

"There are a number of things we're looking to accomplish with this site," Kali began with a self-important air. "Many people hear about Ma through word-of-mouth, but if they're not local, it's very hard for them to find out more information about her. So the first thing we would like it to do is provide information about Ma and her message."

I nodded, taking notes as she spoke.

"In addition, we'd like to start making some of Ma's taped lectures available for purchase online. Not all of them, of course," she added, "but some of the basic ones so people who can't come here right away can still hear her message."

"In addition to that, we'd also like the web site to serve as the central communication system for the community," Jeremy jumped in. "Given that half of our people are still in California, we need a more efficient communication medium. Ma wants to eliminate paper mailings and have everyone to be linked via e-mail and her site."

I paused for a moment. "But not everyone has a computer."

Ma looked at me with a focused gaze. "It will be necessary for them to get one, then. People often fight evolution, technological as well as spiritual. But I'm not willing to slow myself down for them at this point. We need to make use of the tools that God has made available to us. If they want to study with me, they'll have to catch up."

I was surprised at the intensity of her stance, but I didn't say anything.

"Some people have also requested that we make the lectures available as online audio files," Kali started up again, "which Ma thinks is a good idea."

As she continued outlining Ma's vision for the Internet, I found myself automatically calculating the hours it would take to build a site of such complexity. What she was talking about would be at least a five thousand dollar project. Between my credit card debt and my rapidly dwindling savings, it would be a huge help to my budget to have a freelance project like this.

"So, can you do it?" Kali asked when she was finished.

"Ah, yeah, I think so," I said, thinking as I nodded, my mind already considering how to best organize the various functions of the site. "It's a pretty complex project, but I think I can do most of it." I paused, knowing this was the point where I needed to negotiate my fee. Though I'd never had any problem with that before, I felt strangely uncomfortable asking them about money.

"Um, can you tell me what kind of a budget you have for the project?"

Jeremy and Kali exchanged glances.

"Actually, we are really looking for someone who can donate the work," Kali replied. "Jeremy mentioned that you weren't working now, that you might have the time. But if your situation is such that you're not in a position to do that, we'll need to find someone else."

"Oh!" I replied, caught in the sinking feeling that I'd just made a huge mistake. I knew most of Ma's staff were volunteers, but I hadn't expected they'd want me to work for free on this kind of a project.

"Oh, right, of course," I stuttered, trying to recover. I really needed the money, but I felt horribly audacious for even asking about it. I worried that I'd offended them, and I felt a sudden wave of panic that I might lose the opportunity to work closely with Ma.

"Yeah, I can donate my time, that's no problem," I hastily agreed. I tried to think of some way to cover my faux pas. "I meant that because that the site is so complex, there might be some things that need to be outsourced—like the shopping cart. Pre-built ones often offer a lot of useful features that I'm not able to code. What I meant is, is there a budget for things like that?"

"We probably can come up with a small budget," Kali said. "If you can get me the specifics, I'll let you know."

I nodded. "Okay."

There was a moment of awkward silence around the table. Finally, Ma spoke.

"How long do you think it will take make this site?"

"Well, it's hard to predict exactly, since these things often contain unexpected challenges. But if I work on it full-time, I'm guessing a month, maybe a little longer."

Ma sat silently as I replied, eyeing me with that gaze of hers. I felt certain she saw right through my song-and-dance about money, and was ashamed of my selfishness.

After a long moment of silence, she nodded. "Good. When can you start working on it?"

"Right away," I replied. We spent a few minutes working out a preliminary schedule, then Ma turned me over to Kali and Jeremy to come up with ideas for the initial site map. As soon she walked out of the room, I slumped in my chair in relief.

I phoned Lucy as soon as I got home.

"Well, what happened?" she said.

"I am now Ma's official web designer," I replied.

"Oh, my God, Michelle, that's awesome!"

"Yeah, I guess so," I said. "Although I kind of wish I was getting paid," I added.

"Nobody on Ma's staff gets paid."

"I know, but it's going to be a lot of work. I didn't realize they were going to want me to do it for free."

There was a long pause. "You've got to be kidding me," Lucy said. "Don't you realize what an unbelievable honor it is to even be asked to work for Ma? Who cares about money when you get to be in her presence like that?"

"I know, I know," I said. "Don't get me wrong, I'm really grateful for the opportunity. It will be really amazing to be able to be over there and see her every day. I'm just starting to run low on cash, that's all. It's sort of hard to work for free when you can't pay the rent."

"Tell me about it. But you know it's going to work out—volunteering for Ma is like the highest work you could do right now. Of course the universe will take care of you!"

"I hope so," I said, really wanting to believe her.

There was another pause. "You have no idea how lucky you are, do you? Not only does hardly anyone ever get asked to work for Ma," she continued, "it's like totally unheard of for someone so new to the group to get a job. Matt couldn't believe Ma was even considering you."

"Really?

"Really. Kali was with Ma for over five years before she got that job. But I of course raved about you to Jeremy, and I guess he believed me enough to go to bat for you with Ma."

"Wow. I had no idea. I guess I really owe you one."

"You bet you do, sister."

Apparently, there was some rare astrological alignment happening in about six weeks with which Ma wanted to time the launching of the site, so she wanted the whole thing done as quickly as possible. That was fine with me, since the sooner I got done, the sooner I'd be able to start a job that actually paid me. I was feeling better about the volunteer thing since talking with Lucy and realizing just how lucky I really was to have been given the position at all; in fact, I'd begun to think that maybe I hadn't gotten a job earlier precisely so I would be available for this one. And I figured that if I worked my butt off for the next month and really pushed the job search on the side, I could get a new position lined up to start soon as I finished with Ma's site. It would be tight, but it would beat sitting around waiting for the phone to ring.

My schedule changed radically then. After months of unlimited free time, I suddenly found myself working very,

very hard. In truth, it felt good to be back at work, to have some tangible project to focus on. I hadn't realized how much I'd missed having that kind of structure in my life, and I was glad to have a specific reason to get up in the morning.

In the beginning, the majority of my time was spent in Ma's office with Kali and Jeremy, working out design ideas and deciding how best to incorporate the various aspects of Ma's vision into the site. I was disappointed to discover that I'd do all the preliminary work with them, and only see Ma occasionally for design approval. Still, as the three of us sat around discussing which quotes to use and which aspects of Ma's message the site should focus on, I couldn't help feeling privileged to be able to work on such a spiritually important project. To be able to give back to Ma in some small way after all she was giving me was deeply satisfying.

While I should have been able to do much of the development work on my computer at home, Ma preferred to have me work in her office so she could keep an eye on things as they progressed. It was harder for me to do it that way, since I work better when I'm alone, but I didn't complain. The truth of it was, I loved being at Ma's house. Every time I walked in the front door, I felt as though I were stepping into a sanctuary. The building was filled with a light and peaceful energy I could never seem to get enough of. Waterfalls gurgled in nearly every room, and even the bathrooms were scented with rose incense. It opened the heart chakra, Ma said.

The office occupied the airy living room of her large home, and in addition to the constant presence of Kali, students were always coming and going to have sessions with Ma or return something to the tape library. Jeremy was often there as well, if not consulting with us on the site, then working on the tape library catalogue. Then there was Tony, who took care of Ma's yard and cleaned her house, and Susan and Shanti, who shared the job of shopping and cooking for Ma.

"Mmmm, that smells amazing!" I said to Shanti early one afternoon as she stood over a wok filled with leeks, garlic, chard, and mushrooms. "What are you making?"

"It's just a simple polenta dish," she said, feeding me a mushroom.

"Yum," I replied, savoring the earthy flavor. "Is Ma a vegetarian?" I asked as it dawned on me that I'd never seen anything other than vegetables prepared in the kitchen.

She nodded. "Almost vegan, actually. Meat is just too dense of a food for her."

"Huh," I said, poking through the cabinets for a tea mug. "I don't think I could last long without meat."

"I didn't used to think so, either," Shanti replied as she pulled a pan of neat polenta triangles out of the oven. "But the more I've opened up spiritually, the more I've been able to get my energy directly from God. I feel so much lighter, not eating all that dead animal flesh."

I thought guiltily about the roasted turkey sandwich in my bag. I definitely had a long way to go before I'd be able to give that up.

Just then, Susan came in with a new bag of groceries.

"What are you doing?" she said, looking into the wok. "Ma's not eating mushrooms anymore."

"Since when?" Shanti replied.

"A few days. The frequency's not working for her."

"Shit," Shanti said. "What the hell am I supposed to do with this?"

"Look, why don't you take a break," Susan replied. "I'll make her a new stir fry."

Shanti let out an irritated sigh and walked out the back door.

"Can you believe that?" Susan whispered to me as soon as she was out of earshot. "She knows Ma can feel the energy she puts into the food—she's going to get fired if she doesn't stop being so negative."

As Ma's office manager, Kali was the commander of mission control. In addition to handling all of Ma's finances and paperwork, she was also the gatekeeper, responsible for booking all of Ma's appointments. I hadn't spent much time working in the background before I realized that she was someone you did not want to piss off.

"That's the fourth time she's called this week," Kali complained as she slammed down the phone. "Doesn't she realize that Ma has more important things to tend to than her constant freak-outs?"

A moment later, Ma arrived to go over her schedule for the day with Kali.

"So, you've got three in-persons and a phone this afternoon," Kali began. "Also, Bonnie is trying to get another appointment, but I'm concerned that she's doing that dependent thing again. She's called four times this week."

"I see," Ma said. "Did you give her the homework I asked you to?"

"Yes, and she keeps telling me she can't do it without talking with you first. She's getting very pushy, and I don't think it's a good idea to encourage her in this."

Ma stared out the window for a few moments before replying. "When is my next opening?"

"You have a cancellation tomorrow, actually. But otherwise not for about two weeks."

"Book her an appointment in a month. Tell her in the meantime to write down everything that she wants to say to me. Have her make a long list, then call her three days before the appointment and have her review it to see how many of those things still matter to her. I expect she'll find the whole exercise quite enlightening."

After Ma left, I turned to Kali. "Do you get a lot of students like that?"

She rolled her eyes at me. "Enough. Most of them fall into one of two categories. Either they're desperately needy like Bonnie and constantly trying to leech energy from Ma, or they're so terrified of her they won't even talk to her at all. Most people have such weird perceptions of her, it's just really hard to deal with."

I thought about my own relationship with Ma, the mixture of adoration and fear. "It's hard, I think," I began tentatively.

"When you've never met anyone like her before, it's hard to know how to act."

"Well, yeah, at first, sure. You were nervous, but not ridiculous about it. That's normal. But now you can relate to her like a person, which is what she is. Some of these other people, though, they've been with her for years. You'd think they'd have figured it out by now."

My first big meeting with Ma came several days after I'd started. Kali, Jeremy and I had spent a lot of time experimenting with different design concepts, and we'd narrowed it down to one we all liked.

Jeremy and I were already waiting in the dining room when Ma swept in behind Kali. She was dressed in pinks, her loose silk dress accented with a deep rose scarf.

"So, what have you come up with?" Ma began.

I pulled out my sketches and a snapshot of a mock up I'd done for the color scheme. We'd settled on a celestial theme in shades of blue, silver and white.

"So, uh," I said, trying to stop my hands from shaking as I lay the sketches out for her, "we were thinking that we could use this basic color scheme for the site, that it would help create a soothing and opening atmosphere. This is an idea I had for the logo," I indicated a sketch of a diffuse galaxy, "and the basic site layout would look like this," I pointed to another piece of paper with thumbnails of each proposed page. "People would start here, and then be guided to follow a certain pathway through the pages. They can go anywhere, but new people will be funneled in this direction."

She looked intently at my sketches. Her salt-and-pepper hair was down, softly framing her face. She was beautiful and fierce, and I was terrified of what she would think.

After an eternity, she looked up and nodded. "Good. Let's get started."

Matt took me out to dinner to celebrate Ma's approval of my design. We went to an Italian place downtown with a sidewalk patio decorated by hanging flower baskets. The location offered an impressive panorama of the Flatiron mountains silhouette.

"Nice view," I said as the hostess seated us at an intimate table for two.

"I thought you might like that," he replied. "The food's not bad, either."

We ordered tapas and pasta, mostly vegetarian as was the custom in Ma's crowd. But I couldn't resist the salmon carpaccio. Though Matt initially said he wouldn't have any, I was secretly pleased to see his resolve break down when the small platter of paper-thin fish arrived.

"So what's it like, working in the presence of one of the greatest spiritual leaders of our time?" Matt asked as we finished off the appetizers.

"It's pretty amazing," I said.

"Do you get to see her often?"

"Um, not as much as I thought I might. She's usually in her room or with students in her office. But I do get to see her in the mornings when she goes over her schedule with Kali."

"So, what's she like? I mean, is she different than you'd expect?"

I considered this for a moment. "You know, she's really just like you'd think she'd be. She's always so calm, so serene. But she's also super-intense. Sometimes when she's in the office it's hard to concentrate, just her presence is so powerful. It's not what she says, but just how she is, I think." I looked at him with a shy smile. "Sometimes when she's there I'll just sit at the computer, pretending I'm working. But really I'm just sort of breathing in her energy, letting it wash over me. There's such a feeling of peace I get from being around her."

"That must be so incredible," he said.

"It is," I nodded. "I feel so lucky."

"You should. There are not a lot of people in this organization who get to go straight to the center of things like that."

"That's what Lucy said," I replied. "But I guess she just needed someone with my skills."

Matt looked at me thoughtfully for a moment. "There were others who could have done it," he said as he reached for the basket of bread and tore off a piece of foccacia. "In fact, there are some people in the group who are pretty upset about the fact that you were chosen."

I frowned at him. "Really? Who?"

"Not anyone you probably know," he said. "I just heard that this guy from California who's been with Ma since the beginning was going off about it. He does web design, I guess, and it was his idea that Ma build a site."

"So why didn't she let him do it?" I asked.

"Well, he's kind of a difficult guy, actually," Matt replied. "Personally, I wouldn't want to work with him, so I don't blame Ma for picking someone else. But since he's been here so long, some people think it's unfair."

I was growing progressively more uncomfortable with what he was telling me. I knew being picked to do this job was an honor, but I had kind of assumed it was because there was no one else around who could do the work. To find out that I'd been selected over at least one other person made me simultaneously happy I'd made the cut and worried about who else I'd pissed off. "But it was Ma's choice. She must have had a reason. Don't people trust her decisions?"

"Yeah, of course. But some people think that maybe you pushed her into it or something. They don't know you, of course, so it's easier to focus on that sort of thing than the very legitimate reasons why she didn't pick this other guy."

"So, what, they think I'm some kind of manipulator?" I asked, anger in my voice. I was really upset to hear that people I'd never even met were making judgments about me, and I hadn't even done anything. At least, I didn't think I had.

"Hey, don't worry about it," he said, reaching over to touch my arm. "You can't let people like that get to you. They have no idea what's really going on. I just wanted you to know, though, since there's a weekend coming up and you might run into some people who aren't very friendly. Just don't take it personally, that's all I'm saying."

There was concern in his eyes, and I felt myself relax a little under his touch. "It just seems so unfair," I said.

"Yeah, well," he shrugged, "one thing about groups like this is that you have people at all different kinds of evolutionary levels. Even though one of Ma's core teachings is about projection, people still do it all the time. The way you just showed up here and went straight to the center of things makes you more of a target, that's all."

I shook my head. "I can't believe other people are thinking about me that way," I said. It was a strange sensation, being the target of someone else's envy. Growing up, I'd always been the one in that role. I was the one who was making snide comments about the skinny girl with the perfect hair and the mother who showed up with cupcakes for the whole class on every holiday, the girl I desperately, desperately wanted to be.

I'd spent so many of my early years feeling inferior to other people, it was hard for me to believe that there was anything about me that another person might be envious of. But even as I was having that thought, I was flashing back to my first session with Ma, to the time when she told me I had more spiritual ability than many of her students combined. Maybe that had something to do with all of this. Did she pick me because of some higher spiritual ability I didn't even know about?

I knew there was no way to answer that question. I chided myself for even having the thought, since it was such an arrogant one. But deep inside myself, where no one else could see, I couldn't help being pleased.

The beginning work on Ma's web site went smoothly, and I was able to finish the first phase of design work a little ahead of schedule. I'd completed the home page and the basic template for the rest of the pages by the time Jeremy, Kali, Ma and I had our next meeting.

This time, we met in the office in front of my computer. Ma sat next to me and Kali and Jeremy stood behind us as I showed Ma the pages I'd created. I was particularly proud of the home page—underneath the celestial galaxy, a beautiful picture of Ma was surrounded by a soft blue empty space in which golden lines from her lectures would arise as if from nowhere, exist for a moment, and then fade back into nothingness.

"Didn't she do a great job on that?" Jeremy said as Ma observed my work.

She did not reply immediately. Instead, she leaned back in her chair, her eyes focused on the screen. My anxiety grew as she remained silent.

"This is all wrong," she began.

My heart sank.

To my surprise, Kali came to my rescue. "But I thought this is exactly what you wanted."

"Kali, you of all people should know the speed with which things in this universe change," she replied. "This is what we had decided upon, yes. But now that I see the site itself, I can see that it is all wrong."

Ma turned to me with her intense gaze, and I forced myself to meet it. "Let me be clear, Michelle. The quality of your work is obviously high. But this layout highlights a particular problem that has been growing here. Over the past few months, there has been a marked increase in the tendency people have to treat me as a guru. People are focusing on me instead of the God in themselves. This is natural, but I do not want to encourage it. This site should focus on the path and the teachings, not on me as the teacher. That picture is going to have to be removed and the layout re-done."

I let out a sigh of relief. I didn't want to have to re-do it, but I felt better knowing I hadn't just gotten the whole thing wrong.

"But Ma, none of us would be here if it weren't for you," Jeremy said. "We have to give them some idea of who you are."

"The small biography page we discussed will be sufficient. But the rest of the site is going to have to be re-worked. I want all references to me to be relegated to the back. This path is not about me."

Kali and Jeremy exchanged glances. "This is going to set our schedule way behind," Kali protested.

"Then we'll have to work harder to catch up. Michelle is clearly very skilled in her work, and I have great faith in her ability to meet this new challenge." She turned back to me. "You can make these changes, yes?"

"Um, of course," I nodded surprised by the depth of Ma's faith in me. I was determined not to let her down.

I found myself working a lot of late nights after that. Ma's rare astrological alignment showed no interest in re-arranging itself to accommodate our development problems. If we were going to make it on time, I was going to have to haul ass.

I called Matt to let him know I was going to have to cancel a movie date that we had. Between his early mornings and my late nights, there wasn't much opportunity for us to get together. He was pretty understanding about it, though. A month wasn't really all that long in the scheme of things, and he knew what I was doing was important.

In some ways it was easier working late, as most everyone was gone by seven and I could get more done when things quieted down. But it took forever to figure out how to incorporate all the changes Ma wanted made, and I often found myself feeling even more stressed than I did back when I had a real job.

One night around ten, when I'd been working unsuccessfully to figure out why a set of links weren't working, I gave up and went into the kitchen to make myself a cup of tea.

I filled the green enamel kettle with water and started rummaging around one of the heavy oak cabinets. There were no less than 30 different kinds of teas in there, both the standard Celestial Seasonings and a number of obscure Indian and Chinese teas I'd never seen before. I was so busy looking for the peach ginger I'd come to like that I nearly jumped out of my skin when Jeremy came up behind me.

"Sorry," he said, a grin on his face. "Didn't mean to startle you." His angelic blond hair was up in a ponytail, and I noticed for the first time he had a small, gold hoop in his left earlobe. His blue silk shirt seemed to make his eyes even more impossibly blue than normal.

I rested a hand on my still pounding heart and took a deep breath. "I had no idea anyone else was still here."

"I wasn't planning on staying this late myself. But I was about to leave when I found a whole series of tapes that had been completely mislabeled. I've spent the last four hours trying to sort the whole bloody mess out."

"Are you finished?"

"Just about. But I needed some sustenance," he said, the mischievous grin returning to his face. As I watched, he stretched on his toes and began poking around in the back corner of one of the cabinets over the fridge until he emerged with a bar of chocolate.

"Hey, what's that doing here?"

"It's Ma's secret stash," he replied, breaking off a chunk and handing it to me.

"But Ma doesn't eat chocolate," I said.

"Not that you'd ever know," he replied, winking at me.

"Is that the kind of thing you learn after you've been studying with her for a while?" I asked as the rich flavor danced on my tongue.

"Yes, this is a part of a very advanced teaching," he said with mock solemnity. "I suggest you keep it strictly between us."

I smiled as I watched him wrap the bar back up and hide it in the back of the cabinet. In the weeks we'd been working together, I'd come to really appreciate this playful side of him.

"So how long have you been here, anyway?" I asked as I pulled myself up to sitting on the counter while I waited for my water to boil.

"'Bout seven years, I think," he said, pausing to remember. "No, eight—I met Ma in '97."

"How'd you find her?"

"I was visiting friends in California, some people I'd lived with in India. They were the ones who took me to meet Ma."

"You lived in India?" My eyes widened.

He nodded. "There was a spiritual master there I went to study with—Sri Ashimanti—do you know him?"

I shook my head.

"Amazing spiritual master. I lived in his ashram for several years."

"That's incredible," I replied, wishing my own life were even half so interesting. "Was it hard? Living in India, I mean?"

"At first it was kind of hard. In the ashram it was very monastic; you had to divest yourself of all your Western desires. But you get used to it. There's something very soothing about living without attachment to material things."

"I can't even imagine. So you just gave up your whole life to be there?"

He nodded. "It's what the master required of his students. I went back to England once, to empty out my flat and such. That was the hardest part, actually. I was so clear about what I was doing, but my parents thought I'd gone insane. They hired people to try to keep me from going back to the airport."

"You're kidding! They tried to have you kidnapped?"

"They wouldn't have called it that, of course," he said with a wry smile. "They claimed they were just trying to help me, get me back on track, that sort of thing. But the reality of it was that they were embarrassed by me. My parents are very socially conscious people," he added, "living their lives based on what the neighbors think. The fact that I chose to study music instead of becoming a barrister was horrifying enough. When I showed up on their doorstep wearing Hindu robes, well, I think it was all just a bit much for them."

I shook my head, just staring at him. He was unquestionably one of the most fascinating people I had ever met.

One day, as I was working on the revision of Ma's biography page, Kali and Ma were having a scheduling meeting in the office, planning the workshops for the upcoming quarter.

"Listen, there's one other thing," Kali began. "The Connors are at it again."

Ma raised an eyebrow. "Oh, really? What have they done this time?"

"It's another letter. They're threatening to call the police if anyone parks in front of their house."

"Interesting," Ma said, appearing somewhat bored by the subject. "Do they have any legal right to prevent our students from parking on a public street?"

"Well, technically, no. But it does get a little tight out there on workshop weekends, and if a student parks too close to their driveway, they could have that person towed."

"Ah, they are such masters of projection. It's too bad they have to fight our presence instead of recognizing the opportunity that God has given them by having us move in down the street." She paused for a moment, then shifted into a more businesslike gear. "Make an announcement at the next couple of meetings about the situation and warn people not to park too close. Tell them also to bathe the house in light—God knows they could use it."

Kali laughed and nodded.

As soon as Ma left, I turned to her. "What was that all about?"

"Just these bonehead neighbors," Kali said. "You know the old guy and his wife in the ugly green house?

I considered for a moment, suddenly remembering an elderly couple I'd seen gardening in front of a rather dated, olive-colored ranch house. "Oh, right."

"They're just really tweaked by the fact that we're here. I think the collective energy of this place makes it a lot harder for them to stay in denial, so they're just hassling us. It's a pain, really, but what can you do? Some people are always going to be threatened by our freedom."

"Aren't you done yet?" Lucy asked as she threw her Chinese silk bag onto the green Papasan chair nestled in the corner of my apartment. She'd come by to pick me up for dinner, but I was still working on yet another revision of the home page design that Ma wanted to see the next day.

"No," I said, leaning back and letting out a sigh. "Ma called me with some last minute changes, so I'm probably going to be up most of the night. I tried to call you," I added, "but your cell wasn't on."

"I forgot it at home. Well, look, even if you're going to be working all night, you've got to eat, right?"

"Yeah, I guess," I mumbled, staring at the screen in front of me, "but I'm not going to be good company, Lucy, really. I'm too distracted."

She nodded. "Yeah, okay," she said, flopping onto my bed. "I was just hoping you'd be able to take a break since I'm not going to get a chance to see much of you for a while."

I looked up. "What are you talking about?"

"I got a job."

"That's great!" I replied, suddenly recalling with a burst of anxiety that I'd done nothing about finding a job myself since I started at Ma's. But I reminded myself that Lucy's situation was much worse than mine. She'd had hardly any money at all when she moved up here, and she'd been living off of her credit cards for over a month. "You must be so relieved. Where will you be working?"

"Full Moon Grill. You know, that place by McGuckin's?"

"That's a good place, isn't it? I've heard it's pricey."

"Yeah, the money should be good," she said with a shrug, "but I have to work Friday through Tuesday nights. I'm not going to be able to attend any of the lectures, and I'll probably miss most of the workshops unless I can find someone to cover my shift. I'm so broke right now I can't afford to let anyone do that anyway, so with you working days..."

My mouth dropped open. "You're kidding! You couldn't even get Tuesdays off?"

She shook her head. "They would only take me if I agreed to work those five nights. I'm so desperate I felt like I didn't have any choice."

"But Luce," I said, "you can't just not come to Ma's classes. This is the most important thing in your life! Think how much you'll be missing out on if you just stop coming."

"Tell me about it. I don't know when I'm even going to be able to see Jeremy," she said, worry creasing her brow. "I'm just hoping after I've worked there a couple of months I can make some changes—get lecture nights off and pick up some lunches instead. But for now, I'm going to have to deal." She looked down, playing with the lace on the bottom of her peach blouse. "I guess it will be a good opportunity for me to practice the teachings in real life," she said, offering half a smile.

"Well, yeah, maybe, but how are you supposed to be able to do that if you don't have Ma's support at the same time?" The idea of not being able to see Ma was really disturbing to me. Ma had been such a stabilizing force for Lucy, I was worried about what might happen to her if she stopped coming to the lectures for any length of time. "I mean, come on, Lucy, you and I are about as new to this thing as you can be. I really don't think it's a good idea for you to just cut yourself off from things like that right now."

Lucy frowned at me. "You're acting like I have a choice, Michelle," she said. "I've already maxed out two of my credit cards and if I don't start bringing in some money soon, I'm not even going to be able to buy food."

I stared at her, still convinced she was doing the wrong thing. "But what about what you said to me earlier when I took this job for Ma? You were the one who told me that the more you commit to your path, the better things work out. Don't you believe that any more?"

She let out a sigh and looked away from me out the window. "I'd still like to believe that, Michelle. But unfortunately, that's not a belief that's going to pay my rent."

At the next lecture, I missed Lucy a lot. Though there was a certain superficial hugginess amongst members of Ma's group, and I'd met a bunch of new people working for Ma, I hadn't really gotten close to anyone besides Matt, Jeremy and Kali. As Jeremy was tied up on the soundboard, Matt was working late, and Kali often didn't come to the weeknight lectures, I felt strangely alone.

During the question-and-answer period, a worn, middle-aged woman in a frumpy blouse and gray skirt raised her hand.

"I don't know what to do anymore, Ma," she began, clearly on the edge of tears. "I want so badly to study with you and come to your workshops, and I've tried so hard to save my money and make the time, but every time I get close, something happens. First my son developed this reading problem and needed all this extra vision care and then my mother got sick and I had to go back to Ohio and take care of her and whenever I get a bunch of money saved something just seems to come up and then I can't afford to come. I just don't know what to do any more," she finished with a choked sigh.

Ma sat silently for a moment, looking at the woman with a penetrating gaze. "You don't want it badly enough, Kathy," she began. "I know you think you do, but you are allowing your life to get in your way. If you were truly committed to walking the path that God has laid out for you, then nothing, I mean nothing, would get in your way. As it stands, you use the people in your life as an excuse not to follow your own path. And until you make a deeper commitment to yourself, there will always be something to distract you."

Ma got up then and walked towards the front of the stage. "This is a problem I am seeing more and more of," she began again. "Things are heating up, getting more intense, and people are flinching. You are giving into your fears instead of rising to the challenge. Money, jobs, family—these are all just excuses that you are using to avoid taking the next step. But you must remember—the only person you truly need to answer to is God. If you are letting these other things get in the way, you need to ask yourself why and re-evaluate your priorities. Remember, evolution is not going to wait for those who are dilly-dallying around."

I caught my breath. This was exactly what I was worried about with Lucy, but it was disheartening to hear Ma say it out loud. I didn't want to believe that Lucy hadn't been able to get a job that would allow her to be here because her commitment wasn't strong enough. She'd been so dedicated in her devotion to Ma and this path, and I wouldn't even be here without her. But really, it was the only thing that made sense. There was no reason why she couldn't have gotten a job with a better schedule, even if she had to go to Denver to do it. What Ma was saying had to be true.

At the end of the lecture, I walked up to Jeremy.

"Can I talk to you for a sec?"

"Sure, Luv, what's up?" he replied as he set down the tape he was holding and focused his attention on me.

"I hate to say this, but I'm worried about Lucy," I said.

He nodded, a grave look in his eyes. "I know. I am too."

"What can we do, Jeremy? I tried to tell her she was making a mistake, but she wouldn't listen to me."

He let out a deep sigh. "She didn't want to listen to me, either. I tried to talk her into taking her old job back, but she said she couldn't, they'd already replaced her or something. She got quite snippy with me, actually, so I think it might be best to just leave it be for a while. I'm sure she'll realize the mistake she's made soon enough."

"I just hate to see her go through that," I said.

"Me too. But you have to let people have their lessons, Michelle," he said, gently placing a hand on my shoulder. "All we can really do is send her light. You and I need to accept that."

His hand on my shoulder felt reassuring, and I nodded. It seemed like he was right—it was her choice, and there was nothing we could really do. But I still felt uncomfortable, just letting her leave like that. I really hoped she wouldn't be gone long.

"Michelle, it's me," my Dad's voice announced on my answering machine. "Your brother's home and I want you to come for dinner. Thursday." As always, a command, not a request.

The next day, I avoided putting off calling my father as long as possible. I wasn't going to go, and I knew he would throw a fit.

"Hey, Kali?" I asked.

"Hmm?" she replied, her head bent over the books for the Seminar Series.

"Do your parents know about Ma?"

She looked up from her papers. "My mom does. My dad died before I got involved. Why?"

"What does she think about all of this?"

She shrugged. "She was kind of worried about it at first, but now she's used to it. Now that she knows I'm not going to shave my head or something like that. Why do you ask?"

"My dad's an atheist," I said, letting out a sigh. "There's no way he would ever understand this. He wants me to come for dinner, but I don't want to go. I just don't even know what I would say to him."

"You should go anyway," I heard Ma's voice command from behind me. I jumped in surprise, not having heard her walk up. "The best way to let others know about the power of God is to live it yourself," she continued. "If he sees you, he will understand."

"I find that very hard to believe."

She smiled at me. "He may not admit it, that's true. But he'll be affected in spite of himself." She paused then, watching me for a moment. "But what you need to learn, Michelle, is that it doesn't matter if he believes you or not. Your job is to live your truth, no matter what anyone around you thinks. This will be a very good opportunity for you to do just that."

In spite of my better judgment, on Thursday afternoon I fought my way through rush hour traffic to the small suburb southwest of Denver where my father still lived. Traffic was so bad it took me almost two hours to get there, and I was so agitated when I arrived that I had to sit in my car for five minutes just to give myself a chance to calm down.

I looked up at the dated ranch house where I'd grown up. The faded brick walls stood apathetically where I remembered them, holding together a motley collection of mostly unhappy stories. I cringed involuntarily, steeling myself before going in.

Danny was sitting on the couch, his feet up in front of the TV. It had been almost three years since I'd last seen him, and I was shocked at how he'd aged. Thin lines had begun to form on his weary face; his skin was pallid. Danny had always been on the skinny side, but now his collarbones poked through his ragged AC/DC T-shirt like he was some kind of Auschwitz survivor. Twenty-four, going on ninety.

"Hey," I said.

"Hey," he replied without looking up from the soccer game he was watching.

"Dad here?"

"He went out to get some bread. Said he'd be back soon."

I sat down on the overstuffed gray recliner that was my dad's official chair and looked at Danny across the miles of misery that filled our tiny living room. Our mother had died of complications from his very premature birth, a fact he'd begun coping with via drugs before he was even out of grade school.

"So, you're staying here for a while?" I asked.

"Only as long as I have to."

I nodded. I wouldn't want to live there either.

"When did you get here?"

"Week ago."

"How was rehab?"

"It was okay."

I waited for him to continue, but he didn't. I leaned back in my dad's chair with a heavy sigh. Danny and I had gotten along okay until he turned six, when my dad decided I was old enough to watch him after school. I resented having to come straight home every to take care of him, even more so because Danny was incredibly skilled at pushing my buttons and did everything he could to annoy me. At first he'd just do little things, like taking my underwear out of my dresser and wearing it on his head. But he got meaner as he got older, and one time caused a huge fight between me and my best friend when he lied and told her he'd seen me kissing her boyfriend. Our relationship really polarized after that. I found myself yelling at him almost constantly, but he knew Dad hadn't given me any real authority, and I was totally unable to control him. The first time I found pot in Danny's room, my father blamed me for not taking better care of him.

The game broke for a commercial, and Danny looked up at me for the first time. "Why'd you move to Boulder?"

I debated how much I should tell him. As I looked at him, I was surprised to see a genuine curiosity in his weary eyes. For a moment it reminded me of when he was really young, before he'd even started school. Every day when I'd come home he'd ask me what I'd done that day, and then he would spend his afternoon playing it out. There was a time, once, when he wanted to be just like me.

"I found a spiritual teacher up there."

He snorted. "You're kidding."

"No, I'm not. My life was falling apart, and she's been helping me put it together again."

"Shit. My sister, the Jesus freak."

"It's got nothing to do with Jesus," I said irritably. "It's about connecting with God from the inside."

"Oh, yeah, Him," Danny said with a laugh, taking a sip of Coke from a dented can next to him.

"You don't believe in God anymore?" I knew he had once, that one of his Mexican nannies had made a point of taking him to church behind my father's back. I'd come home from school one time when he was about four, and he'd ask me if I'd seen Jesus there.

"Why should I?"

"It couldn't hurt, Danny."

He snorted again. "Yeah, right."

"I don't know, Danny, I just thought, you know, at this time when you're sort of in transition, connecting with something spiritual might be sort of helpful."

"Oh, give it a rest, will ya? I stopped believing in God the night I nearly froze to death in a Five-Points alley. You know why? Because I asked for help that night, and I didn't get it. So if there is a God, he can go fuck Himself for all I care."

The image of him curled up against the pavement behind a

Dumpster, half-frozen, tightened itself around my throat, choking off anything I might say in reply. I stared at the worn, gray carpeting. I wished Ma were there.

"Look, just forget it," I said. "And don't say anything to Dad —he doesn't know."

"Yeah, whatever," he said, turning his attention back to the game.

"You're late," my dad said as he walked in the door a few moments later.

"There was a lot of traffic. Rush hour."

"Come help me in the kitchen."

I let out a sigh and followed him. He turned on the oven and took a long loaf of frozen garlic bread out of its wrapper and placed it on the rack. A light green glass bowl that was older than I was sat on the counter, full of Albertson's potato salad. From the fridge he pulled out a plate filled with lamb chops, a food I'd disliked since I was a kid.

"You know I don't like lamb, Dad."

"You can eat it for one night. It's not going to kill you. Go set the table."

I knew there was no point in arguing. I would eat three bites of the gristly meat, then he would yell at me for wasting food. God, why did I even come?

I grabbed plates and silverware and walked into the dining room. A corner of the gray wallpaper was peeling; heavy blue drapes blocked out the light from the only window. My father never opened them because he didn't want the sun to fade the wood of the table he'd gotten from his mother, a heavy, dark thing that was our only antique. I pulled three cloth placemats out of the cabinet, the same blue and gray ones we'd eaten off of when I was growing up.

I heard the screen door slam as my father took the chops out to the grill. I put three place settings at one end of the table. It was a table for eight, and the long expanse of it stretched away from the plates huddled at one end. When I was a kid, I sometimes had the fantasy that if I just set one more place setting, my mother would come. I'd tried it once, but my father had exploded. He screamed at me to get rid of it so loudly and for so long that when I took the extra plate back into the kitchen, I was trembling so hard that I dropped it. The plate shattered, covering the floor with almost invisible shards that for weeks afterwards cut into my feet whenever I went into the kitchen.

"Okay, let's eat," my father said when he returned a few moments later with a plate full of blackened meat. Danny got up, turning off the television set with obvious reluctance. We each took our places, the same ones we had sat in for the last twenty-four years.

I had not even had a chance to put anything on my plate before my father started in.

"Have you gotten a job yet?"

"Yes, I have," I replied, my voice weary, but grateful to at least have an answer.

"Where?"

"It's a freelance position with an educational organization." The fact that it didn't pay anything was a detail I kept to myself.

"Well, how long is that going to last? There's no security in freelance work, you know."

"Yes, Dad, I know that. I just took it until a more permanent position comes along."

"I can't believe you haven't gotten a job yet. You've been out of work for months!"

"Me and thousands of other tech people, Dad. It's a recession, remember?"

"Well, there's got to be something."

I looked over at Danny. He was shoveling food into his mouth, his head down. I was on my own.

"I don't know, I'm kind of burned out on web design anyway," I said. "I might start looking for something else."

"Like what?" my Dad demanded, looking up mid-cut.

"I don't know, something less stressful. Something that leaves me more time to paint."

"You're not still wasting time on that, are you?"

"I happen to love it, Dad. It's not a waste of time."

"But you're not even that good."

His words struck me in the stomach, and I thought for a moment I might throw up. It wasn't the first time I'd heard him say that, but I was surprised at how painful it still was. Out of the corner of my eye, I saw Danny looking at me, an 'I can't believe you even went there' look on his face.

"Well, it's nice of you to be so supportive," I said. "Look, I've got an early meeting tomorrow so I really should go," I continued, pushing my chair back and standing up.

"But it's not even eight o'clock! You haven't even touched your food."

"I'm not hungry. Nice to see you Danny," I said, turning to my brother. "Good luck with everything, okay?"

He nodded, a prisoner's smile on his face.

"I go to all this trouble, the least you can do is stay for a few minutes."

"I'm sorry, Dad. I just can't."

I was shaking by the time I got into my car. I couldn't believe he could still get to me that way. If Ma was right and the evening was a test, I was pretty sure I hadn't passed.

Eight

I awoke groggy on Friday morning. The cumulative tiredness of my late nights on the computer was starting to catch up with me. I glanced at the clock, sitting up with a start as I realized I had a meeting with Ma and Kali in a half an hour.

As I bolted out of bed, my eyes fell briefly on the unfinished painting of Matt propped up in the corner of my studio.

I remembered then that he'd left early this morning for a ten-day climbing trip in Wyoming. Since our last dinner, we'd only seen each other in passing at Ma's classes, but I'd promised to call him before he left. A promise, I realized with frustration as I pulled on my jeans, I had failed to keep.

That Friday was the start of a Seminar Series weekend. I'd been to one other one before, and at first, it hadn't seemed all that different from the regular workshops. But Jeremy assured me that it was—because the level of the student's commitment was so much higher, Ma could magnify the energy in a way that the regular group would never be able to handle.

I was working in the office all the way up until the start of the lecture on Friday night. Ma had changed her mind about using a pre-made shopping cart for the online store because she didn't like the layout of the various ones I'd showed her, so I'd suddenly found myself having to build one from scratch. I was so wound up in the web project that I debated skipping the lecture altogether, but then my computer crashed at exactly seven o'clock. I decided it was an omen and packed up my things for the weekend.

The meditation had already started, so I slipped into the back of the room as quietly as possible. Jeremy flashed me a smile as I took a seat in the back.

I settled into my cushion, too tired to maintain any semblance of good meditation posture. My stomach grumbled, reminding me irritably that I had once again forgotten to eat dinner.

When the gong rang at the end of the meditation, I awoke with a start.

"Welcome back," Ma began, smiling her radiant smile.

"We are going to begin this weekend with a koan. Though you've made a great deal of progress over the last few months, I have begun to sense a growing thread of resistance within the group. Of course, this is natural," she said, a knowing smile playing about her lips. "If spiritual growth were that easy, then everyone would be doing it."

A murmur of laughter moved through the crowd.

"So, resistance is natural, but not ultimately desirable. The best time to address it is early, when the plant is still small and its roots are not deep. So, that is what we will be focusing on this weekend—weeding out your resistance.

"As you are meditating this weekend, I'd like you to ask yourself the following question: what is the biggest obstacle standing between you and God?" She paused then, surveying the crowd carefully.

"Now, as you contemplate this, be aware that your mind may try to trick you. You may come up with a perfectly logical sounding answer that is nothing more than a mask for the real issue. Do not let yourselves be fooled by the first easy answer. We will spend a lot of time in meditation this weekend so that you can thoroughly address this question. Remember, you want to go deep, to the root."

As we settled into another meditation, I could already feel the question working its way uncomfortably through my mind. Though I'd listened to every tape I could get my hands on, and

I'd been working closely with Ma herself for almost a month, over the past few weeks I'd begun to experience some doubts about my success in the whole "connecting with God" department. I'd started out early with an experience Ma described as a "spiritual awakening," and had come to find meditation to be a useful and therapeutic tool, but the reality was that I didn't really feel any more connected to God now than I had when I'd begun all this a few months ago.

I shifted around on my cushion, trying unsuccessfully to find a more comfortable position. When I'd started my journey with Ma, I assumed that I'd simply follow her instructions and my own personal God connection would follow. But that didn't seem to be happening.

The insecurity about all of this I'd been trying to ignore pushed its way insistently forward in my mind. A few weeks ago, I'd thought about asking Kali or Jeremy how they experienced God, just to give myself some better idea of what it was I was supposed to be looking for. But I'd stopped myself. Ma said other people's experiences don't matter, because each person connects with God in their own way. Besides that, I was afraid of admitting to them that I didn't seem to be discovering it on my own.

I returned to the workshop on Saturday morning feeling vaguely depressed. Ma had spoken before about the fact that finding connection with God is not easy, because in order to do so, we have to let go of everything that is comforting and familiar. Even though the direct experience of God is the most unimaginable bliss possible, she said, we fight it because we are afraid of the unknown. But as I settled into my cushion, I found little comfort in the idea that my own difficulties were common ones.

I was tired, and I had a hard time focusing as I sat. Images drifted in and out of my mind, and more than once I started to fall asleep.

At one point, a memory of the Catholic next-door neighbors I hadn't thought about in at least a decade popped into my head. The family had four daughters, clean-cut girls who would put on frilly dresses every Sunday morning and head off to church. I would watch them from my living room window, wondering about the mysteries they were going off to explore.

One time I got up the courage to ask one of the kids about it, a girl who was a few years younger than me. She told me that they were worshiping God, something everyone had to do if you didn't want bad things to happen to you.

Frightened, I asked my father if that was true. He scoffed at what he referred to as "their superstition," and told me in no uncertain terms that there was no God and I shouldn't waste my time even thinking about it.

I hadn't believed him. Though I had never been inside of a church, there were four of them within a two mile radius of my house. It just didn't seem right, that all the people who filled up those buildings each Sunday were wrong. It just seemed like there had to be something behind all of this, even if I didn't know what it was.

One day, after my father had screamed at me yet again for failing to clean the house, I started praying. I didn't know the right way to pray, so I did so silently inside my head, hoping my raw pleadings would find their way to God somehow. But if they did, I never knew about it—because nothing really changed. Eventually, I stopped trying.

An image of Danny flashed inside my mind. *I asked for help, and I didn't get it.* I shuddered, knowing I'd thought the same thing.

It hit me then, a wave of anger more intense than any I'd ever felt before. Where the hell had God been for Danny that night? And where the hell had He been for me, my whole goddamned life?

The rage that washed through me in that moment was so powerful I thought I might explode. My jaw tightened and my fists clenched involuntarily as the red-hot surge of energy pulsed through my entire body. I knew then that I didn't want to connect with God because I was furious at Him. Furious at him for having taken my mother, for having left me to fend for myself with my father, and for never, ever, having been there in my life.

I did not explode from the force of my rage, but I did begin to shake uncontrollably. Tears began pouring down my face, and I fought for breath. I knew the others could hear me in the silent room, but I was too consumed to care.

I pulled my knees tightly to my chest and began rocking back and forth. It was the way I'd soothed myself when I was a child, hidden in my room. I cried thousands of tears, one for every day I'd ever felt alone.

Eventually, the wave of emotion passed. I just sat there, spent, rocking myself quietly. When Jeremy rang the gong for lunch, I felt empty inside, save for a deep ache in my heart.

A few people glanced over at me with concern as they were leaving the room, but I had no desire to talk to anyone. I felt vaguely nauseous, almost like I had motion sickness. I left my lunch behind and took a long walk down the road to the reservoir. The sun shone brilliantly overhead in the flawless Colorado sky; the water shimmered with a sapphire glow. It was so beautiful I had to stop, to breathe in the rich summer air as deeply as I could.

I felt better when I returned to the sanctuary room. I was exhausted, but calm. I settled sleepily onto my cushion, where my thoughts slowly began wandering back the more mundane issues of my life. Instead of locking onto them as I normally did, however, I felt content to just let them float in and out of my mind.

As the afternoon progressed, there began to be more and more space between my thoughts. It was as though my mind was slowing down, preparing itself to turn off. In the widening space between each thought, a quiet emptiness began to grow.

I began to notice a sensation of falling. It was an odd feeling, like I was slipping down a deep tunnel. But for some reason, I was completely unafraid. It was a gentle fall, as though I was buoyed by a force I couldn't see.

As I fell, I began to feel a sense of dissolving. My edges started to blur like they might in a water color painting, lines of color running loose from their previous confines until what I traditionally thought of as me had simply melted away, and in its place there was only pure energy, a ball of shimmering light.

Eventually, the sensation of falling was replaced by the sensation of growing. The light I had become began expanding like a balloon, slowly at first, but then much more rapidly as it moved out past my sense of who I was, the room I'd been in, the planet I lived on and into the universe.

As I grew, I felt uplifted, my heart soaring with a sense of freedom I'd never imagined. Released from the confines of my normal identity, I felt entwined with the pure energy of the universe. As my heart sang out in bliss, I found myself bathed in a cradle of pure love.

The love I felt wrapped itself around and through me at the same time, permeating every breath of my existence. It was then that I knew that I was not alone. Every doubt I'd ever had about my worth or value was totally erased. I knew beyond question that I was loved and adored exactly as I was. It was the most exquisite, wonderful sensation I had ever experienced.

I don't know how long I floated there, basking in that love. I only knew that at some point I began to be aware of my physical body, of the room I'd been in, of the sound of people stirring around me.

It was hard to bring my focus back to the room. When I finally opened my eyes, all I could see was Ma beaming at me, her hands pressed together in prayer, tears at the edge of her eyes.

Ma was apparently not the only one who was watching me. All around me, people were looking at me with a mixture of confusion and amazement.

"Well," Ma said to me, "how do you feel?"

I opened my mouth, but the only sound that came out was a spontaneous giggle.

Ma nodded. "I know just what you mean. Isn't it marvelous?"

I nodded, a wide smile on my face.

Ma looked up from me, then back out at the room. "So you see," she began forcefully, "what is possible when you allow yourself to truly surrender. Michelle has been studying with me only a few short months, yet her commitment has allowed her to have an experience that many of you have been seeking for years. Remember this, the next time you find yourself thinking it takes time. It does not take time. It takes only commitment and courage."

"What happened to her?" interrupted a wiry man near the door. "Is she enlightened?"

"No, she's not enlightened," Ma said, looking back over at me with the intent gaze I'd seen her use when reading someone's energy field. "But she has taken the first step. She'll still have to choose, of course," she paused, "but she's on the path."

It was strange being talked about like I wasn't there. But in many ways, I wasn't. Part of me was still out there, floating in that love. But another part of me was in here, in the room, in the man who was asking Ma that question. I could feel his envy, and his anger at Ma for making such a show of me. I wanted him to know that what happened to me had absolutely nothing to do with him, that his path would take him exactly where he needed to go at exactly the right time. But somehow, I also knew he wouldn't want to hear that.

Ma fielded a few more questions before ending the day with a closing meditation. As people gathered their things together and began filing out, I sat on my cushion, just breathing. The feeling of ecstasy was a little muted now, but a relaxed bliss permeated every cell I had. I felt grounded, centered, and profoundly at peace.

Jeremy came up from behind me and knelt down to give me a hug. All of my senses were still heightened, and the feeling of his body against mine was utterly exquisite.

"Hey, congratulations," he gushed as we pulled apart a moment later. "I was watching you from the back of the room —you were lit up like a Christmas tree."

I smiled. "It's pretty great," I said. "I had no idea I could feel like this."

"So tell me what happened," he said, his eyes hungry with curiosity.

"I don't know, really. It was kind of a rough morning. I became aware of how much anger I had towards God, how abandoned I felt with my mother's death and all. It was really hard, but after lunch, I just kind of let go of the whole thing. The next thing I knew, I was just...it was just all love." I couldn't help smiling as I said it. I knew it sounded cliché, but it was absolutely true.

"Outrageous," he nodded, new appreciation in his eyes. "That is just so incredibly cool."

The sensation of deep peace stayed with me all throughout the remainder of the workshop. I felt completely impermeable —absolutely nothing seemed to bother me. It was an amazing contrast with how I had lived every day of my life prior to that point. The anxiety and tension I had assumed were the natural background music of being human were simply gone. I felt like I had been given the most precious gift in the world, and I was awash in gratitude to Ma for helping me find it.

She was already in the office when I arrived on Monday morning. She beamed at me as I walked in.

"How are you feeling?" she asked.

I shrugged and smiled. "Perfect. I've never felt this peaceful in my whole life."

"You are doing a good job of integrating," she nodded as she surveyed my field. "I am glad to see that your mind is adjusting well." She paused, looking at me again.

"You've made a great step, Michelle, and it's quite profound. I have to warn you, however," she added, the tone of her voice dropping, "that with increased light inevitably comes increased darkness. You are experiencing great bliss now, but you must become vigilant. The darkness will be looking for any way it can to rein you back in."

I stared at her. The feeling of peace in my body was so strong I couldn't for the life of me imagine what she was talking about.

"I know this does not make sense to you now," she said, a serious look flashing quickly across her face. "But I advise you to be careful. The dark side in you will get stronger. If you are not paying attention, it can ruin you."

Before I had a chance to reply, Kali hurried in to gather Ma up for her first appointment of the day. I watched in quiet confusion as she swept out the door.

I sat down at the computer, meditating for a moment before turning it on. As the machine booted up, I marveled at the lights and patterns across the screen. I had never noticed how playful and pretty it was before.

I opened my design files. Friday night's crash had caused a significant chunk of my work on the new shopping cart to disappear. Normally, I would have been extremely upset by this. My body would tense, I'd clench my teeth, and I'd feel angry at the universe for thwarting me.

This morning, though, none of that happened. The information that I'd lost a good chunk of work was just that, information. I took note, but had no emotional reaction, and set about calmly re-creating what I'd done.

At lunchtime, instead of following my habit of working at my desk while I ate, I decided to take a break and go outside. I headed for the fallen log on the back of Ma's lot. It was hot, and the summer mountain sun bathed everything in a vibrant light. I just couldn't get over how gorgeous it all was.

I'd picked up a roasted vegetable baguette sandwich for lunch on my way to work, and I ate it slowly, savoring each bite. My taste buds were working overtime, and the flavors played vividly on my tongue. I felt ecstatically lucky to be alive.

A slight breeze made the grasses in front of me dance. I watched them curiously, feeling their movements inside me.

Ma had said I wasn't enlightened, but she hadn't really said anything about what I was instead. I knew that the love I'd experienced was the connection with God that I'd craved, and that I'd never again be without that knowing in every one of my cells. But beyond that, I had little understanding of what was really happening to me.

Not that not understanding really bothered me. I was too busy enjoying the experience, feeling like I was floating on air, buoyed along by the grace of God. I still felt detached from my emotional reactions, as I had after my first workshop. But now, I simultaneously felt deeply connected to everything around me. My heart overflowed with love and appreciation for everything I came into contact with, and for the first time in my life, I understood what people were talking about when they discussed the exquisite perfection in everything.

I got up, brushed a bit of dust off of my skirt, and began a meditative walk back to the office.

I got into a good working rhythm that afternoon, and I barely noticed the time pass. Kali left around six, and Ma followed her soon afterwards. She was going out to dinner with one of the students who had flown in from California for the weekend. It was rare for Ma to socialize with students, but at the time, I didn't think much about it.

After the sound of tires on gravel had faded, a peaceful silence settled over the house. I pulled an energy bar out of my bag and decided to make the most of it.

I was so engrossed in what I was doing that I didn't even hear Jeremy come in.

"Still hard at work?" he asked.

His words startled me so much I jumped. I turned and saw him leaning against the archway to the foyer, a quiet smile on his face. "Hey. You surprised me," I said. Despite my scolding tone, I felt ridiculously happy to see him.

"Sorry," he grinned. "Just wanted to make sure you weren't working too hard."

"That's very thoughtful," I smiled back.

"Have you seen the moon?"

I shook my head. "I've been inside all afternoon."

"Well, you need a break, then," he insisted, and motioned me towards the door.

I followed him outside. It had grown dark while I was working, but the summer air was sweet and warm. A light wind played with the loose stands of my hair.

As we rounded the back of the house, I was stopped in my tracks by the sight of an enormous full moon. It hung just over the horizon, its brilliant reflection sparkling off the watery surface of the reservoir. I caught my breath, raising a hand to my chest as tears came to my eyes. It was one of the most beautiful things I had ever seen.

"I thought you might appreciate this," Jeremy said softly, standing close behind me.

"Oh, my God," I whispered, breathing in the beauty before me as deeply as I could.

We stood silently like that for several minutes, watching the slow drift of the moon upwards. At some point, Jeremy slipped his arm around my waist, and without thinking I leaned back into him.

I felt his breath, warm along the side of my neck. A few timeless moments passed. Slowly, I turned towards him. In the glow of the moon, he looked even more stunningly gorgeous than usual. I thought my heart might break, he was so beautiful to me.

He reached out and gently touched my face. I closed my eyes, absorbing the delicate sensation. My skin tingled under his touch, and every cell of my body felt vibrantly alive.

I opened my eyes again. As we gazed into each other, I began to lose sense of where I ended and he began. There was only love, expressing itself through him and me so that we might rediscover ourselves together.

As he leaned down to kiss me, Lucy's face flashed before my eyes. I felt a sudden jolt of awareness. "Wait, Jeremy—we can't do this," I said, pulling myself back slightly.

He stopped, but held his face close to mine. "Hey, it's all right. Lucy and I aren't together anymore."

"What?" I said, my eyes widening. I couldn't believe she hadn't told me. But then I realized that it had been at least a week since we'd spoken, and I had yet to return two of her calls. "What happened?"

"It just wasn't working out," he said as he delicately stroked my arm. "She's an incredible being, but her commitments are just elsewhere right now. We hadn't really been connecting in a while."

"Oh, God," I said as a mixture of guilt and worry moved through me. "I hope she's okay."

"Oh, she's fine, Michelle. She agreed it was for the best, with her schedule and all. Really, she's okay."

I looked back up at him, wanting very much to believe him. I knew I should talk to her, but I was torn. I didn't want to leave him now.

He watched me tenderly, observing my struggle. Then he reached out, grasping my hand with a reassuring firmness. "You can trust this, Michelle," he whispered. "You know love is the only thing that's really real."

I relaxed instantly as he said this. I knew what he was saying was true. In some distant part of me, I also knew it wasn't quite that simple. But as he leaned down to kiss me, I suddenly forgot about everything else.

The sensation of his lips against mine was unbearably delicious. The cloud of love I'd been floating on for the past few days was suddenly focused through the most exquisite physical sensation, and nothing had ever felt so good.

After a slow, lingering moment, he pulled back and looked into my eyes. The boundaries between us were porous, as though we were one person. As we gazed at each other, I could feel both his desire and his uncertainty as clearly as if it were my own. It was only then that I realized the unusual lack of butterflies in my own stomach. As much as I was enjoying being with him, I felt so solid in my own experience of love that I knew beyond question that it was in no way dependant upon him. It was a mind-blowing revelation.

A wave of tenderness washed over me as I looked into his eyes. This time it was me who reached out to trace a finger down the side of his face, to gently stroke his hair. He smiled at me, a shyness in his face I'd never seen before. I smiled back, a joyful giggle rising inside me. I reached up to kiss him again.

The moon had risen high in the sky by the time we began heading back towards Ma's house, our fingers laced together as we walked. I felt simultaneously full and empty, a peaceful bliss radiating through me from some deep core.

"I can't believe how comfortable I feel with you," he began. "It's like we've been together forever."

I nodded. "I know."

He stopped then, looking at me closely. "I keep getting flashes of India whenever I look at you. Colored saris and turmeric. I wonder if that was the last time we were together."

As he spoke, an image of a street full of brown children flashed through my mind. Sunlight shining across a river, women bathing in the water. The smell of incense, the scent of cooking fires.

I was not a person who was prone to visions; in fact, I'd never had one before in my life. But these images seemed deeply natural to me. Like we were leafing though an old photo album together, remembering a particularly lovely vacation. The sense of eternity in our connection was so present in the space between us that when he asked me to spend the night with him, of course I said yes.

Back at his house, Jeremy lead me up the stairs to his bedroom as though we were about to embark on a sacred ritual. But as we stepped through the doorway, the dreamy bliss we'd been floating in exploded into passion. I couldn't get enough of his skin, his hair, his solid physical body, and he pulled at my clothes with equal zeal. This was the point where I usually got nervous, painfully aware of the ways in which my extra ten pounds prevented my body from matching the cultural ideal of beauty. But Jeremy explored my curves with an almost reverent awe, nothing but hungry approval in his eyes. I surrendered my self-consciousness on the altar of his devotion, and let myself be the object of his worship.

I awoke the next morning wrapped in a cloud of warm bliss. Jeremy lay sleeping beside me, his chest rising and falling in an even rhythm. We'd hardly slept at all, but I was floating so high on the currents of new love I felt like I could climb a mountain.

I slipped out of bed and down to the kitchen to put on some tea. I was rummaging through the fridge, looking for things to make pancakes with when my sleepy companion joined me.

"Good morning," he said

"Hi," I replied, greeting him with a lingering kiss.

"I spent the whole night dreaming of goddesses," he began. "I guess that's what happens when you have one in your bed," he added, holding my face in his hands.

I blushed, smiling in spite of myself. "Don't build me up too much," I chided. "Otherwise you'll not know what to do with me when I prove to be human after all."

"Oh, I don't think there's any danger of that. It's your humanity that makes your divinity so beautiful, after all," he continued, taking my hand and brushing the top of it lightly with a kiss. "Never in all my life have I been with a woman who so radiates the Divine," he added with a dreamy tone in his voice.

His chivalrous worship was intoxicating. I wasn't used to having this kind of attention, and I felt a familiar shyness surface within me. But Jeremy's focus was unwavering. As I looked into his eyes, all I saw reflected back was complete adoration. I took in a deep breath and held his gaze, letting myself relax into his acceptance.

"So, my queen," he started, "what would you like to do today?" Though we were both expected at Ma's, neither of us was technically required to be there. I felt a brief urge towards responsibility, but immediately abandoned it in favor of remaining in our magical cocoon.

"Let's go to the mountains," I said. "It's so beautiful, and I've spent hardly any time there since I arrived."

"So be it."

We ate a leisurely breakfast of pancakes and fruit, then threw together a few things into a daypack and headed out. After a brief stop at the gourmet market for brie, peaches and crackers, we turned up into the mountains.

Boulder's mountain hiking trails were usually quite heavily used, but only a few cars filled the trailhead lot on this weekday morning. He'd chosen a path that followed a small stream up into a steep canyon, and the morning sun was still burning the night's dew off the mountain grasses as we began our climb.

The rocky trail began with a vigorous ascent, and I was soon breathing hard. We fell into an easy silence. Being with him felt so natural that I had no urge to fill the space with conversation. Instead I found myself meditating on the rhythms of his body as he walked ahead of me, the muscles moving under skin, the loose strands of blond hair escaping his ponytail, the shadow of sweat forming on the back of his t-shirt.

When we reached the top of the canyon, the trail met up with a wide gravel Forest Service path. We turned south along it for a few steps before he guided me towards a side path so narrow I wouldn't have seen it on my own.

We slipped into the nurturing embrace of the thick pine forest. After a few minutes in the shadow of the trees, our path met up with a small, meandering creek and we soon found ourselves walking through a mountain paradise. The water gurgled softly by our feet as the forest gave way to a small mountain meadow filled with knee-high grasses and the surprise of tiny wildflowers.

He led me to a spot near the edge of the water where three large boulders lay flat in a patch of sun. I took off my pack and my shoes and stepped into the water, the cold snowmelt stream making my feet forget about their complaints.

Jeremy waited for me on the largest of the rocks, watching me as I splashed water over my face and neck. When I returned, he handed me a slice of a fat, juicy peach. It was so messy the juice began running down my wrist before I could even get it in my mouth, but he solved this problem by taking my hand and delicately licking the runaway juice from my arm.

I pulled him towards me, my blood-filled body hungry for his. We lay together on that rock for what seemed like eternity, watching the soft, puffy clouds floating gently overhead.

Eventually, he sat up and reached for his backpack. Out of it, he pulled a small wooden flute. I nestled my head in his lap as he brought the flute to his lips and unleashed a sweet, clear melody into the warm summer air. As the watery notes floated gently around us, I prayed this magic would never, ever end.

Nine

"Where were you yesterday?" Kali asked as soon as I stepped inside the office the next day.

"I, um, well," I said, unable to keep the smile off of my face, "I was with Jeremy."

Kali turned to look at me more directly then, her eyebrows raised. "Well, that explains why he wasn't here either. How long has this been going on?"

"Let's see—about thirty-six hours, I think?"

She watched me for a moment before her face broke into a rare smile. "Well, congratulations, I guess," she said.

"Thanks," I replied. "It's happened so fast, but it feels amazingly right."

"I'm sure it does," Kali said. "Jeremy's a pretty amazing guy."

"He really is," I gushed. "I can't believe how lucky I am."

She gave me a sideways glance. "You do seem to be on top of the world, don't you."

I was about to reply when I heard Ma's voice.

"You are dating Jeremy?" she said, startling us both. I whirled around to find her standing in the doorway to the kitchen. I wondered how long she'd been there.

I nodded, the large smile instantly returning to my face.

She did not smile back. Instead, she looked at me with her penetrating gaze, as though trying to read some deep inner part of me. I shifted uncomfortably, wondering what she was thinking, but I was unable to read anything in her face.

After a moment, she simply turned and walked out of the room.

Between working on the web site and spending every spare moment with Jeremy, most of the week had passed before I finally got around to calling Lucy. I'd been putting it off, uneasy about what she would say when I told her about me and Jeremy. Despite his repeated assurances that everything would be fine, my stomach did little somersaults as I dialed her number.

"Hey, it's me," I said when she answered.

There was a long silence on the other end.

"Lucy?"

"What?"

"I was just calling to say hi. It's been a while, you know, and I wondered how you were doing."

"Pretty shitty. But that shouldn't be any surprise to you."

I felt my heart sink. She already knew.

I took a deep breath, trying to center myself. "Look, Lucy, I'm sorry if you're upset—"

"Upset? Why the fuck should I be upset? Just because my best friend is screwing my boyfriend? Why on earth should that make me upset?"

I was shocked to hear her refer to Jeremy as her boyfriend. "He told me you broke up, Lu. He told me you talked about it."

"Oh, sure, if you call him dumping me talking about it," she snapped. "You should know, Michelle, that this was not a mutual decision. It was his."

I closed my eyes, wanting desperately to not hear what she was saying.

"I didn't know that," I whispered.

"Of course you didn't. You've been too busy jumping to Ma's every command to make time for plain old regular people like me."

"Lucy—"

"Why are you even bothering to waste your time with me? If I'm not spiritually committed enough for Jeremy then I'm sure you don't have any use for me either. Why don't you just go back to your little isolated inner circle where you don't have to deal with the dirty, messy real world like the rest of us?"

The next thing I heard was a dial tone.

Her words had ripped through me like a sharp knife. I wanted to be angry at her for her meanness, but I knew she had every right to feel the way she did. I dropped the phone onto the bed, wondering idly at what point my head had begun to throb. My heart ached, and I felt a terrible sense of loss.

I stared at the ceiling, wondering how on earth I let this happen. I felt a flash of anger at Jeremy for not having been more honest with me about what had really happened between them. Really, I should have known better than to just listen to him without checking it out with Lucy first.

But I couldn't stay angry with Jeremy. What I felt with him was too strong, too powerful to be a mistake. Lucy had to understand that on some level—she had to know she was just being unreasonable. Of course she was upset it hadn't worked out with her and Jeremy, but he and I were meant to be together. The connection he and I had—there was no denying that. She was just letting her own ego pain get in the way of seeing what was really best for everyone. Really, it was Lucy who was being the selfish one.

I felt calmed by this line of reasoning. But then my thoughts turned back to her, and I knew she was crying. In the same way that I'd felt Jeremy's emotions that moonlit night, I was suddenly awash in hers, anguish and rage swirling around over a deep, stabbing sense of betrayal.

Eventually, I drifted off into an uncomfortable sleep. I awoke an hour later, disoriented and groggy, when Jeremy showed up.

"Hey, are you okay?" he asked, concern on his face as he sat down next to me on the bed.

I struggled to sitting, the throbbing in my head increasing as I moved.

"Lucy's not very happy with me."

He shook his head. "Yeah, she's just having a really hard

time letting go. I've tried to explain it to her, but I think she just has to go through it, you know?"

It sounded so reasonable when he said it, like it was all just her process. Still, I didn't feel any better.

"Why didn't you tell me she was so upset?" I asked. "You made it sound like she was fine with the whole thing."

"Well, she was sad and all, but I didn't really think it was that big of a deal. We'd kind of drifted apart the last few weeks since we barely saw each other, and she agreed that it was just getting too hard. So I really thought she was okay."

"Then why is she so mad at me?" I asked, rubbing my fingers on the sides of my temples.

"I think finding out about you and me made it more final. She called me a couple of days ago, wanting to see if we could try again, but I told her no, because I was in love with you. I guess maybe that's when it really hit her."

I cringed, knowing how badly it would have hurt her to find out about us that way. "Oh, God," I muttered.

"Hey, sweetheart, don't do this to yourself." He reached out, turning my face up so I could look at him. "Lucy and I just weren't right for each other, and she knows that, even if she doesn't want to admit it. It sucks that she's in pain, but you and I have been brought together by God—can you honestly have any doubts about how right this is?"

I looked into his eyes, feeling the depth of my love for him, and shook my head. This relationship was everything I'd ever wanted, something I'd spent my whole life hoping for. I knew it was right, even if Lucy didn't want to admit that. It wasn't my fault she was unwilling to let go.

Rationalizations aside, the conversation with Lucy marked the end of the uninterrupted bliss I'd been experiencing since the workshop. After over a week of floating through my life on a cloud of divine peace, the sudden, crashing return to the world of the everyday emotions was profoundly disturbing. I felt like I'd lost something terribly precious, and I was desperate to get it back.

A few days after the call to Lucy, I had a meeting with Ma to go over some changes to the web site. I kept waiting for her to comment on the fact that I'd regressed, but she didn't say anything. Finally, I couldn't keep it inside any longer.

"Can I ask you a question?" I began.

"You may."

"I'm not sure what's happened, but I don't feel like I'm in the same place as I was after the workshop anymore. It's like, it feels like I've lost it, somehow."

Ma looked at me with a tender gaze. "Did you really think it was going to last forever?"

I looked back at her, surprised. "Well, I don't know. I mean, I guess so."

"It's a common illusion. But that's not the purpose of these experiences. We have them to remind us of the truth, to help us see the pathway home. But the real work involves integrating them into everyday life."

I considered this. Though I felt relieved to hear that I hadn't screwed up somehow, I was depressed by the idea that I wasn't going to be able to live my life from that place.

"But I liked the bliss," I confessed.

"We all do," she said with a smile. "Most people think the process of growing into God is much more dramatic and glamorous than it really is. But the truth of it happens in the day-to-day, in the washing of dishes and the parking of cars. It's about remembering God moment to moment, even when there are no fireworks to remind you."

It was clear she was speaking from personal experience. For a brief moment, I saw a glimpse of the path she had walked, not just the Ma who was my teacher, but the Ma who had been a student in her own right. I felt much closer to her then, touched by an awareness of her humanity as I realized that in some ways, she was just like me.

She watched me for a moment, then said, "You've come down from the high of the experience, but you haven't lost it. I can see that it's still inside of you, just in a different place. Do you not feel that?"

I closed my eyes and took in a breath. As I tuned into my internal experience, I noticed for the first time that, underneath the surface layer of everyday emotions, there was a sweetness I hadn't felt before. It permeated my whole body, seemingly radiating from the center of every cell. Though it wasn't as dramatic as the euphoria I'd been bathed in previously, it was more solid somehow. Solid, and deeply satisfying. I felt my body instantly relax.

"Yes, that's it," Ma confirmed as she watched me tap into the feeling. "You still have it, but your work will be remembering that."

I nodded, a new kind of understanding inside of me. Though I couldn't say exactly what, something suddenly made a lot more sense.

I woke up on Saturday morning at Jeremy's house. He was just stepping out of the shower as I pulled myself to sitting.

"When did you get so ambitious?" I asked with a yawn.

"Believe me, I'd much rather stay here in bed with you," he replied, coming over and giving me a slow, rich, good morning kiss. "But I promised Shadowdancer I'd help him sort out the glitch he's having with his sound equipment, remember?"

"Oh, right," I nodded. "Well, I guess I can spare you for a morning."

"I'll call you as soon as I'm done," he promised. "Feel free to hang out as long as you want. There are some blueberries in the fridge."

Despite his invitation, I opted to head back home as soon as I'd had a shower of my own. I'd spent so little time there lately that the place was a mess, and I knew if I didn't do something about it soon it would be beyond redemption.

I had barely started cleaning the bathroom when the phone rang.

"Oh, my God, you are actually still alive!" I heard Megan's voice exclaim from the receiver when I picked up the phone. "It's been so long since I'd heard from you I thought you'd gotten sucked into the Boulder vortex."

I smiled, happy to hear her voice. She had worked for another design firm in my old office building in Denver, and we'd been regular lunch mates.

"Yeah, sorry, Meg, I've been a bad friend. I've just been working really hard on this web project for the group here, and it's taken up pretty much all of my time."

"Well, hey, at least you're working. That's more than I can say. I could sure use a job right now."

"No way, you got laid off, too?"

"Like two months ago. I didn't mind too much, since this witchy manager had started working there, and it was great to have some time off. But I haven't been able to find another gig, and the job scene's just really bad here."

"Ugh," I replied, trying to repress a surge of anxiety about my own impending need to find a job.

"But enough about me," she said. "How's Boulder?"

"Pretty good, actually," I said, wondering just what I should tell her. She didn't know the first thing about Ma. "There's a guy..."

"Guys are good, guys are good. What's he like?"

"Oh, you know, gorgeous, talented, brilliant, nothing special."

"You sound ecstatic."

"It's pretty cool."

"How long?"

"A couple of weeks maybe?" I said, struggling to remember. Time was something I'd gotten less good at recently.

"Okay, so we've still got the new blush thing going on," she said, a touch of cynicism in her voice. "Save me the details until we know he's going to last."

"Believe me, Meg, he's a keeper."

"Yeah, yeah, whatever. Have you heard about Joan and Michael?"

I spent the next hour on the phone with her, catching up on Denver gossip and all the news of the outside world. I always liked talking to Megan because she was so good at making me laugh, but it was strange to have a conversation with someone that in no way included Ma. It made me realize just how separate I'd become from the rest of the world these last few months.

"It's really good to hear your voice," I said as the conversation was winding down.

"Yeah, you too. Don't be such a stranger, okay?"

"I promise."

"Hey, listen," she added, "does that group you're working for need any additional help?"

"No, sorry. We're pretty much done. Besides, it's all been volunteer, anyway."

There was a long pause. "You've been working for free?"

"Yeah, well, good cause and all."

"You have got to be kidding me. Why would you let someone take advantage of you like that?"

"She didn't take advantage of me," I said. "I thought I could learn a lot by doing it, and since I wasn't working, where's the harm?"

"Yeah, well, it's your time. So listen, come down to Denver soon, okay?"

"Yeah, definitely," I replied, though I had no intention of following up on that. I was a little offended by Megan's comments, and after I hung up, I thought briefly about calling her back to defend myself more thoroughly. She had no idea what honor it was to be able to work with Ma, that this was about so much more than the money. But I didn't call her back. Without knowing Ma, there was no way she was going to understand.

I was able to finish putting the final touches on the shopping cart a few days later. It was a relief to feel that things were finally starting to come together for the website. There was still more to do, but we had almost a week before the alignment, so I decided to leave the office early for a change. After several weeks of working twelve and fourteen hour days, I was tired.

I picked up some tortellini from the deli on my way home. As I stood in the check-out line waiting to pay, my eyes fell on a stack of newspapers. So much for my ambitious plans to job-hunt while I was working on the site. I hadn't even so much as glanced at the employment section since I started working at Ma's.

I considered grabbing a paper on my way out, but decided to just wait for the weekend edition instead. There'd be a better selection then, and I wouldn't have time to do much before then anyway.

My studio seemed especially quiet when I got home. I put on some music and set the small table for one, pulling out a travel magazine to read as I ate. I leafed through a few pages before I came to an article about sailing through the Greek Islands. That was something Lucy and I had wanted to do together for years, and we'd even gotten so far as pricing a couple of different trips last summer.

I felt a deep ache in my heart as I thought about her. I really missed her. She'd been so much a part of my life for so long. Even if she was moving away from Ma's community, it didn't feel right to not have her in my life at all. There had to be a way we could get past this. There had to be a way to heal it.

My eyes fell on the phone, sitting silently on my bed table. I picked up the receiver, then paused, remembering her anger at me. What was she feeling now?

I looked over at the clock. She'd be at work now anyway. I sat there for a few minutes, wondering what to do. What on earth should I even say?

I was about set the phone down, but then dialed her number anyway.

"Hey, Lucy, it's me," I said to her voice mail. "I feel really terrible about all of this. I'm really hoping that there's some way we can work this out. I'd really like to talk to you. Please give me a call, okay?"

For the next few days, as soon as I walked in the door after work, I looked over at my answering machine. But the message light remained dark.

On Tuesday, I ran into Matt at the lecture.

"Welcome back," I said awkwardly, knowing Jeremy must have told him about us. "How was your trip?"

"Uh, great. Good climbing, nice weather. Hot, though."

I nodded. "Nice."

There was a longish pause.

"So, you're doing good?" he asked.

"Yeah, great. I've been working pretty hard, but we're getting close to being done on the web site." I paused. "And I guess you know about me and Jeremy."

"Yeah, he told me," he said, looking down. "Uh, congratulations, I guess."

"Thanks, yeah. Look, Matt," I began, feeling like I had to say something, and hoping the words would show up if I opened my mouth. "I'm sorry it didn't work out with us. This thing with Jeremy, it just seemed like it had to happen—"

"Hey, look, you don't have to apologize. It's not like we were together or anything."

I nodded, looking down. He didn't seem angry, but his eyes were so terribly sad.

"Yeah. Well, I hope we can still hang out."

"Yeah, sure," he said, shrugging. "Well, uh, I'm going to go grab a cushion. See you around."

"Bye," I said as I watched him walk away.

Feeling vaguely depressed, I dropped my things on a cushion and headed to the back table where the water cooler was. As I walked, I noticed Melinda arrive through the rose-colored curtain door. I smiled at her and offered a little wave. She looked away without responding, as though she hadn't seen me. But I was positive she had.

During the question and answer period that night, a woman who was visiting from California raised her hand.

"This has been such a strange time for me," she began, her voice shaking. Sitting next to her was a man who obviously adored her, and he held her hand tightly as she spoke. "We've been trying for over a year now to get pregnant, and I'd gotten to the point where I was about to give up. But then, all of the sudden, we were pregnant. I was so euphoric when we found out, I think it was the happiest I'd ever been in my life."

She paused then, trying to manage her emotions. Ma was watching her closely, a fierce tenderness in her eyes.

"But then I miscarried," she said. "When I saw the blood I knew right away what was happening, and part of me thought I was going to die. But at the same time, another part of me was so aware that this was exactly what needed to be happening, that the timing wasn't really right, and that this was really a blessing."

"When you open your mind to God," Ma said, "it's impossible to see anything but the blessing."

The woman nodded. "I've been studying with you for so long, now, and I didn't really think I was getting it. But in that experience, I realized that I was, that I had, that even when I didn't think I understood, it was still inside me somehow. And I found myself thinking that this is what really matters, to be able to find it in moments like these. And then I began to think that what I really need to be doing is not coming here, but working to find that place in every moment of every day."

As she spoke, I found myself nodding. It was exactly what Ma had been saying to me the other day. It was such a gift to be able to be at Ma's, to bathe in the energy and be shown the pathway with such clarity. But the real test was really living your life. As I watched this woman, I couldn't help but admire her strength and her willingness to do that, to let go of the training wheels and embrace her own life head on.

Ma watched the woman carefully for a long time. "You need to do both, Elisa," she said. "The work we do here is meaningless if you cannot integrate it into the larger world. But at the same time, you must never forget how tricky the mind is. Given the first opportunity, it will abandon higher truth in favor of the smallness of the ego. You need to come here because this is what keeps you honest. It is too easy to get caught in your own delusions without a mirror to keep showing you who you really are. Coming here," she repeated, "is the only thing that keeps you honest."

I was surprised by Ma's reply. I'd heard her speak a lot about the dangers of the ego, but it was odd to hear her say we needed to keep coming here to combat it. It seemed contrary to her normal stance that she was just a temporary guide for us until we were able to see clearly on our own. But then, I didn't really know Elisa—maybe her case was different.

I looked over at Elisa, who was nodding. "Oh, yes. I see," she agreed. She sank back into her cushion, a slump in her shoulders I hadn't noticed before.

A few days later, I was in the office, working out a glitch in the mailing list when I heard loud voices coming from upstairs. As there was hardly ever any noise in the house, I sat up with a start, wondering what was going on.

My wonder turned to amazement as I finally registered the sound of Ma's voice. I couldn't hear well enough to understand what she was saying, but it was definitely her voice. I turned to Kali, confusion on my face.

"What's going on?" I asked.

She sighed. "I'm not really supposed to talk about it. But you're here, so you really should know. Just promise not to tell anyone else, okay?"

I nodded quickly. "Yeah, of course."

"Ma's just broken up with her boyfriend."

My mouth dropped to the floor. "Ma has a boyfriend?"

"Well, not anymore. They had a rather rough breakup a couple of days ago. I suspect that's him she's talking to on the phone."

My brain did a double take as it tried to process this information. Ma hadn't ever said anything about her personal life, but there had never been any acknowledgement that she had one. I had just assumed that she was beyond the need for any kind of human love.

"How long had they been together?"

"A few years."

"I had no clue."

"She didn't really want it to be public knowledge. She didn't want to create any sense of competition or favoritism amongst her students, so they played it pretty low key."

"He was one of her *students*?" I repeated.

"Yeah. But they'd actually been friends before she experienced her transformation. He's been with her since the beginning. They didn't start dating until she'd been teaching for a while, though, and even then, she resisted it. But I guess there were some signs, and it became apparent that there was a divine purpose to it, so she surrendered."

The image of Ma leaving for dinner a few weeks back with the student from California flashed in front of my eyes. He was one of the Seminar Series members, a man named David. He was about Ma's age, and wore his grey hair back in a ponytail.

The voice upstairs grew louder, then abruptly silent. In all of the months that I'd been there, I had never seen Ma express any kind of strong emotion.

"She's really affected by this," I said.

"Well, the intensity of her love is so much greater than ours. She feels things on so many more levels than we do that his actions are a million times more painful to her than we could ever imagine."

"Do you know what happened?"

"Not totally. But I'm guessing he brought up the teaching thing again. He's been trying to talk Ma into letting him teach with her, and she knows he's just not capable of it, that he hasn't evolved enough. But his ego hasn't really wanted to accept that. So I think it was probably about that."

"Oh, my God," I said, shaking my head.

"So, listen, don't tell anyone all this, okay? Ma doesn't want anyone to know."

"Yeah, of course. So you and I are the only ones?"

"And Jeremy."

"Of course."

A few hours later, I settled into my cushion at the front of Ma's lecture hall. Though I tried half-heartedly to meditate, my mind kept sifting through the layers of new information I'd heard that afternoon. I just couldn't believe Ma would be as susceptible to that kind of human emotion as the rest of us. It seemed so contrary to my experience of her—she always seemed so detached, to be able to see the higher wisdom in things. To see her get so caught up in her own personal dramas was a little unsettling. I mean, she wasn't even supposed to have personal dramas at all, right? I thought that was part of the point.

At the end of meditation, I looked up to see Ma sitting serenely in her white chair. She looked as calm and focused as she always did. I felt myself let out a sigh I hadn't realized I'd been holding. It was reassuring to see the Ma that I knew.

There was a long silence as she surveyed the room, reading the energy of the group. I felt a slight edge of nervousness as her eyes passed over me.

"We are going to talk this evening about humility," Ma began. "Which means, of course, that we will also be talking about ego," she smiled as a chuckle moved through the room.

"When you are truly walking the path of God, you are walking a path of humility. In the presence of God's magnificence, you know that you are nothing more than an infinitesimal speck in the universe. Ultimately, this humility is the most freeing thing we can experience.

"The ego, however, is not inclined to surrender to humility so easily. It wants you to believe that you are more than you are, that you are better than those around you. So while the goal of the spiritual path is to develop true humility, one of the dangers of walking a spiritual path is that the ego will try to use that same path to bolster its sense of superiority."

She paused for a moment, watching us carefully. "At the beginning, this can be particularly problematic. I see it most often in new students who are busy making judgments about people who have not chosen to walk their path with them. You've all run into them. Anyone ever been accosted by a new yoga convert?"

I laughed, as did the rest of the room. It was a common problem, especially in Boulder.

"Even a few months of spiritual study is considered sufficient credentials by the ego to begin evaluating and judging others according to the teachings. But seasoned students can fall into this trap as well. It is one of the biggest hazards we face, the fact that the ego likes to think it knows better than the higher wisdom of another's soul."

An image of Lucy flashed through my mind, and I shifted uncomfortably on my cushion. Even before the whole Jeremy disaster, I had condemned her for not making herself more available to Ma's teachings. I realized with painful embarrassment that I had just done exactly what Ma was describing, assuming all sorts of things about Lucy that I had absolutely no business assuming.

"What the ego does not understand," Ma stressed, "is that truly walking the spiritual path does not involve building up the ego. On the contrary, it involves the ego recognizing its place in the grand scheme of things. As those who have had the courage to genuinely open their hearts to the Divine can tell you, the true presence of God is the most joyously humbling of experiences. We stop seeking to feel superior because we understand our place in the universe. We recognize the perfection of exactly where we are, and by extension, where everyone else is as well.

"Unfortunately, it often takes a while for people to come to the experience that brings that understanding. So, the ego has much time to run rampant, building itself up with knowledge and pseudo-understanding. At the core of this is often a good intention—we wish to help others, and we would like to do so in the same way that we have been helped. But there is a profound difference between a desire fueled by ego and a calling granted by God."

A man named George raised his hand. Ma nodded at him.

"As a psychotherapist," he began, "I can totally relate to what you are saying. I've often noticed that the temptation to think I'm better than the clients I work with, but at the same time, I also feel like doing this work is my true calling. I know that my spiritual understanding is by no means complete, but

I'm wondering if just being aware of it is enough to keep the ego in check."

Ma's eyes narrowed as she looked at him. "You are deluding yourself, George," she said. "At your level of understanding you don't have a clue as to what it is to have a true calling. A calling is not something you wake up one morning and casually decide to do. It's something that is forced upon you by the Divine whether you like it or not. It's something that pushes you to the very edges of your resources, beyond what you think you can handle. You are far too comfortable in your life to have even begun to find your calling. The work you are doing is all about your own ego. Don't try to fool yourself into thinking it's something else."

As she spoke, there was an edge of anger in Ma's voice I'd never heard before.

He looked at her, stunned. "But I really do want to help people."

"Only so you can feel better about yourself," Ma snapped. "When you want to help people even when you get absolutely nothing out of it, that is when you know you are doing God's work. As it stands now, you are the worst kind of hypocrite— pretending to help people so you can feed your own ego. You are a parasite, George, not a soldier of God."

I could hardly believe what I was hearing. Ma was always direct in her assessments of what people were going through, but her words had always been delivered with as much compassion as truth. To hear her almost yell at George in this way was so disturbing to me I could barely keep breathing.

I didn't hear much of what she said next as I tried to restore some semblance of internal equilibrium. By the time I returned my focus to the stage, her anger seemed to have passed. She was talking gently to a newer student about how to develop the habit of questioning your motivation for everything as a way of rooting out the places where your ego was in control. She looked just like she always had—calm, serene and in control.

Later that evening, as Jeremy and I were preparing for bed, I was still feeling shaken by the incident with George.

"Have you ever seen Ma get so angry with a student like that before?" I asked him as he pulled his white shirt over his head.

"I dunno, maybe," he said, yawning as he spoke and flopped onto the bed. "Why do you ask?"

"Well, it just seemed so weird," I said as I sat down next to him. "I've just never seen her get so mad like that, and it seemed so harsh."

"Yeah, but you don't know George, either. He's such an arrogant bastard that the compassionate truth route would have just gone right over his head. If Ma pulled out the big guns, it's because she knew that's the only way she'd get through to him. She can see stuff like that, remember?"

"Oh, right." It's true, I had heard people talk about the fact that Ma was incredibly skilled in communicating a message in the way that the recipient would be best able to hear it. Still, it didn't make me feel much better.

Jeremy was watching me closely. "What's wrong, Luv? You look so worried."

"Oh," I said, letting out a sigh. "I just—well, it scared me, I guess. I mean, I can't imagine Ma yelling at me like that. She's so powerful, you know, I think it would just crush me."

He let out a little laugh. "I don't think there's any need to worry about that. You're light years ahead of George, you know; you're not dense like he is. She only does that when someone really needs it for their growth, and you're so open I can't imagine that ever happening with you." He reached over and stroked my hair, and I felt myself relax a tiny bit. But when he took both hands and started gently rubbing my neck, my muscles were still rock hard.

"You're not really afraid of Ma, are you," he said.

I looked up at him. "What?"

His face was full of tenderness. "Who was it that used to yell at you, Michelle?"

I opened my mouth, but before I could get the words out, I collapsed into tears. He was completely right—it wasn't Ma's yelling I was afraid of. It was my father's.

Jeremy gathered me into his arms and held me tightly as I cried. His soft strokes on my hair and back soothed me a great deal, and in a few moments, I was calm again.

"That looked like a good one," he said, a soft smile on his face.

"I had no idea that was in there," I said, wiping the remaining tears off my face.

"That's what's so great about Ma, you know," he said, "she's such a perfect mirror she can bring up just about anything that people need to heal. That's been one of my biggest teachings with her, actually. Whenever I find myself questioning her, I start looking for what I'm projecting. It's amazing how it's always about something else."

I nodded. "Yeah. It's really something how that works."

I was at the gourmet market on the corner the next day after work, loading up on tortillas and cheese, when I looked up and saw Lucy. She was holding her cart tightly with both hands.

"Hi," I said.

She just looked at me.

"I tried to call you," I said.

"I know."

When she didn't say anything else, I realized I was going to have to just dive in. "Look, Lucy, this isn't right," I began. "I know this whole Jeremy thing has been really painful, and I'm really sorry about that. But I don't see why we can't get past this."

She looked away. "No, I guess you wouldn't."

"Lucy, don't do this."

She looked back at me, her eyes narrow. "What the hell do you want me to do? Pretend that it doesn't bother me that my best friend stole the only man I've ever really loved?"

I stared at her, surprise open on my face. I'd never heard her say that before. I'd watched her go through so many men in during our friendship it had never occurred to me that Jeremy had any more meaning to her than the rest of them.

I looked down into my basket. "I'm sorry, Lucy. I didn't realize that."

"No, I'm sure you didn't," she said, bitterness in her voice.

I looked back up at her, seeing the pain in her face for the first time.

"God, Lucy, I really didn't know how you felt, I mean, if I had..." I stopped myself, realizing uneasily that I was not at all sure what I would have done if I'd known.

She stared at me, silent.

I tried again, wanting her to understand my side. "I know how badly that must have hurt, Lucy," I said. "But Jeremy and I, we have this connection—"

"Oh, and he and I didn't?"

"No, I mean, of course you did, but there was a higher purpose—"

"Look, Michelle, you can justify your back-stabbing behavior however you want. But I don't want any part of it." She let go of her cart, turned away and walked out the door.

I looked over at her basket, the containers of yogurt and a box of English muffins. The ache in my chest squeezed tighter around my heart.

Okay, so she loved him—that explained why she was so mad. But I loved him too, and no matter how upset she was, I couldn't believe that what Jeremy and I were doing was wrong. It was too beautiful, too perfect. She had to understand that. And if she couldn't, well...

I took hold of my basket and pushed it towards the checkout counter, leaving her abandoned cart in the middle of the aisle.

I was working intently at my computer the next day when Ma startled me.

"We don't have very much time left before the alignment," she said. "Are you going to be done?"

"I think so. The site is basically functional now. All I'm doing at this point is testing and fine tuning."

"Good." She looked over my shoulder, watching as I clicked

from page to page. "The alignment is at 4:42 AM on Wednesday. That is when we need to launch."

"Really? That's awfully early."

"Make sure you are here by four. I don't want anything to hold us up."

As I was shutting my computer down later that night, it finally began to sink in that the project was almost done. But the sense of relief that I usually felt at the end of a project was strangely absent. In its place was a feeling of unease fueled by the knowledge that I was almost out of money. I still had absolutely no idea what I was going to do next, and I had very little time to figure it out.

On the drive home, I waited impatiently behind a line of cars for the light at Broadway to change. It was rush hour—God, I hated traffic.

I let out an irritated sigh. After six weeks of working at Ma's, I had absolutely no desire to get another job. It wasn't that I minded working hard—I'd been doing nothing but that over at Ma's. But working for her was different. It was energizing to be at her house, in her presence, helping to create something I really believed in. The last thing I wanted to do was sit in some fluorescent-lit office building working on a project I had no connection to.

As soon as I walked in my front door, I pulled out my checkbook. I'd been avoiding balancing it for some time now, knowing I had probably less than a thousand dollars left. But I needed to know how much there really was. I started punching numbers into my calculator. As I added—or rather, subtracted—all the numbers, my stomach began to turn.

The final balance in my checking account was one hundred and fourteen dollars. I stared at the figure, not believing that could be right. I cleared my calculator and ran through it all again. One hundred and fourteen dollars and sixty-one cents.

"Oh, my God," I whispered. "How can that be?" I subtracted all of my checks one more time, hoping I'd made some mistake somewhere. But the only mistake I seem to have made was assuming I had more money than I actually did.

I had barely a week before my rent was due.

"Shit!" I muttered. My stomach tightened even further, and I felt the beginnings of panic in my breathing. I'd deposited my final unemployment check at the beginning of the month. Even if I got a job tomorrow, it would be at least two weeks before I got paid.

I forced myself to standing and began pacing around my apartment. "Breathe, Michelle," I said as I tried desperately to calm down.

There was no way I could ask my father for money. He would simply insist I move back home, a nightmare I would starve to death before considering.

I wondered if Jeremy would be willing to help me. I hated to ask him, but I didn't know where else to turn. He was the only person I knew who had any money, though it suddenly occurred to me I had no idea if he had enough to lend out.

I reached for the phone. But before I started dialing, I realized Lucy had been in just this position a couple of months ago, and she hadn't gotten any help from him. And it wasn't as though he didn't know about her money struggles—she talked about them openly from day one.

I stared at the dial pad. I wondered if she'd ever asked him for help. Maybe he was one of those people who don't like to lend money to close friends. I had a sudden flash of how awkward it would be if I asked him and he said no. God, I would hate for him to see me so desperate. Maybe that's why Lucy just ran up her credit cards.

The thought gave me an idea. I tossed the phone onto the bed and started pawing through my desk, looking for my own credit card files. I had a several cards with high limits, but I'd split the cost of the Seminar Series up between two of them. The MasterCard was maxed out, with ten thousand dollars on it from the Series. The rest of the Series cost was on a Visa, but that one had a limit of eight thousand, five of which I could take out in cash.

My shoulders relaxed a little and I sank into my desk chair. I knew it was a bad idea to use my credit cards to pay my rent.

But I didn't really have any other choice. Starting Thursday, I could devote myself to job hunting full time. As I began to fill out one of the checks that came conveniently every month with my statement, I promised myself it would only be this one time.

I stayed over at Jeremy's on Tuesday night. We set two different alarm clocks to make sure we got out of bed on time.

When the alarm beeped all too early the next morning, Jeremy was already wide awake.

"Aren't you excited?" he asked as I stumbled around, reaching for my clothes in the dark morning.

"Yeah, I am, actually," I yawned. "Though I'm not sure why I should be."

He leaned over and kissed me on the forehead. "It's not every day that you get to participate in a private ritual with Ma. It's really quite phenomenal. You'll see."

Shortly before four, we climbed into his black Pathfinder. The streets were deserted, the silence in the air pregnant with anticipation.

Lights were already on in the office when we arrived. Kali greeted us with a yawn. I set to work immediately, uploading the final pages for the site. When there was just one page left, I stopped.

"I'll get Ma," Kali said.

They returned a few minutes later, Ma dressed head-to-toe in white. She took my seat at the computer and lowered her head as if in prayer. With one hand resting on the monitor, she mumbled something—a blessing I think, though it was too soft to hear.

After several long moments, she looked up at Kali.

"Forty seconds," Kali said, looking at her stopwatch.

Ma rose from the chair and nodded at me. I returned to my seat and began to upload the final page.

Just as I started working, Ma placed her hand on my shoulder. I felt a jolt of energy through my body.

"Ten seconds," Kali said.

The bar indicating the progress of the upload filled out, indicating completion.

"Now."

I pulled up the site. "Okay," I said. "You are launched."

A big smile broke out across Ma's face. "Good. Very good." She turned to me then and looked deeply into my eyes. "You have done a great thing for us. How does it feel, to be an instrument of God?"

I blushed and looked down at the floor. "Pretty amazing."

Jeremy leaned over and gave me a huge hug. "You are just so awesome!"

I smiled, feeling shy as I stood in their midst. Six months ago, I'd never even heard of any of this. Now, I had played a major part in spreading the word of Ma's message. It was almost too much to take in.

"So," Ma began, "what are the next steps?"

"The student mailing announcing the site is ready to go out today," Kali replied. "People will be told to visit the site and sign up for the e-mail list if they want to stay abreast of what's happening. They'll be sorted into Seminar Series and non-Series lists, and the Series lists will get the information first, along with your weekly updates."

Ma nodded. "Good. And the tape catalogue?"

"We still have a ways to go on that," Jeremy replied. "All of the tapes that are labeled are currently offered for sale on the site, and three of them are available for immediate audio download. But it's going to take me quite a while to finish the index and make all of them available for sale."

Ma turned to me. "You have more time now. You can also help with this project."

"Ah, um, yeah, I'd like to," I began. I was flattered that she wanted me to stay on, but I knew there was no way I could afford to. "But I don't think I'll be able to help for very long. I mean, I need to get a job."

Ma looked at me. "Well, you can continue to help us until you find one."

* * *

To celebrate the completion of the web site, Jeremy took me out to dinner that night at a chic nouveau cuisine restaurant on the Pearl Street Mall. The sun was just dipping behind the mountains as we walked down the mall, its angle throwing much of the landscaped brick street into shadow.

I pulled a thin shirt over my shoulders, wishing I'd brought a jacket. Though it was still very hot during the day, the air had begun to turn cool the minute the sun disappeared. I snuggled closer to Jeremy as we walked.

"You're quiet tonight," I said after the waiter had taken our order.

"Yeah, sorry. I got a bit of disturbing news earlier. But it's nothing too serious. Nothing worth spoiling our evening over, anyway."

"Do you want to talk about it?" I asked, looking at him with a touch of worry.

"No, no," he shook his head. "It's nothing really. Just some news about an old friend. I'm not even sure it's true, so I'd rather not speak about it at the moment."

"Okay," I said, confused by his reply. We'd talked about absolutely everything in the first few weeks of our relationship, and it seemed so foreign for him to withhold something from me. I was about to ask him to say more, but I stopped myself. I didn't want to seem nosy.

"So, how much more do you think there is to do on the tape catalogue?" I asked, trying to change the subject.

"Could be a while yet. I've completed the first three years, and the last two were pretty well tracked. But the middle section is badly disorganized. A lot of the tapes don't even have dates. So we'll have our work cut out for us."

I smiled. "I can think of worse fates than being stuck in a small room with you."

He offered half a smile. "Yeah."

It was not the response I was hoping for. Jeremy was usually so present and attentive with me, it was odd to see him so distracted. I began to feel a little bit anxious, wondering if he was in some way upset with me.

"Are you sure you're okay?" I asked.

"What? Oh, of course," he said, suddenly turning to me with renewed focus. "I'm sorry, Michelle, I've just got a lot on my mind. But really, I'm fine."

I watched him closely, relieved to see that there was no sign of anger towards me. But I still wished he would tell me what was going on.

Ten

On Saturday, as Jeremy and I were picking up a few things for breakfast from the gourmet market, I bought a copy of the local paper. We went back to my house, and while Jeremy whipped up some scrambled eggs in the kitchen, I nervously read through the ads.

"God, there's hardly anything here," I said. I was just about to give up when a small ad for a web designer caught my eye. The ad listed a URL for more information.

"Why are you even thinking about getting a job anyway?" Jeremy asked as he served up two plates of scrambled eggs and English muffins. "Don't you want to keep working at Ma's?"

"I'd love to keep working at Ma's," I said as I buttered my English muffin. "I just can't afford to. I need to pay my rent."

"Oh," he said as he reached over and picked up the front section of the paper. He leafed through the pages, utterly unconcerned with my plight. It was then that I realized what it really meant, that he had never had to work a day in his life.

"So, look," I said, "I'd like to hang out today, but I think I really should get a jump on this job application. I'm getting pretty desperate." I felt a brief flash of hope that he might offer to help me, tell me to not worry about the money thing and just spend all of my time with him.

But that didn't happen. "Okay," he said through a mouthful of eggs. "Just call me when you're done."

I nodded, then picked up my plate and took it to the sink so he couldn't see how pissed I was. As I held my plate under the running water, I forced myself to breathe deeply. It wasn't fair to get mad at him, just because he didn't have to worry about money and I did. But I still wished he'd be a little more compassionate about the whole thing.

The ad led me to a website for a downtown firm that offered Internet business solutions. They were looking for an in-house designer to add to their team and the criteria fit my resume almost perfectly. I held my breath as I put together a cover letter and e-mailed my resume off to them. I hoped that this one would work out.

I was just getting ready to go over to Ma's on Monday morning when the phone rang. It was a secretary from the design firm, saying that they liked my resume and asking if I could come in for an interview in a couple of hours. I agreed immediately, saying a silent prayer of thanks as I did so.

I called Jeremy to tell him I wouldn't be in until later, then began going through my closet, looking for something to wear. After several months of dressing in brighter colors and more creative styles, all of my old work clothes seemed dowdy to me. I wanted to dress in a style that was more reflective of who I was now, but I needed this job so badly I wasn't sure I should risk it.

I finally settled on beige pants and a tailored ivory blouse. As I looked at myself in the mirror, I let out a sigh. I looked okay, but I felt stiff and uncomfortable.

I left early, but parking was tight and I drove around for almost fifteen minutes before I finally found a spot on the top floor of a garage. The elevator was broken, and I had to run down six flights of stairs in order to get there on time.

I had just stepped in the waiting room of the old Victorian building when a very perky woman in a bright pink dress popped up to greet me.

"Hi! You must be Michelle," she beamed. "Welcome to our office. Can I get you some coffee? Tea?"

"Uh, no, thanks," I said.

"Okay. Well, have a seat and I'll let Mr. Taylor know you're here." She pointed to an ornate wooden chair and bounced off down the hall.

The secretary worried me. If a person needed to be that upbeat in order to work in this office, this was not likely to be a good fit. I sank into the chair, wishing desperately I was back at Ma's.

A moment later, a well-groomed man in his late fifties came into the lobby. "Michelle? I'm Garrett Taylor," he said, extending his hand. A crescent of gray hair framed his tanned, bald head, and I was relieved to note his smile was friendly, not manic. "Come on back."

His office took up most of the rear of the building. It was a wide, open room with high brick walls and several tall, arched windows that showcased a stunning view of the mountains. He gestured to a seat in front of an enormous mahogany desk.

"So," he began, reviewing a copy of my resume, "you've got quite a bit of experience. I took a look at some of your work online, and it's really very good quality."

"Thank you," I said.

"Tell me, then, what is it that you like about doing web design?"

"Um, well," I began, trying desperately to remember what I'd learned about how to give a good interview, "I find the whole creation process very interesting. Learning what it is that a client needs, and then discovering the best way to develop that for them. I like the problem solving aspect, and just the satisfaction that comes from bringing the whole project through to fruition."

He nodded as I spoke, but he was looking down at my resume. "So your last job was with Kennelworth Design. What happened there? Why did you leave?"

"I was downsized," I said. "The owners decided to shift the focus of the firm and they let all of their staff designers go."

"So you've been out of work for almost six months?"

I nodded.

"That's a long time," he said. "What have you been doing?"

"Ah, well, I took some time off," I began, but then became worried I might sound lazy. "And then I took on some free-lance work," I added.

"That's not listed here. Who was it for?"

"Um," I stalled, anxiety rising in my chest as I realized I was not at all prepared to talk about my involvement with Ma in a job interview. "It was for a small community group."

"Here in Boulder?"

I nodded.

"Who was that, then?"

He was looking at me closely, waiting for me to reply. I felt frozen, unsure what to say. But I'd never been a good liar.

"The Seminar Series School." Maybe he'd never heard of it.

His face darkened. "Ma's group," he said.

I nodded slowly.

"Are you a member of this group?"

"Um, well," I stumbled, "yes, I guess so."

He dropped my resume on the desk with a sigh and stared for a moment at some spot on the wall behind me. My heart sank. Whatever he was thinking, it didn't appear to be anything good.

Abruptly, he pushed back his chair and stood up. "All right then. We've got several more people to interview, and I expect we'll make a decision by the end of this week. We'll let you know."

I stood slowly, already knowing that I wasn't going to get the job. As we shook hands, he met my eyes only briefly before looking away. There was something in them, a complicated mixture of emotion I wanted very much to ask him about. But before I had a chance to say anything, he shut the door in my face.

I walked back to my car with knots in my stomach. I was already familiar with the fact that Ma's group made people who didn't know anything about it uncomfortable—alternative spiritual groups tended to do that sometimes. But this seemed like something different. He clearly already knew about Ma, and what he knew, he didn't like. What I didn't know was why.

* * *

I called Jeremy as soon as I got home.

"How'd it go?"

"Not great," I said, kicking off my shoes as I sat down. "At first it seemed like it was going pretty well, but then he started grilling me about what I'd been doing since I got laid off. When I mentioned the project for Ma, he got really weird on me and just totally ended the interview."

"What was his name?"

"Garrett Taylor."

"Huh. Never heard of him. Well, I wouldn't worry about it too much. Obviously, that wasn't the right place for you to be."

"Yeah," I said, wishing it felt as simple as he made it sound.

I had a hard time sleeping that night. The moon shone brightly through my windows, and I tossed and turned uncomfortably as the moonlight traveling across the room marked the passage of time on my walls.

Sometime after two, I finally drifted off into a restless sleep and into a very strange dream.

I am walking through an ancient city whose walls and buildings are carved out of milky crystal. Each wall shimmers with an iridescent glow, as though they are lit from within.

I am dressed in the white robes of a spiritual initiate. I approach the sacred temple at the center of the city, a building that looks much like the others except it is larger and fronted with a set of intricately carved crystal columns.

Today is the day of a great ceremony for which we have been preparing for most of our lives. An astrological alignment that happens only once every thousand years is occurring, and we are going to harness the energy of the alignment so that it can be used to propel the evolution of humanity forward.

As I walk up the steps and into the great temple doors, several others join me. In the group I recognize Lucy, Danny, and several other students of Ma's.

*We move through the public outer halls of the temple—
wide, bright spaces whose altars are filled with candles,
flowers and other offerings of the common people. A sentry
standing at the end of a long hall sees us approach and opens
a heavy stone door that leads us into the inner chambers.
There, we await the arrival of the high priestess.*

*My heart smiles in recognition as she enters. Though she
doesn't look like Ma, there is no doubt that it is her. The light
that shines from her eyes is unmistakable.*

*The high priestess is dressed in velvet robes of deep wine,
an intricate pendant of lapis lazuli over her breast. She
radiates power, a regal woman who towers over us as we
kneel before her. She begins by leading us through a series of
prayers and ritual preparations. Then, just as the ceremony is
about to begin, she stops to address us one last time.*

*"From this point, there is no turning back," she says. "You
must be totally committed, every cell of your being focused
completely on God. The power we are going to embrace is so
strong that even the slightest waver will cause your complete
destruction. There is absolutely no room for mistakes."*

*Despite her warning, I am unafraid. I have been prepar-
ing for this moment my whole life. I know I am ready.*

*Slowly, the high priestess begins the ritual opening of
innermost chamber of the temple. It is a room that has never
before been opened in my lifetime.*

*As she completes the final steps for the opening, I take in a
deep breath. The doors move slowly apart as we stand in
triangular formation behind her. Much to my surprise, a
great burst of laughter escapes the lips of the high priestess.
Then, instead of the carefully planned ritual entry, she leaps
forward into the chamber.*

*A violent burst of light levels her before her feet even touch
the ground. I have only enough time for my heart to scream
before we are all destroyed in a fire of light.*

I awoke suddenly, drenched in sweat. Most of the dream
had already receded from my consciousness, and in its place

remained only a few cloudy images and a feeling of deep, unexplained dread.

I sat up and turned on the light. I took a few deep breaths, but my heart was still racing. I tried to remember the dream, but the last fragments of it disappeared completely as I focused on them.

I got up to get myself a drink of water. I felt better as I moved around. The stress of my unemployment must be getting to me, I decided. I took a long gulp of water, and promised myself I would spend the next morning doing some serious job hunting.

When I awoke up again a few hours later, I was totally wiped out. I remembered my middle of the night resolutions to spend the morning job hunting, but between my exhaustion and my sense of defeat from the day before, I couldn't bring myself to even open up the want ads.

As I mulled over the previous day's interview, I couldn't help wondering if it was all some kind of sign. I'd felt so uncomfortable and out of place downtown, with all of its rushing stress and perky smiles. Maybe I was just barking up the wrong tree with my job search. I tried to meditate on it for a little while to see if I could get more clarity on the issue, but that didn't seem to help.

A shower helped me to wake up a bit, so after a late breakfast I headed over to Ma's to help out Jeremy in the library. Even if I wasn't getting paid to be there, I was grateful to have some place to go where I could do something productive. Fortunately, there was plenty that needed to be done.

I climbed the stairs to the small, cramped bedroom in the back corner of the house. The walls had been lined with so many shelves you couldn't even see out the window, and almost every single shelf was covered in thousands of hours of tapes.

After greeting Jeremy with a kiss, I settled onto a mediation cushion with a walkman and a stack of white cassettes. Jeremy had started me off with some of Ma's lectures from the period right before she moved to Colorado. As I listened, I made notes of the general themes she covered for the index. I did learn new things as I went through Ma's tapes, but I was also surprised to notice how much of the material was familiar to me. I hadn't realized just how much I'd already learned in the short time I'd been there.

The next day, Kali called me at home late. Her mother had to have emergency surgery in the morning for some kind of heart problem she had, and Kali was flying back to Ohio to help out. She would be gone for a week and asked if I could fill in for her.

I was very happy to help. As much as I liked spending my days with Jeremy, the library got to be kind of stifling after a while. But I felt uplifted just being in the office, with its high ceilings and expansive views. If only I could get a paid job working there, everything would be perfect.

Kali had left me a very organized list of what needed to be done, and I gratefully lost myself in the details of Ma's office work. I'd finished up most of what she had left for me within the first couple of days and even had time to do a little fine tuning on the mailing list.

On Thursday, I was answering an e-mail from an annoying student who didn't understand why he had to have an appointment to speak with Ma when I was startled by the arrival of a messenger.

"Delivery for Carlotta Simmons," he said, holding a thick, white envelope.

The name caught me off guard. I'd seen Ma's real name on a few things in the office, but I'd never heard anyone actually speak it before.

"I'll sign for it," I said.

"I'm sorry, she needs to sign for it herself."

I stared at the messenger, a youngish man in chinos and a white oxford.

"She really can't be bothered right now," I replied. "Can't you just leave it with me?"

He shook his head. "If she can't take it right now, I'll have to come back. I need to serve her in person."

All of my insides began to wobble. "Ma's being sued?"

"Look, I really need to just give this to her in person," he said again, shifting to his other foot. "Can I see her, or not?"

"Um, wait here," I said, pointing to the bench in the foyer.

I headed upstairs, my hand tightly gripping the banister for support. We had strict instructions never to disturb Ma when she was in her room, and my stomach busily tied itself into knots as I approached her door.

I took a deep breath, then knocked as quietly as possible.

There was no answer. I knocked again, a little louder this time.

"I'm meditating," her voice said through the closed door.

"It's urgent."

I heard the rustle of fabric and footsteps as she approached the door. "What is it?" she said, a touch of irritation in her voice as she flung open the door.

"There's a messenger for you. He says he has to see you in person. I think—I think it's about a lawsuit."

Her eyes widened ever so slightly. But then she blinked, and looked as serene as she always did.

She brushed past me and went down the stairs. I went back to the office, listening to the low voices in the foyer. There was a moment of silence, then the closing of a door.

A moment later, she appeared in the office door. "Cancel all of my appointments for today. And tell Jeremy to come see me as soon as he gets in."

I was still nodding as she swept out of the room.

Jeremy showed up a few minutes later. "Hey, sweetheart," he said as he set down a bundle of tapes on the table near the door and kissed me on the cheek. I looked up at him, worry on my face. "You okay?" he asked.

"Ma's being sued," I replied, my voice thick with disbelief.

The affection on his face was immediately replaced by rage. "That asshole!"

"You know who's suing her?" I asked.

"It has to be David," he said. "He's the only one caught in his ego enough to do something this crazy. Oh, God, what an idiot," he said, slapping his hand against the wall.

"I just can't believe this is happening," I said, shaking my head.

"Unfortunately, I can," he said, a grim look on his face.

"Why? I mean, how can people even think that way about her?"

"You'd be surprised. Everybody thinks they want the light, until they find out that there's work involved. To uncover the light, you have to go through the darkness, and a lot of people aren't ready to do that. So Ma's a convenient target that they can project onto. It's always so much easier to blame someone else than to deal with yourself."

"Oh," I remembered suddenly, "she asked to see you right away."

He nodded. "Okay. But look, Michelle," he added, "don't tell anyone about this. That's just what he wants, for everyone to find out. He's trying to undermine everything she's doing."

"No problem," I agreed. "Do you think he has a case?"

"No. He's just doing it for the shock value, I expect. He's trying to get even with her, bring her down to his level. He's such an idiot," he added, shaking his head. "He never was capable of understanding what an incredible gift she gave him with her love."

As Jeremy walked out of the room, I turned back to my computer. Unable to focus, I watched the clouds floating across the screen saver. I figured it was true, what he was saying, that the whole thing was based in David's projection. But I still couldn't shake the intense feeling of heaviness that had settled into the room.

I did not see Ma again until the lecture the following night. She appeared on stage looking even more radiant and intense than usual.

"We are going to talk this evening about self-responsibility," she began. "If you wish to grow in the arms of God, this is something that you must understand. No one, and I mean absolutely no one, is to blame for what happens to you. Your life is an unfolding reflection of the contract that you have made with God. It is based on your lessons and your soul choices. You may bring other people into your personal passion play to help you work out the lessons you have to learn, but ultimately, they are not in control. You, and you alone, are responsible for what happens to you.

"Now, I realize that this is not a popular position. We live in a society that is quite fond of assuming the role of the victim. A role that, with our increasingly inane legal system, has become very profitable for some," she added wryly. "Do not be fooled, however, by juries who award victims for blaming someone else for their troubles. They, too, are caught in the trap of believing that power lies in the hands of others.

"If you wish to grow spiritually," she continued, "the very first thing you must do is accept responsibility for everything that happens to you. What I mean by this is that you must recognize that each and every experience you have, pleasant, unpleasant, joyful, painful, whatever it may be, each and every experience you have has been carefully orchestrated by your very own soul. I am not implying with this that we are in conscious control of every minute of our lives, on the contrary, it is our souls, not our minds, which do this work. But it is nonetheless crucial to understand your own creative role in the events you experience because if you fail to do so, you will feel at the mercy of the will of others and lose the very opportunity for growth your soul has worked so hard to create."

She leaned forward, as if she were about to share a great secret with us. "You see, the problem with blaming someone else for your experience is that it distracts you from learning whatever it may be that your soul has been trying to teach you. By blaming another, you focus outward instead of inward. And as we well know, the truth is always in here," she said, tapping gently on her heart.

She paused a moment, letting that sink in. "If, on the other hand, you are able to look carefully at the experiences that you are having in such a way as to see the unfolding message from your soul, then, and only then, will you be able to pass through the doorway of healing. You will release yourself from the need to re-create those kinds of unpleasant experiences because you will have resolved the underlying issue. You will be able to move forward. You will be able to get on with your life."

At the beginning of this speech, I listened closely, her words sparking something inside of me. As she continued, however, I found myself having a harder and harder time paying attention. I had the sense that what she was saying was somehow crucial for me to understand, but I had to keep forcing myself to listen. I was distracted by an image of my father's face that kept forcing itself to the front of my consciousness. An image of his disapproving, judgmental face.

During the closing meditation, I tried hard to get a grip on myself. I took deep breaths, trying to set aside thoughts of my father and center myself in the here and now. But I was not successful. Somewhere inside of me a door had opened, and every negative memory I had about my father swirled viciously around inside my head. His constant criticisms of every action I took. The mean comments he made about my boyfriends. All the negative things he said about my paintings. His refusal to pay for art school. I was awash in a sea of his angry judgments, reliving every moment of them.

By the time Jeremy rang the gong, I was so devastated I could barely stand up. I begged off of our standing post-lecture date, telling him I had a bad headache. I was afraid if I told him what was really going on, I'd start crying and never, ever stop.

As I drove home, I fought against the emotional collapse threatening to engulf me. Tears started rolling down my face in spite of myself, and I hit the steering wheel repeatedly as if that might beat them back.

By the time I got home, the tears had been replaced by a full blown rage. I'd spent a lifetime fighting my father's judgments of me, but never before had I really faced them head on. It was unbelievable, the amount of abuse I had suffered under his cruel care. And contrary to Ma's directions, I was consumed with blame.

I threw myself on the bed, my fists pounding at the pillows. I hated the bastard for taking every chance he could to shoot me down. It was his fault my life was such a horrible mess, and I felt that to be true in the depths of my soul.

As I allowed myself to feel wave after wave of the emotions I'd denied for years, a strange kind of relief took hold of my system. Even as I raged, there was enormous, incalculable relief.

Eventually, the energy was spent. I sat up, wiping my eyes. The rage dissolved, I felt slightly disoriented.

I looked around, noticing that everything in my studio appeared slightly more vivid than usual. My eyes fell on the easel I'd set up in the corner, and without thinking, I got up and walked over to it.

I sat down in front of the easel, brushing my fingers lightly across the unfinished painting of Matt. A clear line of thought began arising in my mind. I understood then that the reason I'd never followed through on my desire to paint had nothing to do with my father. He was just a convenient excuse. The real reason I'd never gotten serious about my painting was because I was afraid to.

The awareness was a quiet one. There wasn't much emotion attached to it, just a kind of knowing. To paint meant to be seen. To be seen meant risking disapproval. It was a risk I had simply been too frightened to take.

I picked up a brush. I traced the soft bristles across the palm of my hand, then brushed them lightly back over the surface of the canvas. I was painting the canvas, and God was painting my soul. If he was willing to take that kind of risk in creation, why shouldn't I?

I didn't really get an answer. Just an image that began to arise in my head, some colors, a shape. I moved the picture of Matt aside and replaced it with a blank canvas. I began to paint and didn't stop until my arm was too tired to hold onto the brush.

* * *

I awoke late the next morning, still in my clothes, my hands covered in paint. I sat up, blinking my eyes hard against the bright sunlight streaming through my windows.

A deep feeling of peace permeated my body. I could hardly believe how free I felt. It was huge, whatever had happened for me last night, and I felt an overwhelming gratitude towards Ma for setting it into motion.

I got out of bed and walked over to my easel. The painting I'd completed last night was more abstract than my usual work. Pastel wisps of color filled the canvas, and in the center was the faintly perceptible outline of a woman in shimmering gold. It was by far the most beautiful thing I'd ever done.

My face broke out into a smile and I took a deep, satisfied breath. Then I went into the bathroom to get the paint off my hands.

I called Jeremy to see if he might want to have breakfast with me, but he wasn't home. I tried his cell phone as well, but there was no answer, so I left a message.

It was nearing six o'clock by the time he called me back.

"Hey, how are you feeling?" Jeremy asked when I picked up the phone.

"Much better. Last night was a big one for me."

"Yeah? Great," he replied. His tone was distracted, filled with a distance I wasn't used to.

"Where are you, anyway?" I asked.

"Over at Ma's. We finally heard back from the lawyer, and he's agreed to see us on Monday. But we've got all kinds of crap we need to get together before the meeting, so I've been here most of the day just plowing through stuff."

"Sounds like you could use a break," I said. "Want to get some dinner? I hated missing out on our date last night," I added, "and I was hoping I might be able to make it up to you."

"Oh, thanks, but I don't think I should. I've only found a quarter of what we need, so I think I'll be here pretty late."

"Oh, okay," I said, trying to hide my disappointment. "I didn't realize there'd be so much to do for that."

"Yeah, neither did I."

"Is there anything I can do to help?"

"No, I don't think so. Thanks for asking, though."

A moment of silence hung in the air.

"Well, you know, if you need a break, or you get done early, call me, okay?"

"Oh, of course. Definitely. As soon as I can break free."

I called Jeremy late on Monday afternoon.

"So how did the meeting with the lawyer go?" I asked.

"Not too bad," he began. "Ma said the man's energy is very dense, but he really knows his field, so she agreed to use him. His initial opinion is that the suit's pretty bogus—more of a harassment thing than anything that would stand up if it went to trial. But it's going to cost a lot to defend against it, and if he presses forward, it could get ugly. David doesn't have a lot of money, so we're guessing his lawyer is working on contingency. Our main strategy at this point is to put together a response that will show all the holes in their case in the hopes that his lawyer will bail on it. But that's going to require a ton of work, and Ma doesn't have that much money to spend on it either. So I agreed to help with some of the legal research to try and keep the costs down."

"Have you done that kind of thing before?"

"My parents are barristers, remember? I worked a couple of summers in my dad's firm. They'd be thrilled to see me doing this now."

I smiled. "I wish I could help you."

"Me, too. But Ma doesn't want to suck energy from the group by having a lot of people focus on it, so I'm on my own."

"Sounds like you're going to be pretty busy," I said.

"Yeah, I will be for a while. Looks like you'll be on your own in the library."

"It won't be half as much fun without you," I said. "But maybe I can rearrange my schedule so we can get a little bit of time together when you're not working. Maybe sometime in the next couple of days?"

"I'm not sure. I'll be spending most of the week down in Denver doing research, so I might even just get a hotel and stay there."

"I could come down there, maybe meet you after work. You know, there's this great vegetarian restaurant in Cherry Creek we could go to."

"Uh, maybe. I'm not sure how late I'll be working, and I might be pretty wasted when I'm done. Let's maybe talk in a couple of days—I should have a better idea of my schedule then."

September 1st dawned with a light frost on the grass. I wondered if winter would be any worse in Boulder than I was used to downtown. I turned on the heat and made myself a cup of tea, snuggling into my bathrobe as I sat down at my desk to shuffle through some paperwork.

I pulled out a stack of bills. In addition to the cash advance I'd taken out for my rent, my credit card bill also had three weeks worth of groceries and gas. I grimaced at the large numbers on the statements and leaned back in my chair, staring at the ceiling. I had to do something, I knew that. I really didn't want a web design job, but it was the only thing that would pay enough to get me out of the financial hole I was in. Mustering my resolve, I forced myself to turn on the computer and started going through the on-line want ads. I went through both the Denver and Boulder papers, but there was nothing new.

I let out a sigh. Though I was uneasy about the fact that there were no new prospects to even pursue, what I mostly felt was relief. It just seemed like such a bad time to get a job anyway, what with Jeremy all tied up downtown and me being the only one working at the library. I didn't really want to let them down right now.

I ripped off another one of the cash advance checks and wrote it out for twenty five hundred dollars. I didn't like doing that, but I already had so much debt at this point it didn't seem like another month's worth was going to matter all that much.

Once I actually got a job, I'd be able to handle the payments easily enough. Even if that didn't happen soon, I could always do temp work if I needed to.

Eleven

The rest of the week passed without so much as a phone call from Jeremy. The tape library seemed especially small and oppressive without him, and in spite of listening to Ma's lectures almost constantly, my mood steadily worsened as the days passed.

Friday marked the start of a weekend workshop, and as I walked into the lecture hall, I was looking forward to finally seeing Jeremy. But to my surprise, he wasn't at the sound table when I got there. Irritated, I sat on a cushion near the back, hoping to see him as soon as he walked in. But as I went to turn off my cell phone, I noticed a message I'd missed earlier. He'd called me from Denver, saying he'd gotten tied up in some emergency project and might not be back until Sunday. I let out a frustrated sigh as Kali showed up and rang the gong to start the lecture.

I took a few deep breaths, settling into my meditation cushion. I was trying so hard to be patient—I knew how important the work he was doing was, but it was just so hard to understand why he couldn't find any time for me at all. It really wasn't fair.

When the gong rang again, I opened my eyes to see a fierce-looking Ma staring out at the crowd. She was wearing a black silk wrap edged with red and pink flowers. In all the time I'd been there, I'd never before her wear black.

"We have a problem," she said in a tone so sharp I immediately flinched. "I have been speaking with you for months now about how crucial this time is for the evolution of the planet, and how important it is for each one of you to give everything you have in your quest for God. What I have been noticing, however, is that many of you are holding back.

"Now, I have been doing this long enough to know that sometimes resistance is a part of the path, that there are blocks that must be addressed before movement can occur. What is happening now, however, is that some of you have indulged your own resistance so totally that you are now impacting the rest of the group. By refusing to move forward," she added, holding a long pause, "you are holding the rest of us back."

As she spoke, I felt the hair begin to go up on the back of my neck. I knew she'd seen me in a pretty negative space the last few days, and I wondered if she was talking about me.

"I have tried very hard to create an environment in which you all can grow into your full potential. But it has reached the point now where I have begun to feel that I am wasting my time with you. Too many of you are allowing yourselves to remain stuck in issues that you should have resolved by now. I cannot help you if you are not willing to help yourselves."

A rush of guilt washed through me. I'd thought I was doing the best I could, trying not to blame Jeremy while at the same time acknowledging my disappointments with our current situation. But maybe that kind of negativity had more force than I realized. Was I really someone who was holding the group back?

"Many of you do not realize the power of your own darkness," Ma continued. "You think you are just having a bad day, but you do not realize the daggers you send out with every negative breath you release. I have been under attack by many of you for several weeks now. I can of course protect myself from your unconscious assaults, but even I cannot mitigate the energy distortion you create for the rest of the group when you embrace such negativity.

"As your teacher I can no longer allow this kind of thing to continue. So, I am now forced to present you with an ultimatum. Over this weekend, I will be watching each one of you carefully. If you persist in projecting your negativity outward, I will have no choice but to ask you to leave my Seminar Series."

Loud gasps erupted from the room. A rising feeling of panic threatened to overtake me. I had no idea how on earth I would continue on my spiritual path without Ma's guidance, and the thought of not having the support of her and this group was so frightening to me I could barely breathe.

During the closing meditation, I found myself fervently praying for help in healing my negativity. When the meditation was over, however, I was still so edgy I nearly fell over backwards when Matt came up behind me and touched me on the shoulder.

"Hey," he said, helping steady myself. "Sorry about that."

"Don't worry about it. I'm just a little freaked out by all this. I had no idea my negativity was impacting people so much."

"You?" he replied, looking at me like I was crazy. "What the hell are you talking about? She didn't mean you; you're like one of her star students. I'm sure she wasn't talking about you," he said again, shaking his head. "She was talking about me."

"You?" I said, unable to imagine anything negative coming out of Matt.

"Yeah," he said, nodding. "Look, I haven't wanted to admit it, but I've had a pretty hard time with the whole thing with you and Jeremy. I've been really stuck on it, actually, pissed off at both of you—though more him, I guess, since we've been friends for so long. It's been really a drag since we live together and stuff, and it's just been eating me up inside. So I think I've been one of those people she's talking about, but I really don't want to be any more. She's right, you know, that kind of negativity is just brutal, and I've got to get over it. So I wanted to start by just apologizing to you."

"For what?"

"Just for, you know, being kind of resentful and unavailable. I mean, you offered to be friends and I just kind of blew you off."

I smiled at him. "I can't say that I blame you."

"Yeah, well, it's my loss since you're cool and fun to hang out with. So, maybe we can try again?" he asked, a touching hopefulness in his voice.

"Yeah, I'd like that," I nodded, feeing suddenly grateful for a second chance I didn't even know I'd wanted.

Matt's reassurances aside, I remained unconvinced I wasn't one of the people on Ma's hit list. I had been really negative the last few weeks, and I knew she could see that. I returned the next morning full of trepidation, as though I was about to take a test I was not at all sure I was going to pass.

To my surprise, Ma's dark mood seemed to have passed during the night. The energy in her voice was upbeat and inspired that morning, and she bathed us liberally in the warmth and love we had come to count on. At one point, she even smiled directly at me.

I felt a little better after that. I began to think maybe Matt was right, that she hadn't been talking about me. But I was still uncomfortable enough that at lunch, I followed Kali out of the room.

"Can I talk to you?" I asked as we walked into Ma's kitchen.

"Sure, what is it?"

"I was pretty unnerved by Ma's talk last night," I began.

"Yeah, Ma doesn't let the students see that side of her very often," Kali said as she pulled a plastic container full of noodles out of the fridge. "Most people don't realize just how much darkness she has to deal with in her position, but it's substantial. She's constantly transmuting it, but sometimes it gets so intense she has to address it in class. It's the only way some students will ever face it."

"So, like, what kind of darkness?" I was too embarrassed to tell her I was worried about my own.

"Oh, everything, really. People are just always projecting onto her." She paused for a moment, then lowered her voice. "It's particularly heavy right now, with the whole David thing—he's been talking to some of the other students, trying to turn them against her. It's not working, of course, but it does make her work much harder."

"So that's who she was talking to last night."

"For the most part. There are a few others who have been giving her a hard time, but it's mostly some of David's friends."

A huge sigh of relief escaped me. She really hadn't been talking about me. Though I no longer felt like I was in immediate danger, I resolved to make sure I didn't let myself get that negative again. I wasn't about to risk getting kicked out.

I was in the library on Monday afternoon when Kali came in holding the side of her face.

"Are you okay?" I asked. It was rare to see Kali show any kind of vulnerability, and she looked absolutely miserable.

"My tooth is killing me," she said. "I have an appointment for next week, but it's gotten so bad I can't wait. My dentist is going to try to squeeze me in today, but I've got to leave now. Can you cover the office for me? Ma's got two more appointments this afternoon and I'm not sure I'll be back before five."

"Yeah, sure, Kali, of course," I replied. "Is there anything else I can do?"

She shook her head. "I'll call you when I know what's going on."

I headed down to the office, relieved to have been given a reprieve from the small library. I slid into Kali's ergonomic kneeling chair and set to work opening the mail.

Towards four o'clock, Shanti showed up in the office.

"Where's Kali?" she asked.

"She had an emergency appointment," I said. "What's up?"

"Did she leave a check for me?"

I frowned at her. "She didn't say anything about that. What kind of check?"

"My reimbursement for Ma's groceries," she said. "I really need to get that to the bank today. Are you sure it's not here somewhere?"

"Um, I'll take a look, I guess," I said. I began poking around on the desk, looking for something with Shanti's name on it. There was nothing in Kali's outbox, and I shuffled through several of the piles without any luck. I was about to give up when my eyes caught sight of some papers from the lawsuit at the bottom of one of the piles. I quickly covered it back up, not wanting Shanti to see it.

"I don't think it's here, Shanti," I said. "It's not like Kali to forget things, but she was in a lot of pain this afternoon."

"Shit," she muttered. "I really need that money. Can't you write a check for me?"

"I'm not authorized to," I said. "Besides, the checkbook is in a locked drawer and I'm not even sure Ma has a key. She's in session until after five, anyway, so I think you're going to have to wait."

After promising to have Kali call her as soon as she came back, I shooed her out the door. When I turned back to the desk, my eyes fell on the pile of papers where I'd seen the suit. I knew I shouldn't look at it. It was Ma's private business, after all. But the urge to read it was overwhelming. Despite all of Jeremy's assurances that this was just a nuisance suit with no validity, I wanted to see it for myself.

I took a quick glance around to make sure no one was watching, then dug the suit out of the bottom of the pile. To my utter shock, the lawsuit I held in my hands was not the current one between David and Ma. This paperwork was dated 1998, and had been filed against Ma by some people named Kathy Battalia and Jacob Silver.

As my eyes moved across the page, my stomach turned in slow somersaults. They accused Ma of causing them great harm and suffering by running a psychologically oppressive cult. They claimed she had restricted their freedom, violated their trust, verbally abused them and milked them financially. Her actions, they said, caused them severe emotional trauma and financial ruin and they were suing for monetary damages in excess of a million dollars.

By the time I got to the end of the suit, I was shaking. I re-read the charges, trying to get my brain to make sense of them. Was this really my Ma they were talking about?

"Kali's not back yet, huh?" Tony, the gardener, called out from the doorway.

I jumped, shoving the papers under Ma's appointment book.

"Ah, no," I said, breathless, hoping he hadn't seen what I'd been doing.

"Alright. Could you leave her a note to call the guy about shutting down the sprinkler system? Looks like winter might be coming early this year."

"Uh, yeah, Tony, sure," I said, scribbling the note down on the message log. "I'll let her know."

As soon as he left, I let out the breath I'd been holding and tried to calm myself down. I couldn't believe what I'd just stumbled across. My God, could any of that actually be true?

I pulled out the papers again and read the charges one more time. It really sounded outrageous, but to see it there, printed in black and white like that was just so disturbing. While what Ma was doing here was clearly not an oppressive cult—if anything, Ma actively discouraged people from getting too involved—I suddenly realized I really had no idea what had been going on back in California. A sick feeling started growing in me as I realized no one had ever satisfactorily explained why Ma had moved here. Had she somehow been forced to leave?

I stared blankly at the papers, unable to reconcile what it said on them with what I had experienced personally as a student of Ma's. After all, I'd never seen anything even remotely involving a restriction of freedom—this was an open community, and half our people didn't even live here. Everyone came and went as they pleased, and Ma made it clear we were all responsible for our own choices. As for violation of trust, I could hardly imagine that. Ma had the highest integrity of anyone I'd ever known, and was impeccable about keeping her agreements and her word. That just didn't sound anything like her.

I guess it was true that her classes were on the expensive side, but that was all voluntary. I'd never seen Ma take money from anyone except for the training she gave them in return. And it wasn't like she pressured people into it. Yeah, she had encouraged me to sign up for the Series, but it was such an important step in my growth, and I didn't regret it for a second. So I didn't see how anyone could claim that as milking.

As for verbal abuse, well, she had always been nothing but compassionate with me. Despite my desire to gloss right over that, though, one thing kept me from dismissing that charge completely. I kept thinking back to that evening that she attacked the psychotherapist in class, the one Jeremy said was so arrogant. I had been really frightened when I saw her do that, and the whole thing still kind of bothered me. Was it possible that was something other than a true teaching? Did she used to do more of that in the past?

My reverie was interrupted by the appearance of Carolyn, who had just finished up her session with Ma. She came into the office and sat down to write out her check. While she was busy doing that, I discreetly slipped the lawsuit back to the bottom of the pile where I'd found it.

"Here you go," she said, handing me a personal check for three hundred dollars.

"Thanks," I said, looking at it closely. Three hundred dollars really was a lot of money for an hour. I looked back up at her. "Did you have a good session?" I asked.

"I really did," she nodded. "She really helped me to see how my unresolved feelings for Ted were holding me back. I just can't believe how insightful she is. Isn't she just incredible?" she said, letting out a sigh.

I knew exactly how she felt. She was talking about the Ma that I knew, the Ma who had helped me in so many ways.

"Yeah. She really is," I said.

"I just don't know what I would do without her," Carolyn said. "Can I make another appointment for next month?"

After booking her next session, Carolyn breezed out the door, a radiant, relaxed smile on her face. I took another look at the check. Well, there was no question it had been worth it for her.

When I left the office an hour later, I was uncomfortable to be walking out of there with knowledge I didn't know what to do with. I called Jeremy as soon as I got home, hoping I could talk to him about it. While most of what I'd read in the suit seemed totally bogus, I had to know if there was any truth to any of it. I needed to find out what had happened.

There was no answer on his cell phone, but I kept calling until he finally answered it at close to ten o'clock.

"I'm so glad I finally reached you," I said.

"What is it Michelle? You sound worried."

"Well, it's probably nothing, but I was filling in for Kali today, and I stumbled across some papers on her desk about another lawsuit, one from several years ago. Did you know about that?"

There was a pause before he answered. "Yes, I did know about that," he said. "She left that on her desk? Bloody hell."

"Well, it was pretty well covered up," I said hastily, not wanting to get Kali in trouble. "I only found it because I was looking for a check for Shanti. But Jeremy, what was that all about? The accusations were so harsh. I mean, there's no truth to that, is there?"

"Oh, don't be ridiculous, Michelle," he said. "How could you even think there was any truth to those ludicrous complaints? That woman was completely psychotic—she'd been on medication for years. Ma thought she could help her, but the woman was just too far gone, and she just totally turned on Ma out of nowhere. The whole thing was completely made up."

"Oh, thank God," I said, simultaneously relieved to hear it and embarrassed to admit I'd been worried about it. "I mean, that's what I thought. But it was just so disturbing to see it there, you know, in black and white like that. Especially," I added, a detail nudging itself into the forefront of my mind, "since there was more than one person involved."

"Oh, you mean the guy? He was a really sleazy character. He found out about it and just jumped on the bandwagon, trying to get some money out of Ma. Trust me, Michelle, there's absolutely no truth to any of it."

"So it was dismissed, then."

"Well, no, actually. They didn't have a case, but Ma's lawyer advised her to settle since it would cost so much more to fight it in court. They shouldn't have gotten anything, but she paid a few thousand dollars to make the whole thing go away."

"I see," I said. I was relieved to hear his perspective on the whole thing, and it did make sense, that an unstable person might try to do something like that. It was quite a few years ago, after all. But something inside me remained unsettled.

"There haven't been any other suits, have there?" I asked.

"What are you talking about? Of course not. I can't believe you'd even ask that kind of question."

"I'm sorry, I know. It's just strange for me to see all this negativity around Ma. I'm just so surprised that people could think about her like that. It's so contrary to what I know of her."

"Well, you shouldn't let yourself be so easily influenced by this kind of garbage. You know what Ma is, Michelle. Don't waste your time with all of this."

"Yeah, you're right. I don't know what I was thinking," I said. "So listen," I added, hoping to change the subject, "are you busy tomorrow night? I'd love to finally have some time with you."

"Yes, so would I," he said, "but it's going to have to wait a bit. We've got a key meeting with the attorney on Wednesday morning and I've got a ton of research to do before then. But let's talk later in the week. I should have some time then."

"Okay," I said.

"Sleep well, my love," he said softly.

It wasn't much, but it helped somehow.

I spent the rest of the week working in the tape library, keeping my phone on vibrate so I'd be sure to get it when Jeremy called. But by Friday afternoon, I'd still hadn't heard from him.

I called him three times before I finally got him on the phone.

"Hey," I said.

"Oh, hey," he replied. He sounded far away.

"How'd the meeting go?"

"Okay. He said we're on the right track, but he still needs a lot more information. So it looks like I'm going to have to keep working down here for a while yet."

"Oh," I said. "That's a bummer."

"Tell me about it."

"Well, do you want me to come down there tomorrow?"

"No, I really can't spare the time," he replied.

I'm not sure what it was—some combination of distance and edge in his voice, but I finally lost my ability to be patient. I was tired of being constantly put off. "Well, Jesus, Jeremy, you've got to take a break sometime. We haven't spent any time together in like two weeks."

"I've been really busy, Michelle."

"I know that, Jeremy," I said, trying to control the anger that was rising in me. "But there's more to the world than doing lawsuit research. I mean, what do you expect me to do, wait until this case is over before I get to see you again?"

"I'm surprised at you, Michelle," he said, his voice measured. "I would think you of all people would understand how important it is to support Ma right now."

"I do understand that," I said. "Why do you think I'm spending all of my time working in the library for free instead of looking for a job like I should be? It's because I want to help out, too, you know."

"Well, then you should be more patient."

I took a deep breath, trying to calm myself down. "I have been patient, Jeremy. But I am also your girlfriend and I think I have the right to see you every now and again. You're putting me off indefinitely and I don't think that's good for our relationship."

"Well, maybe we have very different ideas about relationship," he said. "God is always going to come first with me, and Ma needs my service right now. You need to understand that."

"I do understand that," I said. "But how long do you expect me to wait?"

"Look, Michelle," he sighed, irritation in his voice, "I don't have a lot of time for this right now. I think Ma was right about your attachment issues—you really should be dealing with that on your own. I just can't—"

My heart skipped a beat. "What do you mean, Ma was right about my attachment issues?"

There was a long pause. "Ma mentioned to me that your energy was becoming very negative, and that your attachment issues were being triggered by my absence. She didn't think it was a good idea for me to indulge you with that."

"What?" I said. "You've been discussing me with Ma?"

"I discuss everything with Ma, Michelle. She's my teacher, remember?"

I sat there with the phone pressed against my ear, feeling more mortified than I could ever remember feeling before. I had been judged and failed, just like I was afraid of.

"Oh, God," I muttered.

"Listen, Michelle," he continued, "I'm sorry I don't have a lot of time to deal with this right now. But I've got to get back to work. I'll call you when things lighten up, okay?"

I just nodded. "Yeah, okay."

I sat there with the dead phone in my hand for a long time. So Ma had noticed my energy after all. Maybe my negativity wasn't bad enough to get me kicked out, but it could very well cost me Jeremy if I didn't deal with it.

The sun had begun dropping behind the mountain, and as the darkness settled in through my studio, I thought hard about Ma's comments. It wasn't difficult to figure out what she was talking about. I'd had very little in the way of positive male attention when I was growing up, and I did tend to get clingy with men I was really attracted to. Jeremy's absence was really triggering me. I was starting to worry that he wasn't just busy, that he was really avoiding me. It was a very familiar line of thought.

As I sat there, half-meditating, the guy who lived in the house behind me stepped outside and started fiddling with his grill. A moment later, a woman appeared holding a plate full of chicken. She was followed by a young girl, maybe four years old, holding a skewer of vegetables in each hand. Her father lifted her up so she could set them on the grill. He held her tightly as she did so, making sure she didn't get too close. Then he set her carefully back on the ground, where she took her mother's hand and went back inside.

I felt a pang of jealousy as I watched that cozy scene, and there was an enormous longing in my heart to be a part of it.

As I sat there, my craving for the kind of emotional support and security I'd never gotten at home began to grow. I wanted someone to hold me carefully and make sure I didn't get burned. I wanted someone to stroke my hair, to tell me that Jeremy still loved me and that everything was going to be okay. It was a kind of comfort I'd never had, and I wanted it desperately.

A wave of sadness passed through me, and soon I was crying. I wanted Jeremy to be the source of that comfort for me, but that wasn't really his job. No wonder he was irritated with me. I needed to give him some space, figure out how to find that comfort for myself.

As I sat there, an idea began forming in my mind. I got up from my cushion and began rummaging around in the back of my closet for my box of photographs. When I took off the lid, the picture of my mother was right on top.

I picked it up, wiping some dust off the edge of the frame. It was a formal, black-and-white shot, her shoulder-length blond hair impeccably curled in a sixties style. She had a slight smile on her face, as if she was remembering a secret joke.

I pulled the photograph close to my chest, feeling my heart ache. As I sat there, rocking myself gently back and forth, a memory of her floated through my mind. I must have been about three, and she was drawing a bath for me. She held me on the edge of the tub, her arm tight around my waist, as I poured an entire bottle of bubble bath under the faucet.

I'd always loved bath time with her. I looked at the picture again, the longing for her still sharp in my heart. Well, maybe she wasn't here. But I had a bathtub, and I decided to use it.

I set the photograph on the bathroom counter, then began searching in the cabinet for some bubble bath. I found a dusty bottle way in the back corner, still unopened. After blowing the dust off the top of the lid, I sat on the edge of the tub and turned on the water, pouring the pink liquid under the faucet in a steady stream. I used twice as much as necessary, and a mound of bubbles grew rapidly past the edge of the tub.

I dropped my clothes on the ground and slipped into the warm water. My muscles instantly relaxed in the water's embrace. I took a long look at my mother's smiling face, then closed my eyes.

Though it didn't immediately lessen the craving for the feeling of strong arms around me, in some small way, the bath really helped. As I lay there soaking, everything seemed to be a little bit easier. Okay, maybe Jeremy was really busy right now, but I knew he loved me. Our relationship was solid, the best one I'd ever had. Everything was going to be okay. I let out a sigh and sank deeper into the bubbles. Of course everything was going to be okay.

Twelve

Late on Sunday afternoon, the phone rang. I leapt across the bed to answer it, hoping it would be Jeremy.

"Michelle, it's Kali."

"Oh. Hi."

"There seems to be a problem with the web site. No one can access it, and I've just learned that some of our e-mails are getting bounced. We need you to come in and take a look at it."

"It sounds like it might be a server problem," I said. "Have you tried calling them?"

"No. I'm swamped, and I don't think it would do much good anyway, since I don't understand that stuff. You really need to come in."

"Okay. I'll be over in a little bit."

As I pulled my car into Ma's driveway, I was surprised to see Jeremy's Pathfinder. I'd thought he was still in Denver— maybe I'd get to see him after all.

"What are you doing working on a Sunday?" I asked Kali as I slipped into my old chair in front of the computer.

"Just helping Ma out with this lawsuit stuff," she said with a frustrated sigh. "As if I didn't have enough to do with running Ma's entire organization."

I felt a twinge in my stomach as she spoke. I'd offered to help—why hadn't they asked me?

"So I got a call about an hour ago from Shanti telling me the site was down and had been all day," she said. "Her e-mails have been bounced and God knows who else's."

"Right, okay," I said, switching on the machine. "I'll see what I can find out."

Everything seemed to be okay on our end, so I contacted the server's tech support. While I was waiting for an agent, I turned my attention back to Kali.

"How long has Jeremy been here?" I asked.

"I don't know. He was here when I got in," she said, not looking up.

"Where is he?"

"They're in a meeting."

"Oh." I wished I could go upstairs and see him, just to say hi. It was so hard, not having spoken with him since that last difficult conversation. I hoped he would come down before I left.

After waiting on hold for close to an hour, I learned that the server we were on had crashed.

"They're in the process of moving everyone to new servers," I told Kali, "but they can't say exactly how long it's going to take. They hope to have us back up and running no later than tomorrow."

"Okay," she nodded as she gathered up her things for the night. I turned off the lights and we walked out to the parking area. "I'll call you in the morning if it still looks like there's a problem," she said as she got into her car.

I waited for a moment before getting in my own. I was hoping Jeremy would come down and say goodbye, though he had no idea I was even there. After several empty minutes, I got in my car and drove away.

I was halfway home before I realized I'd left my cell phone at Ma's house. I thought about just getting it in the morning, but I didn't want to not have it in case Jeremy called. So I turned around and headed back towards the reservoir.

It was just getting dark as I turned down Ma's street. It was that time of night when lights were glowing from the windows of the houses, but people hadn't yet shut their drapes. As I witnessed the various domestic scenes I passed, a melancholy feeling took over me, a sensation of being an outsider to such warm moments. But then I caught sight of Ma's. Lights blazed from the upper floor of her house, a beacon against the darkness. In some small way, at least, I knew I could call her place my home.

As I turned in the driveway, a movement from one of the upstairs windows caught my attention. I looked up to see Ma and Jeremy standing in her bedroom. One of his hands was resting lightly on her arm, the other was gently holding her face. Before my brain had a chance to process what I was seeing, he leaned over and kissed her.

She did not resist. After a long moment, she pulled away and then brushed his third eye with her lips. Then they turned, arm in arm, and walked out of my sight.

As I watched this, the blood drained out of my body and was replaced by ice. My shocked mind simply stared at the now empty window, my hands gripping the steering wheel as I felt something shatter inside me.

I sat in my car for a long time. It couldn't be. It couldn't. But the image of the two of them kissing refused to disappear from my brain, playing itself over and over in my mind.

Maybe he was just trying to comfort her. No, that was a real kiss, not a casual one. It couldn't be.

I stared at the house, now dark in all rooms except one. I closed my eyes, fighting back a tidal wave of thoughts I wasn't capable of facing. I couldn't have seen what I thought I did, I reminded myself. I must have been imagining things.

I got out of my car, looking up at Ma's window as I did so. It remained empty. I walked into the office to pick up my phone. There was no sound from anywhere inside the house. I knew Jeremy was still there, upstairs in Ma's bedroom. *In Ma's bedroom.* How could that be?

I shook my head, as if I could snap myself out of it. I must have been imagining things. I got back in my car and started driving. Turning onto Jay Road, I cut off an SUV. I hardly noticed as they swerved around me, honking.

I wasn't sure at what point I had started crying. My mind was so numb I only noticed it when I walked in the door of my house. They were the kind of tears that leak out of you, the ones that escape from behind the dam you are doing everything in your power to hold up.

The phone rang almost immediately after I shut the door. I stared at it through watery eyes, suddenly frightened of who it might be. As I stood there, debating what to do, the machine picked up.

"Hey, Michelle, it's Matt." His voice was deep, solid, and comforting. "Listen, I was wondering if you wanted to catch a movie tomorrow night. There's an Indian film playing at Crossroads—it's supposed to be good. Give me a—"

I picked up the receiver. "Matt?"

"Hey, Michelle, you're there. How's it going?"

I started crying in earnest then, my body overcome by heavy sobs.

"Michelle? What is it? Are you okay?"

"I—oh, God, Matt," I heaved. I tried to say something else, but all I could do was sob.

"Michelle, just hang on, okay? I'll be right there."

Ten minutes later, he knocked softly on my door.

"What the hell happened?" he asked, taking me by the shoulders as I dissolved into tears once again. Gently, he led me over towards the bed and sat down next to me. "Jesus, Michelle, what is it?"

I struggled to catch my breath. "Oh, God, I'm not even sure. I mean, I think—I don't know. I just—"

"Hold on, okay? Just take a deep breath."

I did so, my body shuddering in the process.

"Okay, now start from the beginning."

I took in another gulp of air before speaking. "I was over at Ma's today—there was some sort of problem with the web site. I was surprised to see Jeremy's car there because he'd said he was in Denver all week and I haven't seen him in like two weeks, but he was upstairs with Ma, and you know we're not supposed to disturb them and everything..." I reached for more air as he rubbed his hand on my shoulder. "I left with Kali but then I had to go back because I forgot my phone and when I got back to the house I saw—" My voice trailed off as I froze, terrified to say anything else.

"You saw what, Michelle? What did you see?"

I turned to him, my frightened eyes staring into his. He was genuinely worried as he watched me struggle with what to say next. Part of me was screaming inside that I should just keep my mouth shut, the implications of what I was about to say threatening me from all sides. But some other part of me was pushing hard to say it anyway, and I gave in to a swell of momentum from deep inside me that soon had control of my vocal chords.

"I saw Ma and Jeremy kissing," I said, my voice barely above a whisper.

"What?" he said, shock visible on his face. "Where?"

"In the window."

"Are you sure?"

I looked away from him. "I think so."

"Christ, Michelle, that's crazy," he said, getting up and walking a few steps away from me. "That just doesn't make any sense. I mean, Ma can be pretty affectionate, you know, maybe it was just that kind of kiss."

I shook my head. "He kissed her, the same way he kissed me. It was a lover's kiss, I'm sure of it."

"But why would she do that? Ma doesn't need that from him. She hasn't been with anyone since her transformation."

I stared at him. "You didn't know about David?"

"What are you talking about?"

"David Michelson, from California. He and Ma were lovers. For years."

"Who told you that?"

"Kali."

Matt got up and began pacing around my studio. "Why the hell would Kali tell you that?"

"Because it's true, Matt. I found out about it when I over-heard Ma arguing with him on the phone. Kali told me not to tell anyone, that Ma didn't want to create jealousy amongst her students. He's suing her, you know."

"What?!"

"I saw the papers. That's why Jeremy's been spending so much time with her. He's helping her prepare for the suit. At least, that's what they told me." I said, wondering then just how much time it took to prepare for a lawsuit, anyway.

Matt walked back and forth across my small kitchen. "None of this makes any sense," he said, shaking his head. "I'm sure this is all just a big misunderstanding. Ma is so far above all of that, there's just no way it can be true. I'm sure you've misunderstood," he said, more to himself than me.

"I don't know, Matt," I said, staring at the floor. "I can't believe it, either. But I'm pretty sure what I saw."

He looked at me from across the room with a gaze that made me uneasy. I felt my stomach tighten as I realized he might not believe me. But then he walked over and sat down next to me, putting a comforting hand on my shoulder.

"I'm sure whatever it was you saw looked pretty bad," he said, looking at me earnestly. "But think for a minute, Michelle —this is Ma we're talking about here. Remember?"

I looked away. I wanted him to believe me, to acknowledge what I saw as real. But there was also a big part of me that wanted him to be right, that wanted all of this to be a huge, horrible mistake.

I let out a sigh. "I don't know. I don't know what to think."

"Look, there's got to be some kind of explanation. Jeremy told me he'd be home tonight—I'll talk to him about it then. We'll get this all cleared up, you'll see."

My stomach lurched as he mentioned Jeremy. Oh, God, what would he think if he heard this from Matt?

"I don't know, Matt," I said. "That could be really strange, you know. I mean, maybe I should talk to him about it myself." It was the last thing in the world I wanted to do, but I knew the alternative was worse.

"Well, yeah, I guess. If you think that's best."

In spite of myself, I nodded. "Yeah, let me talk to him. Don't say anything, okay? Just—just ask him to call me as soon as he can. It doesn't matter how late."

"Yeah, sure," he nodded. His face was so calm and reassuring, for a moment I wondered what I was so concerned about. He had to be right, there had to be some kind of reasonable explanation. I hoped to God it was so.

I waited until past midnight for Jeremy to call me, but the phone remained silent. My mind spun in fast circles around different reasons why he hadn't called. Matt was usually in bed by ten, so maybe he couldn't give Jeremy the message because he'd come home to late. Or maybe, I thought as my stomach twisted itself into even further knots, Jeremy hadn't come home at all.

Several times I picked up the phone to dial his cell number, but I couldn't bring myself to do it. I was supposed to wait for him to call me, and the prospect of breaking that agreement so I could ask him if he was cheating on me with Ma was not an appealing one. God, what had I gotten myself into?

I lay awake long into the night, trying to come up with some reasonable explanation for what I had seen. It was dusk—maybe what I had seen was a trick of the light. Or maybe it was some kind of blessing she was giving him—except for the fact that he kissed her. Or maybe I was just totally losing my mind.

I awoke late the next morning to the sound of the phone ringing.

"Hello?"

"It's Kali. The web site's still not working. I was wondering if you were coming in today."

"Um, I'm not really sure there's anything I can do at this point. We're just waiting for the web host to fix it."

"Is it possible you can come in to check up on it? Ma's very concerned and wants to know when it's going to be fixed."

I was still trying to figure out my reply when she added, "Ma would also like to see you. She said there's something she needs to discuss with you."

My stomach lurched. "What is it?"

"I don't know, she didn't tell me. She just asked if you could come in at eleven."

Oh, God. Did Matt tell Jeremy? I started to panic. Oh, shit. What was I going to say to her?

I forced myself to take a deep breath. Maybe he hadn't told her. Maybe this was about something else altogether. I gulped some more air. Either way, it didn't really matter. No one turned down a meeting at Ma's request. I had to go.

"Um, okay, I'll be there."

By the time I walked in the front door of her house an hour later, the knot of tension in my stomach was so thick I wondered if I was going to throw up.

Kali lead me down the hall to Ma's office. She was standing with her back towards me, looking out the window as Kali led me inside and shut the door.

After a small eternity, she turned to look at me. She was staring at me with her penetrating gaze, and I knew she was reading my energy. I was afraid of her, of what she could see, of what she might say.

"I am concerned about you, Michelle," she began quietly. "You are one of my most gifted students, but as I have warned you, that gift comes with a price."

After a long pause, she began again. "I have been watching you carefully over the last few weeks. Not long ago, I began to notice signs of instability in your field. I suspected that you were having trouble integrating the consciousness shift you made last month, and it appears that this is in fact the case."

I felt my heart sink. I knew there was truth to what she was saying. It had been weeks since I'd felt anything even remotely like the bliss I'd found, and I'd been struggling hard with all different kinds of negativity.

"You know, Michelle," she said, "most people don't realize just how dangerous and difficult this path is. They see the love, they see the bliss, and they think that's all there is. But the darkness doesn't let us go so easily. It will fight to the death to keep us in its clutches." She paused for a long moment before she said, "I am afraid that it is fighting hard for you."

The fear I had been feeling ballooned into full blown terror as she spoke. My God, what was she seeing in me?

"When people get close to the light, it is not uncommon for them to experience a backlash," she continued. "For some, this shows up as a return to familiar patterns of negativity and dysfunction. But for others, it can take a darker turn as the ego fights to regain control. In some cases, the ego will stop at nothing to prevent its own death. Even," she added, "if that means sacrificing its own sanity.

"As you have learned, Michelle, the mind is a very powerful thing. When threatened, it can play all kinds of tricks to bring itself back to safety. Including," she said softly, "seeing things that aren't there."

I stared at her, the implications of her words washing over me like freezing rain. Was she saying I was actually going crazy?

"I have learned this morning that you told Matt Taver that Jeremy and I are in relationship with each other. Is that true?"

My throat was so dry I wasn't sure I could speak. I felt my words crack as I opened my mouth. "I only told him what I saw last night," I whispered. "That I saw you kissing."

She watched me for a long time. "I am very worried about you, Michelle. I knew that Jeremy's absence was triggering some deep issues for you, but I did not expect you to be so consumed by them. It appears that you have begun letting the darkness take over your rational capacities. I warned you that this could happen as you increased your experience of the light. You must be very careful now."

I closed my eyes, feeling an intense pressure inside of me. It was though the ground was crumbling away beneath my feet, the gaping abyss below waiting to suck me down. I fought the urge to collapse, to just give in and let it all be over.

As I struggled, Ma walked up to me and gently cupped my face in her hands. "It's alright, Michelle," she said softly. "I can see what's happening to you. I won't let you fall."

My heart lurched in longing for the love she was offering me, and tears began rolling down my cheeks.

With infinite tenderness, Ma wiped them away. "It's alright, Michelle," she repeated. "You can get through this. But you must begin to realize the depths of your own darkness. I don't know what it was you think you saw last night," she continued, "but I assure you, Jeremy and I are not in a romantic relationship. He has been spending time with me solely to assist me in preparing for that frivolous lawsuit. We are not lovers."

As she spoke, a thought exploded through my brain.

She's lying.

The knowledge radiated through me like an electric shock. My eyes flew open, and I stared into her face, inches from my own.

The look in her eyes was not the soft and tender one I had imagined, but rather hard and calculating. Before I knew what was happening, I said, "That's not true."

"What did you say?" she said as shock flashed quickly across her face. Her hands fell away from me, and she took a step back.

"I said, that's not true," I repeated, comprehension slowly dawning as the thought sifted through the layers of my brain. "Oh my God. Jeremy hasn't been spending all these nights in Denver. He's been spending them with you!"

"Michelle—" Ma began, but I didn't let her finish.

Disbelief was rapidly being replaced by anger as I finally let myself see what I had been hiding from. "It makes so much sense now," I said. "You told him to back off from me so you could have him for yourself! Oh, God," I said, shaking my head, "I can't believe how stupid I've been!"

"You have no idea what you are saying, Michelle," Ma said, her voice dangerously calm. "You are making up fantasies about Jeremy and me because you are unable to face the reality that your attachment issues are strangling your relationship with him. My comments to Jeremy were made only for your highest benefit. I had hoped to spare you more pain."

I shook my head, my anger now mixed with amazement at her blatant attempt to manipulate me. "That's thoughtful of you, Ma. But tell me honestly, how much stock would you place in the wisdom of a teacher whose lessons to her students seem calculated to benefit her own agenda so perfectly?"

She stared at me, fierceness in her eyes. "You are caught up in the emotions of the moment, Michelle, and you are not seeing anything clearly. There cannot be any healing until you allow yourself to move through these base feelings and open your heart back up again. Only then will you really be capable of seeing the truth behind all of this."

I met her gaze levelly. She was trying to stare me down, but there was enormous tension in her body. Behind the mask of spiritual master, she was frightened.

I stared at her, wondering how on earth I'd never seen that before. As I watched, the radiant master I adored dissolved, and in her place stood an aging actress fighting hard to be taken seriously. In that moment, I felt something inside me snap.

"I think I've seen things clearly enough, Ma," I said. "You may think your act is still working, but the only one you're fooling here is yourself."

I turned for the door, slamming it loudly behind me as I left. I started shaking as I rushed down the hall. Kali looked up at me as I passed the office, but I just kept going.

As I drove away from Ma's house this time, there was no doubt in my mind about what I had seen. I was so angry it was hard to drive, and it took every ounce of my energy to keep my car on the road. But I needed to get as far away from that house as I could. My grip on the steering wheel tightened so much that my fingers turned white.

I pulled my car up in front of my house a few minutes later and killed the engine. I lowered my head onto the steering wheel, forcing myself to breath regularly. As I sat there, a rush of images began pouring into my mind, all of the things I'd noticed about Ma over the last few months and had tried to ignore. Her angry outbursts. Her outrageous fees. Her hidden secrets. Her judgments of others. The contradictions in her teachings. All of these things I'd noticed, and all of these things I'd tried to justify away.

I looked up, my view of the street in front of me warped by my tears. It was all so clear. I'd wanted her to be what she said she was so badly that I'd worked overtime to avoid seeing the truth. But this, well, this just made it all very obvious. I had just spent the last six months of my life worshiping a charismatic woman who was lying and manipulating people for her own ends.

Eventually, I pulled myself out of the car and walked inside. The rage had subsided a little, but in its place was a profound feeling of betrayal, a pain so deep I couldn't feel where it stopped. It was worse, even, than when my mother died. As painful as her death been, I knew she hadn't done it on purpose.

There was a message blinking on my machine.

"It's me, Matt. Listen, I talked to Jeremy. He told me what must have happened last night, and everything is okay. You've probably already talked to Ma, but if not, call me."

I stared at the phone. He sounded so calm. I hated to be the one to tell him. But he needed to know the truth.

I dialed his number. "Matt?"

"Oh, hey, Michelle," he said. "You know, I talked to Jeremy last night. He said that Ma's been having some problems with her back, and he was doing some work on her, massaging her neck or something. That must have been what you saw last night. I knew it was something like that."

I closed my eyes and sank onto the bed. Though it should have been no surprise, hearing that Jeremy was covering for them cut me deeply. It ripped away the last shreds of denial I had about the man I loved, and new wave of excruciating pain washed over me. He'd chosen Ma over me.

I shut my eyes tightly, trying to squeeze back the tears.

"It's not true, Matt," I said softly.

"What? Come on, Michelle. Jeremy wouldn't lie to me."

"Ma just lied to me, Matt. So I suspect Jeremy is just as capable of lying as well," I added, suddenly realizing just how many times he probably lied to me over the last few weeks. A burst of anger flashed through me. "I saw them kissing, and they're both trying to cover it up."

There was a long silence on the other end.

"Look, Matt, I know it's hard to believe. But there's a lot of weird stuff going on around Ma that most people don't know anything about. She wants to keep it that way, so she just accused me of being crazy. But it's not true, Matt. I'm not crazy, and I saw them kissing. You've got to believe me."

There was no reply for a long time. "Listen, Michelle," he began, "I don't know what you saw. But I just can't believe what you're telling me. I know you've been struggling with the separation from Jeremy, but attacking Ma isn't going to help."

My head began to pound. Of course that's what Jeremy would have told him. It sounded so logical. Honestly, I couldn't really blame Matt for believing what Jeremy had fed him. A new wave of tears welled up inside me, and I fought to keep them back.

"Look, Matt," I said, "you can think whatever you want. But I'm sorry, I just can't do this anymore. I can't worship someone who is as full of shit as you or me."

There was silence from the other end of the phone. I waited a moment, and then hung up.

Unable to hold myself up any longer, I collapsed onto the bed. I cried for a long time, but the tears were hollow ones, and they didn't make the slightest dent in the pain.

I have no idea how long I lay there. I only noticed that the sun's rays had begun sliding long across the floor when the phone rang. I eyed it warily, not imaging it could be anyone I'd want to hear from.

The machine picked up.

"Michelle, it's me," my father's voice began. "Danny's gone. I caught him drunk a few days ago. Haven't seen him since. I thought you should know."

A click, then silence.

I closed my eyes and rubbed my forehead. Really, it was amazing Danny had lasted this long. I could picture the scene. He'd have been drinking cheap beer in front of the TV; my dad would have lit into him as soon as he saw the empty cans on the coffee table. It wasn't hard to understand why Danny preferred the streets—empty of God and the judgments of the father, I'm sure they were much quieter.

I rolled over onto my back and stared up at the ceiling. In Danny's world, there was no God. I'd tried to convince him there was one in mine. But that world had just collapsed around me. I wondered idly who was right.

Eventually, I fell into a restless sleep. When I awoke the next morning, I was blanketed by the quietly lucid awareness that my life had entirely fallen apart.

The very act of getting out of bed felt like stepping into a wide, empty chasm. Every aspect of my life over the past six months had in some way revolved around Ma, her teachings or her community. But now, in an instant, all of that had gone up in smoke.

I sat on the edge of the bed, my head buried in my hands. I was awash in a horrible feeling of loss, a kind of anguish more intense than I could ever remember feeling. The grief over having lost my teacher, my lover, and my community was entwined with an even greater anguish over everything I'd given up for them—my life in Denver, Lucy, and thousands and thousands of dollars I currently had no prayer of ever repaying.

Worse than the grief was the crushing voice of judgment that wasted no time in brutally reminding me how horribly I had screwed up my entire life. If it was possible to make a worse set of choices, I had no idea what they could possibly be.

I forced myself up from the bed in the vain hope that I could escape those thoughts. But they followed me around with each step I took. I collapsed back into tears before I even made it into the bathroom.

An hour later, I pulled myself up off the floor. I knew I had to do something, something to keep me from falling totally apart. I tried to distract myself by reading, but I couldn't keep my mind focused on the words. I took a bath, but the soothing water had little effect. Eventually, I tried just sleeping, but I could only do so much of that before I was unpleasantly awake again. So I spent most of the day just lying in bed, trying very, very hard not to think.

* * *

Day passed into night passed into day. In the rare moments when I did get out of bed, I moved mechanically through my shrunken world, mostly just to use the bathroom and feed my body the occasional bowl of cereal.

Eventually, a soothing numbness began to take the edge off of my raw nerves. The gaping hole of pain was still there inside me, but its edges had begun to close over. If I kept my thoughts carefully away from anything having to do with my current reality, I could make it through several hours without crying.

Around ten o'clock on the third morning, I heard a knock at my door.

"Michelle?" my landlady's voice called out. Her face was peering in the window—I didn't want to talk to her, but I knew she'd already seen me. I ran my fingers through my dirty hair and shuffled over to the door.

"Oh, hi, Linda," I said.

"You look awful!" she said. "Are you sick?"

"Um, yeah," I said. It was a comfortingly easy answer. I'd never talked to her about Ma, and I wasn't about to start in on that topic now.

"Do you need anything?" she asked as she looked me over with worried eyes. "I just came down here to check on you because your mail was piling up, you know, and you hadn't said anything about going out of town. Can I get you some Vitamin C, or some soup or something?"

"Oh, gosh, Linda, that's really sweet of you." I was touched by her concern, but I wanted to end the conversation as quickly as possible. "I think I'm through the worst of it, though. But thanks for offering."

"Well, if you're sure," she said, clearly not believing me.

I smiled at her, my first one days. "Don't worry, I'll be all right," I said as I reached for the pile of mail she had brought down with her.

"Okay, then. Well, call me if you need anything."

I nodded as I shut the door. What I needed was a new life. But I didn't think she'd be able to get that for me.

I tossed the mail on my desk. As I did so, I caught sight of myself in the mirror—it had been days since I'd so much as even brushed my hair, let alone bathed. No wonder she was concerned. Ugh. I really needed a shower.

My muscles relaxed as soon as I stepped under the warm water. I scrubbed every inch of myself, as if washing away a lifetime's worth of dirt. Then I just stood there, letting the water cascade over me until the temperature turned cold.

After getting a comb through my hair and putting on some loose clothes, I went into the kitchen. I was feeling hungry for the first time in recent memory, but I was stopped by a picture of Jeremy that hung on the fridge. I'd taken it the day of our first hike together, and the bright sun shone on his blond hair as if it were gold. He looked like such an angel, the bastard.

I pulled the picture off the fridge, wiping away tears as I did so. Really, I should have seen it coming. He'd dumped Lucy for me, and me for Ma. It made perfect sense.

It had been over a week since we'd spoken. There had been no formal end to our relationship, but I held no illusions about that. The fact that he'd made no effort to contact me spoke volumes.

I thought about calling him then, just to have some sense of completion. And to see when I might be able to pick up the sweater I'd left in his room the last time I'd been there. But the image of his bedroom, and the expensive white sheets on the bed where he'd first made love to me, ambushed my fragile defenses. I leaned over the counter, unable to hold back the tears.

I only let myself cry for a few minutes. I forced myself to take deep breaths and calm down. I threw the picture in the trash, and decided I wasn't really all that fond of the sweater. I clearly wasn't ready to talk to him.

There wasn't much food in the fridge, but I was able to pull together breakfast out of a couple of eggs, half an onion, and some toast. It was the first real meal I'd had in days.

After washing the dishes, I turned and looked over the mess of my apartment. I spent a few minutes straightening things up, then turned to the pile of mail Linda had brought. Without even looking, I could see that there were several bills in it. I felt my heart sink, the undertow of emotion threatened to pull me back in. But I turned and forced myself to walk away before I could start crying.

I knew I had to get out of the house. But I didn't really want to see or talk to anyone. I looked out the window, up to the mountains. It was a beautiful, warm fall day. Maybe a hike would do me good.

The trail around the lake near my house wound its way up the side of the mountain, and I was soon breathing hard as my muscles worked to carry me up the steep path. The effort was therapeutic, pulling the blood out of my brain long enough for my thoughts to begin to clear.

I hiked for a long time, merging onto a trail that climbed up to the top of the ridge and back into the forest. It was cooler in the woods, and the air felt good against the beads of sweat forming on my skin. I thought maybe I could just keep walking forever, walk right out of Boulder and into a whole new world.

Eventually, I stopped to take a break and a sip of water. A squirrel jumped out from behind a tree in front of me and scampered away. Despite myself, I smiled. I really needed this.

As I rested, I ran my fingers along the bark of a thick tree, breathing in the woodsy smell of pine sap. It was Ma's teachings about being in the moment that had first allowed me to really appreciate the magic of the forest. It had made such a difference in my life, the way she taught me to see things. I closed my eyes, steeling myself against the pain I knew was trailing on the heels of that thought. How could it be? How could that woman have taught such beauty, but done things that were so ugly?

I started walking again, hoping to outdistance the question. I hiked deeper and deeper into the trees, but the thoughts just kept coming. If my perception of Ma was really that distorted, then how clearly could I have seen anything over the past six months? My mind ran over all of the experiences I'd had since I started studying with her—the insights, the understandings, the altered states, the bliss. Had any of it even been real? Had I just created my own delusionary world based on the ravings of some crazy middle-aged woman who was no more spiritual than the rest of us?

I didn't wait for an answer, but just kept moving as fast as I could. The trail had taken a steep turn up, and I followed it back and forth up the side of the mountain until it came to an abrupt end at the top of a rocky ridge.

The view was incredible, the tree-lined slopes rolling away below me like emerald velvet. I collapsed onto a boulder to catch my breath. I don't know how long I sat there, feeling nothing except the pounding of my heart and the cool mountain air against my skin. I closed my eyes, taking in a few deep breaths. As I did so, the first thing I noticed through all of my internal chaos was the quiet feeling at the center of my cells I had come to equate with God.

It was the seed that had been left inside me after the original feeling of overpowering bliss from the Seminar Series weekend had receded. It had never really disappeared, but it had been weeks since I'd remembered to tap into that connection. Yet here it was now, unasked for, quietly asserting itself as I sat on the edge of the cliff, preparing to throw everything I'd learned in the last few months over it.

The feeling was sweet and calming. It expanded as I focused on it, filling me with a kind of soothing, internal embrace. As I took in another breath, my doubts about the truth of what I'd experienced began to dissolve. Here, alone in the woods at the top of the ridge, I knew that however false Ma might have been as a teacher, that my own experience of God was real.

I felt tears begin to run down my cheeks. They were quiet ones, made of a mixture of gratitude and grief. They washed my face gently, cleansing away the dirt and the sweat until there was nothing left to clean.

I'm not sure how long I sat there, crying first, and then just sitting. It was only when I noticed the sun had begun to sink towards the mountain that it dawned on me I should go home.

* * *

It was dark by the time I got back to my studio. I headed towards the bathroom, my muscles aching for a warm tub. Before I got there, my eye was caught by the photograph of Ma I'd placed on my bookshelf shortly after moving in.

It was an 8x10 portrait of her, a black and white one I'd put in a silver frame and surrounded with dried rose petals. It was one of my favorite pictures of her—she was sitting regally in the white chair, a mysterious smile on her face.

I walked over and picked up the frame. It didn't seem possible, that the woman in this frame could lie. How could she, when she was the one who started me on this path in the first place? In spite of everything, she had been instrumental in helping me connect with a part of my life I hadn't even known existed. And in that, she had given me a huge gift.

I ran my fingers around the edge of the frame, letting my eyes rest in her soft, deep gaze. I felt a sharp pang of longing to have everything back the way it had been a week ago. Tears formed again on the edge of my eyes. It was never going to happen, I knew that. And I hated her for it.

I turned the picture over and pulled it out of its frame. I hated her. And I loved her. I thought my heart might split in two.

A tear fell on the picture, and then another. I put my finger in the puddle; the paper under it was turning sticky. I looked at the picture again, looked deeply into her gray eyes. Then I ripped the photograph in half.

I awoke the next morning feeling strangely calm. Although I was nervous about how I was going to put the pieces of my shattered life back together again, it felt easier now. Scary, but not impossible.

I began by sweeping the rose petals that had surrounded Ma's picture off the bookshelf. I didn't want any reminders of that. Even without the petals, though, I could still see the hole where the photo had been.

I stared at it for a moment, knowing I needed to find something to put there. I looked around my studio and realized the painting I'd done of the abstract figure in golds and pastels was still sitting on my easel. I picked it up and set it on the bookshelf, letting it lean against the wall.

I stepped back for a moment, allowing myself a rare moment of admiration. I usually disliked almost all of my work, but this piece was different. It was so much more than just a painting to me, having been birthed out of my realization about the creative side of spirituality.

I sat down on the bed, a whole series of thoughts unfolding in my mind. Maybe I didn't know anything about enlightenment, but what I felt while painting was not all that different from what I'd felt sitting on that mountainside the previous day. When I was painting, there was a peace inside me that just wasn't there otherwise. It was something I'd always known, but had forgotten when I got caught up in the day-to-day world of corporate design.

Whatever direction I decided to take my life from here on out, I knew that painting was going to have to be a large part of it. I'd been putting it off for way too long. Maybe I'd have to get a design job to get myself out of debt, but no matter what I did, I was going to start painting regularly again. If I could resurrect nothing else out of my wreck of a life, I knew I could at least do that much. I made a promise to myself—and to the quiet feeling of peace inside me—that I would do at least a painting a month from now on.

After that, everything became much clearer. The decision to move back to Denver was as obvious as my move up to Boulder had been. I liked Boulder, but I was done here. There was no reason for me to stay.

Before I set about searching for a new place to live, though, there was one more thing I had to do. Late one afternoon, I headed down to the restaurant where Lucy had been hired a few months back. I hadn't seen her in over two months, and I hoped she was still there.

It was early, and the place wasn't open yet. I knocked on the glass door, trying to quell my nervousness as I did so. A busboy let me inside, and as I stepped into the dining room, I was relieved to catch a glimpse of Lucy's black braid as she kneeled in front of a set of wooden shelves, stocking wine glasses.

"Lucy," I said.

She looked up, surprise, then wariness, on her face.

"What are you doing here?"

I took a deep breath. "I came to apologize."

"What happened?" she replied, turning her eyes back the glass rack, "Jeremy break up with you?"

I bit my tongue, trying not to react. She had every right to be pissed.

"Yes, he did. He's been sleeping with Ma," I added.

"Oh, my God," Lucy said as she turned back to me, eyes wide. She watched me for a moment before dropping her polishing cloth and standing up. "What happened?"

I shrugged. "It's a long story. I'll tell you when you have more time. But listen, I'm moving back to Denver. I wanted to let you know."

"Really?" she said.

I nodded.

We stood silently for a moment, watching each other.

"So, uh," I said, "would you be interested in getting some lunch tomorrow?"

"Ah, I've got a shift."

I didn't say anything, waiting to see what would happen. I wasn't really expecting her to forgive me immediately, but I hoped there might be an opening at least.

We were interrupted by her manager. "Look, Lucy, I think I'm going to let you go. There's only one reservation on the books and it's been dead all week. You're section one, so why don't you just take the night off?"

She nodded at her manager and turned back to me. I could see her thinking, weighing her options. "Um, well," she said after a moment, "I guess I'm free now."

I broke into a smile. "Great. Where should we go?"

Twenty minutes later, she joined me at a bright blue table in a funky, brick-lined restaurant on East Pearl. We passed the first few minutes with the menu, but after placing our orders, an awkward silence descended heavily on the table.

After fidgeting with the silverware, I pulled together my courage and dove in. "I can't even begin to tell you how sorry I am, Lucy. I feel horrible about what's happened between us, and I really want to see what we can do to get through this."

She stared down at the table. I sat there, waiting for her to reply. But she remained silent.

"Please, Lucy. Say something."

When she finally looked up, there was an uncharacteristic sadness in her eyes. "What do you want me to say, Michelle? I was really hurt by what you did, and I can't just pretend it didn't happen."

My heart twisted itself into a guilty knot. I leapt to defend myself.

"I don't expect you to pretend it didn't happen," I said. "But I hope that you can understand that I really, really didn't mean to hurt you."

"How could you think I wouldn't be hurt?" she said, a sharp edge in her voice.

"I acted based on what Jeremy told me, that you guys had broken up," I said. "Yes, it was stupid—I mean, it was just wrong for me not have talked to you first—but I didn't know then that he was such a liar."

She turned away, her gaze out the window. I squirmed in my own discomfort, realizing just how lame my rationalizations must have sounded. There was a sharp stab of pain in my heart as I let myself really feel for the first time just what I had done. I had betrayed my best friend. For a guy.

If there was a worse crime between women friends, I didn't know what it was. I stifled the urge to run away and hide.

"You're right, Lucy, really," I said, keeping my eyes fixed on the bright blue of the table. "There's no excuse for what I did." I squeezed back a tear and struggled to keep my composure. "I'm just not used to that kind of attention, you know, any of it, what I was getting from Ma as well as Jeremy. I've never been the special one before, and I guess it kind of went to my head. I really wasn't trying to hurt you. I honestly didn't even know you'd be upset. But I should have. I really should have."

I took in a breath, wiping away the tears from the edge of my eyes.

"I'm sorry, Lucy. I'm sorry I hurt you so badly."

A few seconds of silence passed before I heard her voice. "So what happened?"

I looked up at her. She still looked sad, but her face seemed a little more open.

"Um, well," I said, suddenly realizing just how much there was that she didn't know. How much there was that most members of Ma's group didn't know. I started with the story about David, and kept talking until I'd told her about my confrontation with Ma. By the time I finished, her eyes were wide and her mouth was hanging open.

"You have got to be kidding me!" she said. "My God, I had no idea any of that was going on!"

"She does a pretty good job of keeping it all under wraps."

Lucy shook her head. "You know, I'd found myself wondering sometimes just how good of a teacher she could be if two of her top students could behave like you guys did. But Melinda kept telling me you can't judge a teacher by the quality of the students, because some of the best teachers are the only ones qualified to handle the most fucked-up people. But, Christ, I had no idea all of this shit was going on."

She took a sip of water, stirring the liquid with her straw, a thoughtful look on her face. "Even though I haven't been there in a while, I kept thinking I was going to go back. I mean, I've never met anyone like her before, and I really wanted to learn more from her about how I could be a better person in this whole crazy, fucked-up world. But with what you're telling me, now it all just sounds like some freaky cult or something. I can't believe I got suckered in to something like that!"

"I know," I nodded. "Sometimes I still find it really hard to believe, despite the glaring evidence in front of me."

She paused a moment before replying. "I guess I owe you an apology too, then."

I looked at her, surprised. "Why on earth should you be sorry?"

"I'm the one who got you into this. None of this would have happened if I hadn't dragged you to that first meeting."

"That's not really your fault, Luce. Maybe you told me about it, yeah, but I saw what I wanted to see."

She let out a wry smile. "It looked so good from the outside, didn't it?"

I nodded. "Yes. It did."

There was pause. "So how much debt do you have?" she asked.

"I'm not really sure, since I'm afraid to even look at my bills. But it's got to be close to twenty thousand, maybe even more."

Lucy's eyes widened. "You're kidding! That's more than twice what I've got."

I smiled at her. "So I win, huh?"

"Totally. You got way more screwed than I did. Congratulations."

Despite myself, I laughed. We might still have a long road ahead of us to get back to where we'd been, but this wasn't a bad start. Impulsively, I reached across the table to grab her hand. She squeezed mine back tightly, and as she did so, tears started running down her face. It wasn't long before I was crying too, and I moved my chair over so we could hug. We were still holding each other tightly when the waitress set down two plates in front of us and discreetly walked away.

I headed out early the next morning over to the corner market in search of a latte and the Denver paper. It was a warm fall day, and I sat at a table outside the market, wanting to make the most of the gentle sun. I turned to the employment section, circling a list of possible design positions. To my relief, there were several.

Before I turned the page, however, I let my eyes to drift over some of the other job categories. A position working in a downtown Denver gallery caught my eye. I was about to pass over it, sure the pay would be horrible. But then I stopped, listening as something inside told me to circle it anyway.

On impulse, I called the number from my cell phone. The woman who answered said they needed someone three nights a week. I felt my excitement grow—that might be perfect. I could still get a design job, but get my foot in the door with the art scene.

She asked me a few questions over the phone before asking if I could come down the next day with my resume. I quickly agreed.

The gallery was in Cherry Creek, an upscale neighborhood near my old design firm. It wasn't a huge space, but they were well established and their taste in painting mirrored my own. I got into a great conversation with the owner about the quirky visual style of one of their more prominent artists, and she hired me on the spot.

"Well, I guess you probably don't need this, then," I said, indicating the resume we'd been too busy talking about art to discuss.

"Oh, I guess I should have a copy," she said, reaching for it across the table. She glanced through it quickly. "Wow, you do have a lot of web design experience."

"It pays the bills," I said.

"You know, we've been talking about doing a little more with our site here. Several of our artists have started to get some national recognition, and we'd like to do more to feature them. Would you be interested in working on something like that?"

"Oh, definitely," I said. "I think that would be a lot of fun. Although," I added, "my rates for doing that type of work are quite different than the compensation we agreed to for staffing the gallery."

"Oh, of course! This would be a totally separate project. Besides, I can't imagine you would charge us more than the last firm we hired, and they didn't even know the first thing about painting. So I'm sure we can work all that out. Let me talk to my partner, and we'll discuss it further when you come in for training. How does that sound?"

"Great," I said, a big smile on my face. "I'm looking forward to it."

I walked out of the gallery feeling enormously pleased. I'd still have to find more work, but just knowing I had some money coming in was a huge relief. I decided to celebrate by getting a pastry from the gourmet cafe I used to hang out in when I worked at Kennelworth. I bought myself a blackberry tart and settled into a small, white streaked marble table near the window.

The tart was really good. I leaned back into my chair with a satisfied sigh. I'd forgotten how much I loved this little café. We used to come here almost daily when I worked at Kennelworth. I wondered what all of my old co-workers were up to now.

I really should call them, I realized. I had already sent my resumes off for the ads I'd seen in the paper, but I wanted to do something more. I was going to be a lot more pro-active in finding a job this time. I made a note to call each of my former officemates as soon as I got home.

It was mid-afternoon. I knew I should probably get on the road soon to avoid the traffic, but I'd hoped to do a little legwork on finding some housing while I was down here. I decided to make a quick stop at the gourmet health food store to check out their housing board. To save money, I had decided to look for a roommate situation until I'd made some headway with my debts.

I walked over to the market, breathing in the crisp fall air as I did so. Fall had always been my favorite season. Even though it signaled closing time for much of the natural world, I'd always associated it with new beginnings. New school clothes, new notebooks, and fresh, sharp pencils, ready to draw a whole new world.

I was walking up to the main entrance of the busy market when I stopped dead in my tracks.

Walking out of the sliding glass door, wearing a green employee apron, was my brother.

"Danny!"

He stopped and turned towards me. "Shit, Michelle," he said. "What the fuck are you doing here?"

"Looking for a place to live. What are you doing here?"

"I got a job, man," he said, a wide grin on his face as he spread out his hands and took a small bow. "At your service."

I stared at him, my brain having a hard time reconciling that information with what I though I knew of his current life. "But Dad told me you relapsed."

"Dad is full of shit," he said. "I was having a beer, big deal. He doesn't really understand that there's a difference between beer and heroin."

"So why did you leave? Where did you go?"

"I had to get the fuck out of there. He was riding me so hard I would have relapsed if I hadn't left."

I nodded slowly. I could understand that.

"I'm living with my girlfriend now," he said.

"You have a girlfriend?"

"Yeah. Over there." He pointed through the door to one of the checkout stands where a short, heavyset girl with a buzz cut and metal rings in her ears was chattily ringing up customers. "She helped get me this job, too."

I stared at him, a surprised smile on my face. He looked so different, it was hard to get over. He was heavier, which was part of it. But then I realized something else—for the first time in I don't know how long, he actually looked relaxed.

"Well, way to go, Danny."

He shrugged.

We looked at each other for another moment, the silence building up into awkwardness.

"So, does Dad know you're okay?" I asked.

He looked away. "No."

"You should tell him. I'm sure he's worried sick."

"Look, Michelle, if you want to tell him, be my guest. But don't tell him where I am. I don't need that bastard breathing down my neck. My life's okay now, and I'm not gonna listen to him tell me what a loser I am."

I nodded. "Yeah, I got it. Okay."

Another awkward moment passed.

"So, listen, I should get back to work."

"Okay. Well, it's good to see you."

"Yeah. You too."

I turned to walk away, but then shifted back to face him. "So, do you, like, want to get together or something?"

He looked up from the stack of baskets he was compiling. "Do you?"

Our eyes met as we both asked ourselves that question. We were strangers, really—it had been years since we'd had anything resembling a real connection. And we'd never had much in common to start with, aside from the fact that we had both escaped from the same childhood nightmare. But that, I realized as I looked at him, was something.

I shrugged. "It would be nice to meet your girlfriend."

He put on a half-smile. "Okay."

I scribbled my cell number onto a sheet of paper. "Give me a call. I'm moving back down to Denver soon."

He nodded and stuffed it in his pocket. I walked away and headed towards the community board, knowing he probably wouldn't call. But that was okay. In some part of me I hadn't known I still had, I was just incredibly relieved to know he was okay.

As I turned my car onto Speer Boulevard, I dialed my father's number.

"Dad, it's me."

"What is it?"

"Listen, I wanted to let you know I saw Danny."

"What? Where?"

"Um, I just ran into him on the street," I lied. "I just wanted to let you know he's okay."

There was a moment of silence from the other end of the phone. "Why hasn't he called then?"

"Well," I said slowly as I moved my car through the traffic towards the exit to Boulder, "I think he probably just needs some space for a little while. He said you were kind of hard on him, you know, and that was making it difficult for him to stay sober."

"Hard on him! What the hell is he talking about?" my father practically shouted. "I've done everything I can for you kids and all you can seem to do in return is complain about it! All I was doing was making sure he didn't screw up again. I'm his father, for Christ's sake. I have that right! Why can't you understand that?"

I counted to ten and took a deep breath.

"Well, Dad, I'm not sure what to tell you. This is a hard time for him, trying to go straight and everything. I think he's just doing the best he can right now."

"That kid is never going to amount to anything," he grumbled.

I resisted the urge to get angry with him. "You never know, Dad," I said as my eyes settled on the mountains ahead of me. "I think we're all just doing the best we can. Sometimes, that's all you can ask for."

Traffic was heavy on the way home, and I was looking forward to taking a hot bath as soon as I walked in the door. But as I turned down my street, my heart skipped a beat. Matt's Cherokee was parked in front of my house—with Matt sitting on the bumper.

A wave of fear rose within me, and I fought the urge to turn around. I hadn't had contact with anyone from Ma's group since the blow up, and I automatically steeled myself against what seemed likely to be some kind of attack.

As I pulled up to the curb, he stood up and shoved his hands into his pockets. I bit my lip as I stepped out of the car.

I hadn't even shut the door before he began speaking.

"I owe you an apology," he said.

"What?" That was not at all what I was expecting him to say. I felt my guard drop a tiny bit.

"You tried to tell me what was really going on over at Ma's, and I didn't believe you," he said. "I'm really sorry about that, Michelle."

My brow furrowed. "Are you saying you believe me now?"

He let out a sigh. "I haven't seen much of Jeremy lately, but he stopped by this afternoon to pick up a few things. After he left, I found a folder that he'd forgotten on the entry table. It contained a bunch of legal documents pertaining to a lawsuit between Ma and David. Just like you said.

"But that's not all I found. As I was leafing through the file, trying to make sense of what I was seeing, I found a love poem, addressed to Jeremy and signed by Ma." He paused for a moment, looking past me to the mountains at my back. "You know, he hasn't slept at home in weeks. Earlier I'd assumed he was staying with you, but after last week, that theory didn't hold much water. I'd been wondering about it, but, I dunno, I just didn't want to put the pieces together."

"You and me both," I said. I could see the sadness in his eyes, and my heart ached in sympathy for him.

"Jeremy came back a few minutes later," Matt continued. "I guess he'd realized what he'd forgotten. I confronted him about it immediately, but, Jeez, what an asshole he was when I did that," he said, shaking his head.

"How so?"

"He started going off about how it wasn't what it looked like, how what was happening between him and Ma was just part of some advanced spiritual practices that most people can't understand, and how your relationship with him was really over, but you'd become so mentally unstable you couldn't really accept that."

I felt my throat tighten. "Oh, God."

"Oh, don't worry," he said. "I wasn't about to let him get away with bullshitting me again."

I looked at him, relieved to know he didn't think I was crazy. "So what happened?"

"We had a few words. Got some stuff off my chest that had been bothering me for years, actually," he said with a grin. "I won't bore you with the details, but the end result was that I evicted him. Gave him three days to get out of my house."

"Are you serious? Oh, my God, Matt, that's huge!" I was enormously pleased to hear Jeremy got a dressing down, and even more pleased to know that Matt had taken my side when it would have been so much easier to keep buying the lie. But even if he had chosen to believe me over Jeremy, there was still the bigger issue of Ma. "You know," I added, "that this is all going to get back to Ma."

He nodded. "I know that," he shrugged. "It's okay. I still think Ma's an amazing teacher, but even before I knew about all of this, it seemed like things were getting a little weird. I didn't want to believe it at first—well, you know how that is," he said with a slight smile. "But with all this going on, and the way Ma's lectures have been starting to feel a little off, I think maybe it might be time for me to graduate from The Seminar Series."

I shook my head. "Wow. I'm impressed."

"Don't be. I'm just sorry it took me this long to figure it out. I'm really sorry I wasn't there for you earlier, Michelle," he said.

"Don't worry about it, Matt," I said, touched by his concern. "I doubt I could have been there for me, either."

He looked searchingly into my eyes for a moment. Then he reached down, took my face in his hands and gave me a deep, passionate kiss.

I was completely surprised. But with the touch of his lips, all of the attraction I'd ever had for Matt came rushing back to the surface. Every single nerve ending in my body began to tingle under my skin, and my heart leapt.

After a moment, he pulled back, and let his forehead rest against my own.

"I've always wanted to do that," he said.

It took me a moment before I could get my brain to function enough to speak. I was too busy grinning and blushing. But, finally, I composed myself.

"I'm really, really glad you finally did."

Matt picked me up wearing a brown sport coat and the khaki pants that didn't have any holes in them. His hair was back in a ponytail, and he'd even managed to shave.

"Well, look at you," I said, taking a moment from my raging anxiety to admire my very cute boyfriend.

He shrugged. "Since I'm going to have the guest of honor on my arm, I figured I'd better look good. Shall we?"

He opened the door for me to his Cherokee, and I slipped inside. We were on our way to the cocktail reception for my first art showing ever. I was one of three artists who were sharing space at a small but respected gallery, and I was soon going to see my first critical reviews. I'd worked hard on the eleven paintings that were on display, and I was proud of the progress I'd made since committing seriously to my art after leaving Boulder a year and a half ago. But it was one thing to paint something. It was quite another to let it be seen.

"So, how are you doing?" he asked as he pulled away from the curb.

"I'm kind of a wreck, actually," I said.

"Your work is amazing. You have nothing to be worried about."

"That's easy for you to say," I grumbled. "You're not the one who's about to get naked in front of a bunch of strangers."

"Do you want some juicy gossip to distract you?"

Curious, I turned to him. "Okay."

"Ma's moving to Montana."

"What? How did you find that out?"

"I ran into Panther at the bookstore this morning. Kali told him that Ma was running out of money, trying to fight this lawsuit thing, and wanted to protect what she had left."

"That's still going on?"

"You know those things drag on forever. I guess she's thinking about settling just to get it over with, but she doesn't want to do that while her money is tied up in that house. So she's downsizing and moving the whole circus up to Bozeman."

"Wow," I said. I hadn't even thought about Ma in months, but hearing her name brought up an odd mixture of emotions. In a way I was relieved to hear she was leaving; some part of me relaxed just knowing I wouldn't someday run into her on the street. To my surprise, however, I also felt a little bit sad.

I stared out the window, watching the traffic snake its way along the road. It wasn't as though I really wanted to see Ma again. But I also couldn't help thinking about how much my life had changed since I met her. Despite everything that had happened, things were a lot better for me now than they had been two years ago. I found myself wondering if that would still be true even if she hadn't come into my life. But really, there was no way to know that.

"Well, here we are," Matt said. "Shall I let you off?"

My throat tightened. "Yeah, thanks."

I pushed my way into the gallery, both worried and relieved to see that there were only a few people there so far. I walked over to the owner to let her know I'd arrived. She handed me a nametag and glass of wine before turning to greet one of the other artists.

I looked nervously around. A well-dressed couple was walking up towards one of my paintings. As they started discussing it in voices too soft for me to hear, my breathing went shallow, my stomach tied itself in knots, and it was all I could do to keep from running out the door. After gulping my wine in two sips, I bolted for the bathroom.

I leaned over the sink and splashed some water on my face, then straightened up and looked at myself in the mirror. The water I'd just splashed hadn't done much for my make-up, and last night's pre-show insomnia had left dark circles under my eyes.

Despite how I felt, I was surprised to notice that my eyes looked calm. As I looked more deeply into them, my face began to look foreign to me, in the same way that a word said over and over begins to lose its meaning. My earlier judgments about the person I saw in the mirror began to dissolve, and in their place was a quiet curiosity about the face staring back at me.

As I continued to look at the image in the mirror, I noticed that the eyes looking back at me were filled with love. I was soon awash in a feeling of warm tenderness, and I felt things in my body begin to unwind. As I relaxed, the person staring back at me from the mirror smiled.

"What are you doing?" Lucy said as she swirled into the bathroom, looking drop dead gorgeous in a low-cut, vintage red dress. "I'm not going to let you hide in the bathroom all night!"

"Sorry, Lu. I was just trying to calm myself down," I said.

"Well, get your butt out there and meet your adoring fans!" she said, taking me firmly by the arm and steering me out into the gallery.

She half-pulled me across the room towards several people who were standing in front of the abstract painting I'd done in Boulder of a shimmering human image against a pastel background. I felt the butterflies start to swirl around again.

"This is just so beautiful," a woman in a black suit jacket and taupe pants was saying. Lucy raised her eyebrows at me and shoved me towards her.

The woman looked up as I approached. She pointed at my nametag. "Oh—are you the artist?"

"Yes," I said, "I am."

Acknowledgements

Many thanks to the following people for their kind encouragement and support in the creation of this book: Debra Ginsberg, Barbara Schmidt, Alex Lovejoy, Cynthia Morris, Wendy Mazursky, Scott Fischette, EJ Essig, Leyla Day, Kirsten Warner, Aaron Young, Megan Prelinger and Connie Shaw. I am also deeply grateful to Steven Sashen for loving me, encouraging me, and fixing my computer whenever it was broken. Finally, special thanks to Marty Hall for believing in me until I was strong enough to do so for myself.